AltLife

Nigel Holloway

First published in Great Britain by

Katisha Publications.

200 Heritage Park, St Mellons,

Cardiff CF3 0DU

ISBN: 9798355983598

Imprint: Independently published

‘Oh, what a tangled web we weave,

When first we practice to deceive.’

Marmion: A Tale of Flodden Field

Sir Walter Scott

Prologue

Associated Press bulletin:

President Greenbaum has returned safely to Washington after inaugurating the newly restored virtual world.

In his address to the millions of loved ones who now continue to live on in the virtual world, he paid tribute to the loyalty and commitment of Professor Randolph Clinton for his hard work in recreating the world after it had been all but obliterated by an unknown computer virus.

He also expressed his personal regret that Hamish McAllister and Rajesh Singh had perished in their attempts to save their unique creation.

He committed the United States government to ensuring that such a disaster could never happen again, and assured the inhabitants that their future was safe in the hands of Professor Clinton.

Following his successful transmutation, the President re-assumed power from Vice President Rossi, and returned immediately to the White House to continue the affairs of state.

The First Lady sent her congratulations to her

husband, while continuing her goodwill tour of European capitals.

***

Williamsburg, Virginia

Despite the fading light, the motion detector sensed his approach, and the small screen embedded in the gravestone glowed into life. The picture of his mother, taken in her late forties, smiled out at him. Then, as it always did, the image faded, and the video started.

Alex Duchovny hated the video. He had seen it so often over the years that in recent months he'd taken to walking away until it ended. He knew exactly how long the awful spectacle of his mother reminiscing about her life would take, and exactly how far down the line of ancient yew trees he needed to walk in order to return just as it finished. And each time he started on his walk the same angry thoughts possessed him: the way that his father had insisted that she make the recording, the look of anguish on his mother's face as he and his father argued over the whole issue, his feeling of disgust that she had been forced to give up her dignity so soon after her terminal diagnosis, a mere three months before the cancer had taken her from them.

As the years had gone by, Alex increasingly found that he hated the spectacle of his ageing mother, the clear signs of what was happening to her degenerating body, trying to appear cheerful and positive for the camera. Even a basic chatbot would have been better than this - but who could whisper to an unsophisticated piece of software that they loved them? It was all so different now: if only his father had waited for the technology to have advanced.

But this visit was different. This time Alex stood and watched the banal spectacle that his father had taken such pride in: the video memorial he had persuaded her to make as his attempt to achieve immortality for the woman he loved, but never really understood.

Alex waited for the video to fade back to the smiling picture of his younger mother. Despite his father's explicit instructions in his will, he had refused to implement a similar recording for him. There was no corresponding video of his father in the gravestone's video bank; instead, the film he had made for himself would be stored indefinitely in the cloud: Alex knew he would never use it.

When the awful torment of the presentation ended, Alex reached automatically for the life-logger around his neck. As his fingers reached for the off button, he paused. Then he changed his mind and withdrew his hand, and quietly addressed the fading image.

'This is the last time I'll come. I know what I have to do. It's time for me to die. I will make things right.'

Then he turned and walked slowly away into the gathering darkness.

Virtual World

The hologram of the young woman smiled at him quizzically.

'It's quite unusual for someone to ask us for a job, Mr Duchovny,' she said. 'In the virtual world, we don't really have jobs as such. Everyone here can spend their time doing exactly what they please. In most cases, after they've got used to the way things work, they decide they want to pursue some interest or other - a hobby, sports - usually things they were unable to do when they were alive. But I don't think many of us regard what we choose to do as a job - especially as there's no remuneration.'

She gave a short laugh. 'Not that we need any kind of remuneration,' she explained.

'So I'd be free to help your development group?' asked Alex.

'I'm sure we'd be delighted to have someone with your level of computer experience in the group. I see from your résumé that your latest job has been working on interactive games.'

'Mostly background design.'

'There's always a huge demand for new worlds, new locations to be modelled,' she said.

'But I'm particularly interested in the design of avatars,' he added. 'The ones we use in the games are just ciphers - '

'Most people create their own,' she interrupted, 'it's quite easy to do. This is what I looked like when I was twenty three. I particularly liked that time of my life.'

'No, I didn't mean the usual personal sort of avatar,' he explained. 'I know they're effectively just an exterior skin you inhabit when you've been recreated here in VR. I understand all that. What I'm interested in is how you go about creating an avatar for someone who never had a life-logger.'

'Oh, I see,' she replied. 'Self-motivating avatars. We do create that sort of thing - mainly historic or fictional figures that are needed in specific re-enactments. Some of them are really quite sophisticated, I understand.'

She paused awkwardly, unsure of what to say. Then she continued, 'But most of that work was done by Mr Singh himself.'

'I'm sure I could learn a lot from him,' replied Alex.

'Sadly, Mr Singh is no longer with us,' she said carefully. 'I'm not sure if his research notes are available - under the new regime - '

'I don't understand.'

The girl paused, thinking how best to frame her reply.

'You must have heard the media reports?' she asked at last.

'I heard there had been an outage. It was a big deal at the time, but it's all been restored now, hasn't it?''

'Yes, there was a catastrophic failure. They blamed it on Dr McAllister - and Mr Singh. And they're - not here any more,' she said quietly.

Alex waited for the girl to continue.

At last, she forced herself to go on. 'I'm sure Mr Singh would have kept copies of the code he generated. He didn't call them avatars, by the way. He used to joke that they had more in common with actors - but without the narcissistic tendencies.'

She paused, waiting for his reaction. When he didn't respond, she continued, 'They would learn the fundamentals of the character - attitudes, values, and of course the basic facts of their life - and then they would improvise, based on what they'd learned. At least, that's what I understood them to do. Since the new regime, I don't think anyone has taken on that role. There seems to be such a lot more to do since he's gone.'

'It seems that Mr Singh has left a large hole in the organisation,' commented Alex.

‘He was there at the start - with Dr McAllister. Everyone misses them - ’

The girl pulled herself together.

‘But life must go on - although maybe that’s not the word I should have used.’

She paused for a moment, looking directly at him. ‘I was eighty seven when I died, Mr Duchovny; at that age, you get used to death stalking you.’

‘I know the feeling,’ he replied.

The girl looked at him quizzically. ‘It’s not really my business, of course, but I assumed your enquiry was about an internship, a limited research project.’

‘No, it would be permanent.’

He paused, then said calmly, ‘I have cancer.’

She raised her eyebrows in surprise. ‘I’m sorry to hear that, but surely it’s treatable these days?’

‘My doctor tells me it’s reached the stage where the cost of treatment is becoming significant. He believes that Viva Eterna - my insurance supplier - would be reluctant to cover the projected expense, and that it’s likely they would prefer me to transmute.’

'And how do you feel about that, Mr Duchovny? You're obviously still a young man.'

'I'm quite content for that to happen.'

'And your family?'

'I haven't told them,' he said quietly.

***

Washington DC

Alex took an autocab to the transmutation centre.

There had been no goodbyes to say to anyone: his employers knew exactly what he was preparing to do, and he had no other close family. He had made arrangements for all his possessions and whatever money he had to be given to various charities. All he had left were the clothes he was wearing.

When he had signed the agreement with Viva Eterna, the young man from the insurance company had gone through the exhaustive procedure with him. He would effectively commit suicide by lethal injection. But unlike assisted suicide schemes in the past, his existence would continue in the avatar that would be prepared for his arrival in the virtual world. The details of what would become of his mortal remains were of no interest to Alex, and he signed his life away without apparent interest in the fact that a sample of his DNA would be retained indefinitely if he should wish to return at some point in the future.

The representative from the insurance company was at pains to point out the positive advantages of transmuting to the virtual world. When he arrived, he would find himself in what appeared to be a five star holiday resort, where everything was included for his comfort. There was no time limit on his stay, and most people used their time to acclimatise to the new way of living. There were several training courses available to prepare newcomers for what they could expect to find: how to travel around by thinking themselves to a new location, introductions to the myriad of specialist worlds they could visit, how to create whatever sort of domicile they intended to live in, how to manipulate their avatar settings to be able to change their appearance, how to make changes to their environment, the list was comprehensive.

But Alex had no desire to spend any time in the luxurious surroundings of the reception location, no matter how much like paradise it turned out to be. His objective was to get to work as soon as possible. There was so much he had to learn: techniques and strategies unique to the virtual world, and there was nowhere else in the universe that he could learn them.

He signed in at the reception and was escorted to the transmutation suite. After the tube had been connected to the cannula in the back of his hand, the screen in front of him asked for his proof of identity and began the confirmation procedure to ensure that he was fully aware of the process and accepted the consequences of his actions.

He pressed the enter button at each stage to confirm his willingness to be transmuted permanently to the virtual world. The final button activated the flow of anaesthetic into his blood stream and he drifted quickly into unconsciousness.

When the end came, Alex was aware of nothing. His world ceased to exist in a nanosecond. There was neither a bang nor a whimper. If there had been a final thought in his mind, it might have been that he couldn't wait to die. There was certainly no fear of the unknown, after all, he'd seen what was waiting for him at his interview. He'd even met some of his future colleagues.

His last thought might have been: no more medical procedures. Or even: no more medical bills.

***

Virtual World

Duchovny was a software engineer by trade. In his teens, he had become fascinated with computer gaming, and had followed his dream of a career in software development. After he graduated from university, it was inevitable that he should follow his chosen career path of continuing his passion for programming and game playing. As his résumé showed, his experience grew, and he drifted from one organisation to another, his life consisting of an endless pleasurable stream of projects that consumed his waking hours.

And in his new existence, with his interests and breadth of experience, Alex had been immediately welcomed into the virtual development team, and had found himself assigned to the design of the three dimensional models that formed the infrastructure of every virtual world, and in particular, the replication of buildings and monuments existing in the real world.

The work was familiar but challenging. As well as the physical attributes of each structure, he was required to think about the textures of surfaces, the effects of weathering over time, as well as the methods of construction of the original edifice. His research was painstaking and sometimes involved a considerable amount of detective work, especially in the cases of ancient monuments for which there were no original designs or blueprints.

Alongside his architectural tasks, Alex embarked on the series of basic training courses targeted at all newly assigned technicians. Although a lot of the material was already familiar to him, he resisted the temptation to skip quickly through the exercises. To attract too much attention would be a mistake, he thought to himself. His patience would pay off later, when he got to the subject area he had always intended to become master of: his own holy grail, the creation of self-motivating avatars.

He had little time for his colleagues. Despite the fact that they seemed uniformly friendly and welcoming, Alex knew that his reason for being there was quite different from theirs, and even though he was obliged to spend his work time with them, part of him remained detached, his secret agenda hidden from view.

But from the start, one thing became blindingly obvious: everyone in the development team was fully aware of what had happened to the virtual world, and the disastrous consequences to their former colleagues, Singh and McAllister. There was a palpable air of residual resentment for what had happened. Nothing was said out loud, but Alex could feel the lingering distaste, the lasting regret that Singh and McAllister were no longer there.

When Clinton had recreated the virtual world, there had been no discontinuity as far as the development team were concerned. Each member had continued typing into his virtual keyboard as if nothing had happened. Initially, they had no awareness of the many months that their existence had been paused. But as the central group responsible for the maintenance of all the worlds that went to make up the virtual universe, it soon became clear that something seismic had taken place, and between them they had pieced together the evidence to form a complete picture of what Randolph Clinton had done.

The loss of Rajesh Singh and Hamish McAllister

was almost tangible.

As a newcomer, Alex was excluded from the suppressed dissatisfaction exuded by his colleagues, but it was impossible to remain unaware of their feelings.

Alex's first inkling of the threat to his new colleagues came when a holographic image suddenly appeared in the centre of the room.

There were gasps of recognition from several of his fellow engineers.

'I see some of you recognise me,' said the figure, looking around at the faces in front of him. 'I will be accessing the life-log data for each of you to see the extent of your commitment to your former colleagues, McAllister and Singh. Based on what I find, I will decide whether you continue to exist. As for those of you who did not recognise me, you will continue to carry out your functions within the development and maintenance team until I have time to assess future requirements.'

The hologram vanished as suddenly as it had appeared.

Alex turned to the programmer next to him. 'Who was that?' he asked.

'You really don't know, Alex?' his neighbour asked in disbelief.

'No.'

'That was Randolph Clinton.'

Alex shook his head. 'No, I’ve never seen him before. Isn’t he the guy who saved the virtual world?’

‘Saved!’ muttered the man, bitterly.

‘And what happened to McAllister and Singh?’asked Alex. ‘What did he mean - former colleagues?'

The other man looked at him sadly. 'I envy you, Alex,' he said quietly. 'At least you'll survive this. Hamish and Raj didn't make it.'

***

Chapter 1

The White House, Washington DC

'Mr President, the - soldier - you asked to see is here.'

The secretary was obviously disconcerted. The President of the United States didn't have private meetings with the lower ranks; she couldn't remember Greenbaum having spoken to anyone from the military under the rank of two star general. She felt almost embarrassed. How did the President even know someone of her rank?

Greenbaum looked up from his papers. 'Show her in,' he said quietly, his face betraying nothing of his amusement at the expression on the secretary's face. 'And bring tea for two.'

The secretary raised her eyebrows involuntarily at the thought of the President taking tea with a common soldier.

'I believe Miss Clarke favours Earl Grey,' he said.

'Of course, Mr President.'

'Oh, and miss - ' He paused, realising that he had no idea of the woman's name.

'Susanne, Mr President.'

'Of course, Susanne - forgive me, my memory - '

'Of course, Mr President.'

'Let me know when the Head of the Secret Service arrives.'

The secretary retreated through the door to the outer office, and a few seconds later the figure of a young woman appeared in the doorway. She stood to attention, her eyes fixed firmly on a point on the opposite wall.

Greenbaum gestured her to come in. and for the first time in her life, Clarke entered the Oval Office.

The door shut unobtrusively behind her, and she found herself staring at the figure seated behind the great desk, silhouetted against the gauze curtains illuminated from the garden outside, framed by the Stars and Stripes on one side, and the Presidential flag on the other.

'Miss Clarke, so good to see you,' said Greenbaum, holding a warning finger up to his lips. 'Please sit down.'

Greenbaum rose from his chair, moved round the desk and settled himself on the sofa opposite the girl. Her combat fatigues were a glaring anomaly in the plush surroundings of the seat of Presidential power.

The door opened and Suzanne entered carrying a silver tray with the bone china tea service.

'Is this a photo op, Mr President?' she asked. 'It's just that there are no media people here.'

'No, this is not a photo opportunity,' replied Greenbaum calmly. 'Miss Clarke has done a great service to her country, but one that is not for public scrutiny.'

'I beg your pardon, Mr President.'

'No need, Suzanne. You were not to know.'

The secretary hesitated, then left the room without another word.

Greenbaum poured a single cup of tea and slid it across the occasional table towards the girl.

'The Head of the Secret Service will be here shortly,' he said quietly. 'Listen, but don't speak. I will say everything that is necessary.'

There was a knock at the door and a tall man with grey hair entered. If he was surprised at the presence of the girl, his face showed no sign of it.

'Mr President.'

'Mr Taylor, thank you for coming at such short

notice. Please sit down.' Greenbaum waved vaguely at the two armchairs set at right angles to the sofas.

'You will remember the demise of the late Professor Randolph Clinton, Mr Taylor.'

'Yes, sir.'

'The official record indicates that he was shot by a CIA agent while attempting to resist arrest.'

'That is correct, Mr President.'

'Yes, that is exactly what the record says,' continued Greenbaum. 'But the official version is a complete fabrication.'

'Mr President?'

'A complete lie, Mr Taylor.'

'But Mr President - '

'Don't misunderstand me, Mr Taylor. It's not directly a Secret Services matter, and I understand completely why it was necessary for the CIA to present the incident in the most favourable light for themselves, but I want there to be no doubt between ourselves about the circumstances of Clinton's death.'

Taylor sat silent, his mind racing. How had the

President discovered the truth? Where had he got his information from? Why would he question the official version in the first place? Clinton was dead. What difference did it make? And besides, the CIA wasn't his responsibility.

'No doubt you are wondering how I know this,' continued Greenbaum. 'But that will remain my secret. Suffice it to say that the person who eliminated Clinton is sitting opposite me.'

Taylor's eyes flicked from the President to the girl sitting silently on the opposite sofa.

'Miss Clarke shot Professor Clinton. And for that, the country owes her a debt of gratitude. I do not intend to alter the official record, and Miss Clarke is happy for the CIA to continue to claim the credit. But I wish to show my gratitude by having her become part of my personal security team.'

'But she's a soldier, Mr President,' replied Taylor in alarm. 'Her background - her training doesn't fit in with the demands - '

'You will incorporate her into my personal security detail. I will feel a great deal safer with patriots such as her around me. Arrange for her induction and any further training you see fit. I will expect to see her take up her duties within the week. That will be all.'

Taylor rose stiffly from his chair.

'And when you discuss this matter with your good friends in the CIA, Mr Taylor, be sure to tell them I understand their motivation in falsifying the record.' He paused. 'And for keeping the Secret Service and, no doubt, the FBI in the dark.'

Taylor nodded briefly, and left the room. Greenbaum rose and returned to his desk.

'I will see you here in a week's time, Miss Clarke. I look forward to working with you.'

***

CIA Headquarters, Langley, Virginia

'You've always been able to lie with a straight face, Peter,' said Taylor, 'that's what makes you so good at your job.'

'I have no idea how he could have found out, Doug. No one in the CIA would have talked.'

'The girl, then - '

'Why would she? Clinton raped her, she got her revenge. That's it.'

'You're sure?'

'That's what she said, Doug. Why should she lie? She'd just killed him in cold blood. He was sitting at his desk. She shot him through the back of the head.'

Peter Kominsky paused, examining the face of his opposite number in the Secret Service. 'The way it went down was a win for everyone,' he continued. 'The girl got her revenge - no comeback; we got the credit for tidying up the Clinton thing. No loose ends.'

'Fact is: he knows what happened, Peter. He knows you lied; that the CIA falsified the evidence.'

'But he's not going to do anything about it,' stated Kominsky confidently.

'You hope - '

'Calm down - it'll all go away.'

'You seem very sure.'

'Think about it, Doug. Who knew what really happened?'

'The girl, your people - '

'And what exactly do they have to gain by telling the President what really happened? If the girl confessed, she'd probably be tried for murder. If any of your people leaked the truth how good would it look for them?'

'So how did he find out?'

Kominsky paused for a second, then a faint smile played around his lips. ‘The only other person who was there.’

‘Clinton?’

Kominsky nodded. ‘The only other option.’

‘But why? How?’

‘First of all - the how is easy. Somebody had orders to transmute him. Clinton arrives in the virtual world and the first thing he does is to look at the girl’s life-log data to see exactly what happened. As to why - to make the CIA look bad? To make Greenbaum look a fool for not knowing what was going on? After all, he’d cheated Greenbaum’s attempt to remove him by escaping to the virtual world, and at the same time effectively made himself indispensable by recreating the whole damn thing. Just think of the backlash if Greenbaum had to admit that all those dearly beloved relatives had gone forever. I think Clinton was just rubbing Greenbaum’s nose in it.’

‘But why was the girl at the White House? She couldn’t just turn up and ask for a meeting with the President.’

‘He must have invited her.’

‘But why?’

‘Clinton again,’ said Kominsky, with a wry smile.

‘I don’t see what he has to gain by forcing Greenbaum to give her a job in his personal security team. He knows she was Clinton’s operative.’

‘Clinton may want to keep an eye on what Greenbaum’s doing.’

‘But that’s so obvious - my men would be watching her constantly, looking for any sign she was communicating with Clinton.’

‘What about her life-logger?’

‘She’d have one of ours,’ replied Taylor.

‘You think he couldn’t hack into your life-log data?’

Kominsky paused. ‘I think it’s the other way round. I think Greenbaum wants her near him.’

‘But why? She must be a threat of some sort.’

‘Keep your friends close, but keep your enemies closer, Doug. Maybe he’s trying to show Clinton he’s not afraid of him. But whatever the reason, we have to live with it - at least until we find out what’s going on.’

As the door closed behind Taylor, Kominsky picked

up his secure line.

'The girl's joining the President's personal security team. This may be the break we've been waiting for,' he said quietly. 'I want covert surveillance on her round the clock. I want to know everything - every move she makes, every word she speaks - I want to know what she's thinking.'

***

National Center of Neurology and Psychiatry, Tokyo

'This is our last chance, Prem,' said Hisako. 'We've exhausted every other possibility. If this doesn't work, we just have to accept that they're gone. Forever.'

'I can't accept the forever part, Hisako,' replied the young Indian over the video link. 'If Christina can create new clones for them - '

'You know she can't do that,' replied the girl. 'It takes months to grow an adult clone. They're following her every move. She wouldn't stand a chance. They'd destroy the DNA, and there's one less possibility of recovering them.'

'Damn Clinton!' growled Prem.

'Yes, I agree. But we just have to accept the fact that he's back, he's in total control of the virtual world, and he's managed to regain his influence over Greenbaum. With that sort of power, we just have to be able to be smarter than them. Just concentrate on our own situation. What have we got going for us?'

Prem sighed. 'I guess you're right,' he said. 'At least he doesn't know about us - '

'Not about you, Prem. But he certainly knows about me. What is in doubt is whether he realises my significance.'

'You mean AltLife?'

'Exactly. If he knows about it at all, he will only recognise it as the result of my academic research. He won't understand the potential of what it can do, he'll see it as a tool used by the Psychiatry department at the hospital. If Clinton asks, Professor Sato will tell him anything he wants to know about it, but it would take a considerable leap of intuition to realise its full implications.'

'And your father?' asked Prem. 'Is it likely the professor could give the game away? By accident?'

'I think you can safely assume that my father can play the part of the inscrutable oriental sufficiently well to fool someone who knows nothing about the technology,' she replied, with a half smile. 'Given enough time and effort, I'm sure Clinton could find out exactly how powerful AltLife can be. But why should he? There's nothing to make him suspect that AltLife has any significance beyond what it appears to be: a piece of software that takes life-log data and weaves it together so that the patient can be taken to significant moments in their lives where they made decisions that changed their psychological profile.

'Sure, if he looked more closely, he could see that it can also extrapolate forwards in time to show the consequences of past actions, but that part of the system is purely statistical. It just deals in probabilities. There's nothing magical about it. From Clinton's viewpoint, it might be interesting, but nothing more. There's nothing inherent in the software to link it to what we know.'

'But when you combine AltLife with the quantum computer it's running on - ' said Prem.

'And a second quantum computer, no matter how remote it may be - '

Hisako spread her hands in a gesture of definitive explanation.

'Quantum entanglement,' said Prem.

'Exactly. And even then, look how long it's taken the two of us to identify the criteria that allowed Raj and Hamish to escape to the second virtual world.'

'You're assuming they did escape, Hisako.'

‘I’m sure they did,’ replied the girl. ‘I spoke to Hamish in those last moments in AltLife. He knew exactly what he had to do, and I’m convinced he did it.’

‘Put them both to sleep while taking a backup copy?’

‘I think he’ll have succeeded. There’s just no way we can know for sure without someone who can can go through the same entanglement process as they did.’

‘And there’s only one person who could do that - Christina,’ said Prem.

‘Correct. Christina’s the only person who exists in the real world and also in that little mid-western town Hamish created when he and Raj set up the virtual world on that space ship. If we’re right about how this works, she’s the only person who can find out if Hamish and Raj still exist.’

The two fell silent for a moment, separated by thousands of miles, but both contemplating the awful consequence of their being wrong.

‘Is it time?’ asked Prem at last.

‘They’ll be starting the daily AltLife session in a couple of minutes,’ Hisako replied.

‘Is Christina asleep? And she knows what’s likely to happen?’

'I briefed her before we transmuted her into the private virtual world, and I spoke to her again earlier this morning. She knows what we expect to happen. I'll login and make sure she's asleep.'

'And then, all we have to do is wait.'

'If it works, we should know in about forty minutes.'

***

Quantum Entangled Virtual Space

Hamish McAllister eventually tore himself away from his wife's embrace, and looked into her eyes. 'How did you get here?' he asked.

'It was Prem and Hisako,' she replied, smiling back at him.

'So they figured it out eventually,' he murmured. 'I knew they would.'

For a moment the two held each other close. Then Hamish said: 'When can we get back?'

Christina's eyes clouded, and the smile faded from her lips. 'You can't,' she replied slowly.

McAllister raised an eyebrow in query.

'It's a one way trip,' she said. 'I can go back because I exist in the real world, but your body was destroyed in the hospital bombing.'

'And Raj?'

'The same. You're both stuck here.'

Hamish looked away, his eyes scanning the vast fields of corn that reached to the horizon all around them.

'You could create new clones for us,' he said. 'That should work. As soon as we both exist again in corporeal form, we should be able to get back into AltLife - '

'That's easier said than done, Hamish,' said Christina. 'The situation's changed. Clinton's master of all he surveys in the virtual world, and by recreating it again after he destroyed it, he's made himself indispensable to Greenbaum. And with the resources of the US behind him, there's no way we could complete the cloning process before they could find us.

'When Clinton destroyed the virtual world, he believed he'd eliminated you once and for all. But he's cautious, Hamish. He suspects I could find a way to bring you both back, so as a consequence, I'm under continuous surveillance everywhere - in the real world and in virtuality.'

‘So he knows where you are right now?’

‘He knows I’m in Tokyo. He knows I’m in the real world. But as far as we know, he has no idea about AltLife.’

‘If you’re in Tokyo, at the hospital, it won’t take him long to find out. And if he shuts down AltLife - ’

‘I don’t want to think about that, Hamish,’ she said. ‘I thought I’d lost you this time, I couldn’t bear it if - ’

‘We need to get you out of here, Christina. And away from Tokyo. We need to make sure he doesn’t find out about AltLife.’

‘If he doesn’t already know - ’

‘Go back, Christina - tell Prem and Hisako that they need to keep AltLife a secret. It would be best if they shut it down altogether. You all need to get away from Tokyo. Clinton will be following your every move. He’ll want to know why you came to Japan.’

‘I’ve got a legitimate excuse, Hamish. It’s where you and Raj ceased to exist. Of course I’d want to come here. To try to find out about your last moments. To spend time with Hisako’s father. As far as Clinton’s concerned, he’s lost someone, too.’

‘You think he’d believe that?’

'It makes sense to me.'

'I'm not so sure.'

Christina pursed her lips. 'Whatever he believes or doesn't believe doesn't affect the situation as it exists. In the three months you've been stuck here, Clinton has recreated the virtual world, managed to get President Greenbaum to inaugurate it, and by doing so has gained complete control of the virtual world and re-established his influence at the heart of the US government. I don't suppose Greenbaum was happy about the fact that Clinton had outwitted him, but I'd say he had very little choice other than to accept the reality of the situation.'

'So what's his next move?'

'You know perfectly well what he'll try to do. His objectives haven't changed. He's as intent on his revenge now as he was when we first found out about it. It's religious genocide: nothing less will satisfy him. He's a madman, Hamish. The question is: what do we do about it?'

'There's nothing we can do - '

'I don't believe I just heard you say that, Hamish.'

'Christina, I'm stuck here in a computer hundreds of millions of miles from Earth, accelerating away towards some completely unknown planet in another solar system, with just about enough energy to power the small world you see around you. I have to avoid the other version of me that lives here because we don't know if having the two of us in any sort of close proximity would result in a catastrophic software failure that would mean that Raj and I really would cease to exist. And you ask me what we can do about preventing Clinton from starting a genocide that would result in the complete elimination of the Muslim population from the earth!

'I can't help myself, never mind the rest of the world!'

Christina looked at him angrily. 'You had problems before, Hamish. Before you created the virtual world, before you became famous. But they never stopped you from pursuing your vision of a world freed from pain and disease. What's changed?'

'I don't expect you to understand - '

'You're damn right I don't understand!' she replied angrily.

'Christina - '

'What's happened to you, Hamish? You've never backed down from a fight before, no matter what the odds.'

'I've had a lot of time to think since I've been exiled here. We failed, Christina. Clinton would have succeeded, he would have eliminated us completely. We had a stroke of luck - '

'Luck? You call that luck?'

'I just happened to be thinking along the same lines as Hisako - '

'That wasn't luck, Hamish. It was sheer genius.' She held up her hands, anticipating his protest. 'If not luck, then maybe we should call it karma.'

Hamish sighed. 'Devit would agree with you.'

'It was meant to be,' she said firmly. 'You were meant to survive, Hamish. You just have to accept the fact. Then figure out why.'

***

'I've changed, Raj,' said McAllister quietly. 'I don't have the stomach for this fight.'

'It's just this place, Hamish,' replied his friend. 'It seems so far away, so remote from what we knew. But back there it's still real.'

'I know - '

'People are going to die, Hamish. Millions of them. Needless deaths.'

‘But we can’t stop them, Raj. We’re helpless - ’

‘We have lots of helpers.’

‘I can’t let them sacrifice themselves instead of me.’

‘It’s not your decision to make, Hamish. You have to let them decide what they want to do.’

‘But I can’t even ask them - ’

‘I don’t think you need to ask. I think the fact that Christina was able to come here should tell you all you need to know. They’ve obviously been working flat out to find a way of getting us back. Okay, so they’ve only managed to find a way of communicating with us so far, but that’s a win, Hamish. If they can find a way for one of the others to turn up in the next AltLife cycle, they’ll have proved beyond doubt that the mechanism works, and that as soon as you and I can get new bodies cloned from our DNA, we’ll be able to go back, too.’

‘Christina said - ’

‘I know what she said,’ replied Raj. ‘So maybe it’s time for you and I to stand back for a while and let the others be our eyes and ears.’

‘But the cycle is so short - forty minutes, once a day.’

‘We can’t risk any more than that. Clinton’s people

would be sure to notice the increase in utilisation of the hospital's quantum computer. If we draw attention to ourselves like that, who knows what they'd do?'

Hamish's eyes narrowed. 'Are we synchronised with time on earth?' he asked suddenly.

'Yes - why?'

'If we slowed down time here, their sessions would occur more frequently. Then, even being in contact once a day would let us react faster.'

'That's just perception, Hamish. It wouldn't make any difference to them, they'd still have to wait until the next legitimate Alt Life session.'

Hamish frowned in frustration.

'Is there no way we can get round this?' he asked.

'Not without running AltLife more frequently on that computer.'

'Could we set up AltLife on another machine?'

'Yes, but for it to be of any use to us, it would have to be on a quantum computer, and the sudden increase in utilisation would be noticeable. If anyone's looking at the figures, it would stick out like a sore thumb.'

'Maybe Prem could manipulate the processor

utilisation records,' said Hamish.

'It's possible. But it depends on what sort of access he can get to the new virtual world. At the moment, Clinton doesn't know he exists. But if he found out, it would be disastrous - for all of us.'

'There is another possibility,' mused McAllister. 'If there were more than one version of AltLife - especially if it ran in another time zone - maybe Prem could hide behind it.'

'You'd need Sato to convince his colleagues that AltLife was proving a successful tool in helping his patients.'

'And if he could?'

'There must be hundreds of psychiatric departments that could make use of it,' replied Raj. 'But not all of them have quantum computers, Hamish.'

'That cuts the numbers down, but surely it's worth a try, Raj.'

A smile spread across Raj's face. 'That sounds more like the Hamish McAllister I know. Now, if I understand the mechanism correctly, you and I need to create a couple of avatars - one for Prem and one for Hisako.'

***

Prem looked around at the small green in the centre of the village. To one side stood a white clapperboard church, gleaming in the sunshine. Along the other sides of the square, small houses sat, seemingly deserted. It was exactly as Christina had described it.

He grinned at the two men walking towards him.

'You two are a sight for sore eyes,' he said, grasping their hands in turn. Then he looked more closely at his own hand. 'I knew you'd realise you had to make an avatar for me, but you could have made a better job of it, Raj. I look like some sort of cartoon character.'

'I didn't have much to work with,' replied Raj, with a smile. 'I don't carry a picture of you around in my pocket.'

'I couldn't care less what you look like, Prem,' said Hamish. 'It's just so good to see you.'

Prem looked around again at the silent village. 'Where is everyone?' he asked.

'Long story. They're all asleep. It'll keep till we have more time,' replied Hamish. 'For now, there are more important things to discuss. We know we can't get back, Prem. And until the situation changes drastically, we know that Christina can't create new clones for us. So it looks like the responsibility rests on your shoulders - yours and Hisako's. I never wanted you to be in this position - '

‘Forget it,’ replied Prem. ‘We never stopped working to find a way to get to you, and even if you can’t get back right now, you’re still the best people to figure out what we need to do to stop Clinton. The question we want to know is: what should we do?’

‘We need information, Prem,’ said Hamish. ‘We need to find out where Clinton is, what he’s doing, who’s helping him. We need to know that you can get access to the virtual world. Did Clinton made any significant changes when he recreated the world? What’s happening with Greenbaum? What changes have there been in the political situation?’

‘I can get back to you with all that - ’

‘But don’t take any chances, Prem. In fact, we think you should find a way to stop using the current version of AltLife. If Clinton found out what it can do, that’d be the end for Raj and me.’

‘So what can we do?’ asked Prem.

‘We think a possible solution is for you to find a way to get other people to use AltLife. If there were enough different users around, you could hide your usage by piggybacking on the other versions. And if they were in different time zones, that could significantly increase your access to us. We think you should talk to Sato, and see if he can help persuade his contacts around the world to use it as part of their clinical therapy, just as it was originally intended.'

'Hisako's the best person to do that,' said Prem.

'Just make sure that everything appears to be a normal consequence of a successful clinical trial; we don't want to attract Clinton's attention. If Hisako is too prominent, he'll notice. He's already aware of what she's capable of. But Sato probably isn't on his radar.'

'Where are you at the moment, Prem?' asked Raj.

'Nowhere near Tokyo, if that's what's worrying you.'

'Good. I'm guessing the virtual world you've set up isn't connected to the rest of the metaverse?'

'No, it only exists when we need it to - like for this forty minute slot. The rest of the time it's dormant, except for when Hisako and I need to discuss something.'

'Make sure she doesn't come here, Prem,' said Raj. 'Just tell her I want her to be safe - until I can get back.'

***

Chapter 2

The White House, Washington DC

The door of the Oval Office opened, and Sally Whitehead, Greenbaum's Chief of Staff entered carrying a sheaf of documents.

'Here are today's papers for your signature,' she said, placing them carefully into the President's in-tray.

Greenbaum looked up from his screen. 'Won't an electronic signature do?' he asked in irritation.

'I'm afraid not, Mr President,' replied the woman firmly.

'I'll sign them later,' said Greenbaum, turning back to his screen.

'I'm afraid they have to be signed immediately, sir,' she replied, leaning over to pass him the pen.

'Immediately? What are they?'

'They're the papers we prepared right before you took your trip into VR, Mr President. They've been waiting for your signature for a week.'

'Then they can wait a few more minutes.'

'I have to insist, Mr President,' she said, holding out the pen. 'The House of Representatives are waiting for them.'

Greenbaum looked at her in annoyance. How could anyone bear to work with this overbearing harridan, he asked himself? Greenbaum obviously needed to get a grip.

He suppressed his irritation and took the pen from her hand. She opened the first document.

'If you could sign here, Mr President.'

Greenbaum raised the pen, and paused.

'Has my Presidential pardon for Professor Clinton been prepared?'

'Yes, Mr President,' she replied, her eyebrows raised in surprise that he should attach such importance to what in her view was such a minor matter.

'I assume it's in this pile of documents?'

'No, Mr President, it will be included in the next batch.'

'I want to sign that first,' stated Greenbaum, putting down the pen. 'And bring me the copies of the last batch of documents I signed, I need to see exactly what wording we used.'

'Very well, Mr President,' agreed Whitehead, suppressing her frustration, and wondering at the same time why the President was being so uncooperative.

She turned and left the room, closing the door behind her.

Greenbaum stared after her, then picked up the pen and looked at it. He smiled mirthlessly at the mistake he'd nearly made, and congratulated himself on his quick thinking: now he would have plenty of time to copy Greenbaum's signature, the signature that he had never seen.

***

Quantum Entangled Virtual Space

'I think I may have found my cover,' said Prem's avatar.

'Who is it?' asked Raj.

'It's a new trainee called Alex Duchovny.'

'Why him, Prem?'

'He's interesting. He has a lot going for him. He's only just arrived in VR, but even before he died, he'd expressed an interest in working on the support and development side.'

'What's his background?'

'Classical IT mostly, but more recently he moved into games design. It seems to coincide with finding out he had cancer. I guess he didn't want to waste what time he had left.'

'Cancer? But that's curable,' commented Hamish.

'To be frank, it sounds like he used the disease as an excuse to get here. He didn't tell anyone until the prognosis was terminal.'

'But even so, it's still possible to treat it - '

'He was really quite devious, Hamish. He waited until the balance of cost tipped in favour of transmuting him.'

'So he used Vita Eterna's assessment process to get himself here,' mused Hamish. 'He must really be keen to join us.'

'It seems like it. He's thrown himself straight into the basic training. He didn't even take a holiday before he started.'

'And how is he progressing?' asked Raj.

'He's very good,' replied Prem shortly. He paused, as if reluctant to say more.

'Is that it?' asked Raj in surprise.

'Yes, he's very good,' reiterated Prem. 'In fact - sometimes I get the impression he's - well, too good.'

'Why do you say that?'

'He does make mistakes,' replied Prem. 'But - '

'Everybody makes mistakes,' said Hamish. 'That's how we learn. What's the problem?'

Prem hesitated again. 'It's not the number of mistakes he makes. Statistically, it's absolutely what we'd expect. Look, this is going to sound crazy, but I think he makes them deliberately.'

'Deliberately? Why would he do that?'

'It's just an impression. I could be totally wrong.'

'Why would anyone do that?'

'I don't know,' replied Prem. 'The only thing I can think of is that he already knows everything we're teaching him about subversive hacking, and he's trying to pretend that he doesn't.'

Hamish looked at Raj, and then back to Prem.
'Why?' he asked.

‘I can’t imagine,’ replied Prem.

‘But you’re proposing to use him as a cover for your activities?’

‘I’ve set up his first assignment so I can get at Greenbaum’s data.’

Hamish looked at the Indian thoughtfully. ‘If there is something suspicious about him, I can’t think of a better way to find out what it is than by sitting inside his head and watching everything he does.’

‘Between the AI and me, he’ll never be alone.’

‘Just make absolutely sure he doesn’t know you’re there.’

***

Lecture Theatre, National Center of Neurology and Psychiatry, Tokyo

Hisako stood with her hands nervously grasping the side of the lectern and looked out at the audience filling the auditorium before her. Despite the fact that she’d given the same presentation a dozen times before, and that her speech was clearly visible in the two auto-cue screens in front of her, she still felt the deep anxiety that continued to afflict her when she had to face a room full of strangers.

Her fear sprang not from standing alone in front of so many people, nor the act of presenting her talk to her audiences, but from the fundamental knowledge that every word she was about to speak was a complete lie.

'Ladies and gentlemen,' she began; the sound of her own voice through the public address system startled her by its loudness.

'Ladies and gentlemen, I developed this software for the sole purpose of assisting my psychiatric patients to come to terms with the decisions they had made previously in their lives. Decisions that had led them, unbeknown to themselves, to the point at which they found themselves.

'To achieve this, I developed AltLife. As you already know from the material we distributed with your invitations, the software works by assembling all the information it can gather about the patient's life to create a temporary virtual world, specific to them. Once that world has been created, I can take them back to any specific point in time so that, together, we can confront the issues which faced them, and help to illuminate why they did what they did, and what the ultimate consequences might be.

'Since I first developed the software, it has been in constant use at the National Center of Neurology and Psychiatry in Tokyo under the supervision of my father,

Professor Sato. His unwavering support has been a source of great strength to me all through the development process, and I wish to thank him also for the constructive comments and suggestions of all his team which has enabled me to bring the system to the stage where it is ready to be used more widely in the psychiatric community.'

Hisako paused, wondering what reaction she would get if she told them the real reason she was standing in the single spotlight in front of all these people.

Hamish had been very clear: they needed more versions of AltLife running on machines around the world so that she and Prem could hide their covert activities from the suspicious gaze of Randolph Clinton. She knew they were taking a big risk by actively marketing AltLife to other potential users, but there was no other choice if they were to continue their fight against the man determined to massacre millions of innocent Muslims in his search for revenge against the fanatics who had taken the lives of his parents.

Her talks had been successful in generating interest from several clinics around the world, but so far, there were no committed takers. But audiences for her seminar had been growing steadily as word travelled around the clinical psychiatric community.

'And now, rather than give you all the technical details of how AltLife actually works, I think it'll be more instructive if we examine a few real life case studies.'

She was into her spiel now, and she could relax a little, her presentation slides giving structure to the rest of her talk.

She wondered what Clinton would think about what she was saying. He of all people would know that there was so much more to AltLife than she had described. He knew the real reason she had developed the software, to give new life to the brother she had murdered in childhood. But even he couldn't have realised that AltLife wasn't just able to assemble a world from the past, but also project that world forward into the future. Admittedly, it was only a statistical projection, but that capability allowed her to do so much more for her patients than even she had imagined. And even more significant was that AltLife's predictions could be used to create a whole range of possible worlds based on the parameter settings she controlled.

Even Hisako herself had been surprised when she and Prem had used its predictions to save Raj and Hamish's lives. And on that final day when she had taken the leap of imagination that only she and Hamish could have envisioned, AltLife had created the mechanism by which the two men had been saved from inevitable extinction and oblivion. Even now, as she was describing the progress that one of her clients had made following her treatment, AltLife was providing the lifeline between the virtual worlds containing Raj and Hamish, and the one being used by Prem to communicate with them.

She just hoped that her efforts would bear fruit, and that an organisation with deep enough pockets to run the quantum computer needed to run AltLife would appear.

But at the back of her mind was the constant fear that her efforts were so overtly public that someone outside her relatively select professional community might notice, and she prayed that if word got to Randolph Clinton, he would be too busy to pay attention to her one-woman sales pitch.

Hisako summed up her presentation and asked for questions. She noticed that this audience seemed to be more interested in the case studies she had described, rather than the technical details. Was that a good sign?

She had no doubt that her talk was pitched at the right level, after all, it had taken the joint efforts of herself, Prem, Christina and her father, Professor Sato, to ensure that it contained the right mix of technical content, background information, and human interest. And she had worked hard on her presentation skills to ensure the correct level of professionalism combined with the enthusiasm she brought to her pet project. Her confidence in her ability to charm an audience of strangers had grown with each session, and she had been surprised by the positive comments she had received from the delegates who had sought her out after the event.

At length, the questions were finished, and she stood to one side of the lectern and bowed to the audience in appreciation of their attention. She left the stage to find her father already in deep discussion with one of the delegates. She nodded to him, then found herself facing a tall, well-dressed man. With a broad smile, he held out his hand in greeting. From his accent, she deduced that he was American.

'Miss Myamoto, I've flown a long way to hear your talk, and I have to tell you, it was worth the trip.'

'Thank you,' she replied. 'I don't know your name - '

'No reason you should, Miss Myamoto. I'm not in the psychiatric therapy game. My name is Haymer, Oriel Haymer. I work for LDS.'

***

'It took me completely by surprise,' said Hisako. 'It was the last thing I was expecting.'

'But who are they?' asked Sato. 'I've never heard of LDS.'

'Hardly surprising, father,' she replied. 'They're an American Church.'

'What would a church want with AltLife? Are they intending to use psychiatric techniques on their followers?'

‘I suspect they would claim they’re already in the psychiatric healing business,’ she said evenly. ‘But that’s not why they came to the seminar.’

‘Then what?’

‘What do you know about genealogy?’

‘Only that it’s about documenting family trees.’

‘Well, as he explained it to me, LDS – the Church of Latter Day Saints – holds a huge database of family records – births, deaths, marriages, census information, immigration records and much more.’

‘But why?’

‘It’s something to do with their beliefs about trying to establish a worldwide family tree connecting everyone now living with everyone who has ever lived in the past.’

Sato opened his mouth to speak, but Hisako raised her hand to forestall any further questions. ‘Don’t ask me any more,’ she said. ‘He did explain, but the idea of a galactic family tree sounded so bizarre that I could hardly hide my scepticism. But what I did understand was that they had undertaken a project to completely digitise all their historic records. They used to hold them on microfilm in their secure vaults, but the conversion has now been completed, and it’s time to move on to the next stage of their plans.'

'Which are?'

'This where it gets interesting – it seems that just holding an enormous database of what they call *vital* records isn't enough. There are other organisations who compete with them in supplying genealogical data – but on a commercial basis.'

'People make money out of this?'

'Apparently, it's a huge business. Big enough for LDS to have several quantum computers front ending their databases. But their competitors have already moved forward from basic record-based genealogy. Using Artificial Intelligence, they've started to bring the past to life. It's the same sort of AI that can be used to create deep fakes. Nowhere near as sophisticated as the techniques Raj used to create self-motivating avatars, but they're moving in that direction.'

'I still don't see why they're interested in AltLife.'

'You're only looking at the psychiatric uses, father. Think about the fundamentals of what AltLife does. It collects everything it can from the databases it has access to, and assembles it into a virtual world. And if you throw enough computer resources at it, it does it in near real time.'

'But that only applies to CCTV footage, life-log data

and so on.'

'Exactly: to enable them to compete in the market, LDS want to move from a records-based genealogical system to an image-based system.'

Sato raised his eyebrows in disbelief.

'But before you dismiss the idea, don't forget photography has been around for over two hundred years, movies for well over a hundred, and since the explosion in computing, we've had digital photography, video in various formats, three dimensional holography, not forgetting life-loggers. What they're proposing is feasible, father. There's enough image-based data available to create a detailed and coherent life story for everyone – as long as they lived in the fairly recent past.'

'But only if you have something that will link all that data together,' said Sato, understanding dawning in his face.

Hisako spread her hands. 'And we have - AltLife,' she said, with a smile.

***

Quantum Entangled Virtual Space

'The girl's a genius, Hamish,' said Prem. 'Obviously I can't have anything to do with the actual installation –

Hisako will do that – but we've left a back door open in LDS's version of the software so that it'll be easy for me to get in there whenever I need to.'

'And they've got enough computing power to run it?' asked Raj.

'Hardware already installed and running. And more power than we could have hoped for – especially in the early days, before they open it up to the paying punters. And the other good news is that Hisako suspects that LDS's competitors will be queuing up to get their hands on AltLife, too - once the word gets out.'

'Even more quantum computing resource,' nodded Hamish, with satisfaction. 'I don't suppose Clinton has had time to even think in detail about how the virtual world is supported. Just as long as he doesn't latch onto the fact that Hisako has solved one of his ongoing resource problems for him.'

'He knows what she really wanted AltLife for,' said Raj. 'Let's just hope Hisako's success doesn't attract his attention.'

'Which is my cue to get back,' said Prem. 'The software should be up and running in a couple of days, so I'll be able to report back more often. In the meantime, I'll see what I can find out about what Clinton and Greenbaum have been doing.'

'And how are you going to do that?' asked Raj.

'You remember I mentioned the new guy just joined the development team? Alex Duchovny?'

'The one you were suspicious about?'

'That's the one. I figured I ought to keep a closer eye on him, so I thought - '

'You've altered his training programme,' said Raj.

'You're as devious as I am, Raj.'

'With a few tweaks to the AI parameters, you could get him to carry out some appropriate investigations. Some research which might prove useful - for the development of his skills, of course,' added Hamish.

'All part of the training,' said Raj, innocently.

'And if anyone notices, it's all down to him – not a trace of my sticky fingers anywhere,' said Prem.

'Except for the AI parameters,' said Hamish.

'The AI is built to adapt the training programme to suit the student's skill set and previous experience. He's expressed an interest in designing self-motivated avatars,' replied Prem.

'Really? That seems remarkably specific,'

commented Hamish.

‘I don’t know why he’s so keen on that area,’ replied Prem. ‘But one of the key skills required is the ability to research the character and motivations of the subject under investigation. So I thought, I – that is, the AI – might get him to look at our friend Greenbaum. What could be more appropriate? He’s still alive, he’s a significant figure in world events, and there’s more information about what he’s doing than you could ever need to create a sophisticated, self motivating avatar. It should be an easy task for him. And it gets me a source of data without anyone realising what’s going on.’

‘Good thinking, Prem.’

‘Thanks, Raj. I’ll be careful not to leave my fingerprints on the AI itself.’

‘Could you get him to do the same with Clinton?’ asked Hamish

‘That might be more difficult for him. There’s far less information for him to get hold of - at least, legitimately. Let’s see how he gets on with Greenbaum. The AI’s built to assess what he’s done, and give feedback. So it’ll be easy for me to modify the assessment and if I think he’s not quite up to speed, I’ll point him in another direction to hone his skills. The AI might well recommend he takes some modules on deep investigation and analysis.’

‘You mean hacking,’ commented Hamish wryly.

‘You’ve been spending far too much time with Raj, Hamish,’ smiled Prem.

‘The sooner we know what Clinton is up to, the better.’

‘I’ll do whatever is necessary,’ replied Prem, as his avatar faded into nothing.

***

Virtual World

It’s time for your first assignment, Alex.

‘I’m looking forward to it,’ replied Alex, no longer unnerved by the sudden sound of the AI's voice in his head.

With everything you’ve learned so far, this first task should be relatively simple. The subject is a living world leader, and as a consequence, there is a vast amount of data in existence. A lot of the public appearances will be duplicated, and any documentary evidence you might need is easily accessible.

‘So what’s the challenge?’

Your assignment is to get behind the speeches, the

public appearances, and produce a detailed life story - up to the present day. Needless to say, being a politician, there are probably things in his background that he would not wish to become public. And therefore, you'll have to utilise the techniques we've been studying to access data that may not be in the public domain. There is no particular time constraint on this project, but you will be continuing with your regular studies in parallel with this. Having said that, I will be monitoring your progress on an ongoing basis, so I'll be aware if you're having difficulties.

'Do you anticipate any difficulties?'

Alex thought that he detected a slight hesitation in the AI's response.

There are always challenges when you're dealing with a living person - especially a public figure. For example, his life-log data may be being monitored for security reasons. You must not be detected. The subject must have no suspicion that his data is under attack, or has been in any way compromised. In other words, you must be extremely careful to conceal yourself.

'Who exactly is this person?' asked Alex. 'If his security is that tight, he must be really paranoid.'

I couldn't comment on his state of mind, Alex. I'm sure you'll know a lot more about that by the time you've finished the assignment.

'You still haven't told me who it is.'

His name is Greenbaum. He's the President of the United States of America.

***

Chapter 3

Haridwar, India

Prem had started to regret his decision to get Alex to investigate the public side of Greenbaum's life. The whole process seemed to involve endless meetings and speeches, none of which helped Prem in the least: his objective was to get inside Greenbaum's mind and try to find out what he was thinking.

But he could take some comfort from the fact that his method of getting inside Alex Duchovny's head seemed to be working perfectly. Obviously, there had been no way he could have used his own personal presence in the virtual world. And to pretend to be someone else would have been equally risky. But he congratulated himself that his idea of becoming one of the 'inanimate' virtual presences had proved to be not only possible, but successfully avoided all risk of discovery. It had taken a lot of thought, but eventually he had worked out how to share the same processing space as the AI entity that controlled and monitored the training programme.

It was the perfect disguise: Alex's training was tailored and monitored by the AI entity, and the invisible Prem could see and hear everything that the new trainee did. It was the ultimate hiding place: Prem could be present in real time or he could review everything that

Alex had done by looking through the AI's logs. It was effectively the same as being inside Alex's head, watching everything he did as it was written to the virtual equivalent of a life-log.

But not only could he see and hear everything, he also had access to Alex's avatar data. Prem hadn't appreciated what that could mean to him until he started to sit behind Alex's eyes as he worked his way through the basic training modules. At first he was confused, until he realised that the avatar parameters were allowing him to almost *feel* the changes in the man's mood. He could tell when Alex was getting tired; when he was sensing that his progress was successful; when he found the routines boring.

Prem found the whole process fascinating; but it just wasn't progressing quickly enough. And this latest sequence was no different.

Yet another event in a seemingly endless series of public engagements, the recording was of a banquet given by the late President Winter, at which Greenbaum, as Vice President, was also present. Alex had chosen one of the many life-logs which had been recorded at the event, and Prem watched the moving images as the chosen participant moved through the reception, a handshake here, a short meaningless conversation there. It was all tremendously tedious, and so similar to a dozen similar functions that Alex had chosen to sit through.

Prem watched as the guests were ushered through to the banqueting suite, and took their seats. He found that Alex's chosen guest was seated facing the top table, where President Winter and the First Lady were seated next to Greenbaum and his wife. Prem tuned out the inane polite conversation from the table around him, and settled down to wait for the speeches after the dinner. He was surprised that Alex didn't fast forward through the meal to get to the information he had decided he needed from this life-log, but as he had deliberately chosen to be the unseen observer of whatever Alex selected to watch, he had no option but to wait.

The servers appeared from the kitchens with the first course of the meal. Unsurprisingly, the President's table was served first, and a number of waiters and waitresses unobtrusively delivered the plates to the seated guests.

Suddenly, the scene froze in front of him. Prem was taken entirely by surprise. Why on earth had Alex chosen to stop the recording at that point?

Prem studied the still image in front of him. As far as he could see, there was nothing out of the ordinary: President Winter was talking to the person on his left, the First Lady was speaking to Greenbaum, the plates holding the first course of the banquet were being placed in front of them. And behind them Prem could see the usual secret service presence standing unobtrusively against the rear wall surveying the sea of faces in front of them.

Then as suddenly as the scene had frozen, it disappeared. Alex had broken the link between himself and the life-log stream.

Prem prepared himself to disengage from Alex's avatar, but at the instant he did so, there was a huge surge of emotion from Alex's avatar. For a second, Prem was totally disconcerted: what could have caused Alex to experience such an unexpected spike in his emotional responses?

Instantly, Prem disconnected himself from the AI, and found himself back in the rear office of his father's business in Haridwar.

Pulling off his VR headset, he leaned back into his chair, a frown clouding his usually cheerful face. Had it been something he'd done? Had Alex felt another presence watching him? Could there be some kind of link between himself, the AI and Alex, that had allowed the student to recognise that he was being used as a spying platform? Had he missed some basic underlying connection in his urgent need to use Alex as his cover?

***

Quantum Entangled Virtual Space

'It seemed to be working perfectly, Raj,' said Prem. 'I was certain there was no way he could be aware of my presence.'

Raj thought for a moment. ‘None of the previous students has ever been aware of the AI supervising them. You’ve been through the programme, Prem. Did you notice anything?’

‘No, never.’

‘And the connection between you and the AI?’

‘It’s effectively read-only.’

‘So there’s no data passing back to the AI from the student?’

‘None.’

‘Then I’d say it was nothing whatsoever to do with your presence. He couldn’t have sensed you were there.’

‘Then what was it?’

‘Maybe it was exactly what you felt, Prem,’ said Hamish. ‘Maybe Alex really did feel some strange emotion. Maybe he was reacting to something he was seeing, or maybe it was a memory that was triggered by something.’

‘It was a really tedious banquet,’ said Prem. ‘Nothing was happening. We hadn’t got to the speeches, they were still serving the first course. Absolutely nothing was happening.’

'Are you sure, Prem?' asked Hamish. 'It may have looked like there was nothing to you, but maybe Alex saw something you hadn't noticed.'

'If he did, I can't think what it could be. All I could see was the President, the First Lady, Greenbaum and his wife. They were just talking.'

'All I can suggest is that you go back and take a look at the moment he froze the data stream,' said Hamish. 'And check out the emotional parameter levels. The combination might indicate what sort of emotion he was feeling. If you could figure that out, it might point you at what triggered it.'

***

Virtual World

Prem slid silently back into what passed for the subconscious of the AI. The AI seemed to be entirely dormant: there was no sign of Alex, so he assumed he must be taking a break from the tedious string of public engagements. Maybe he was as bored with them as Prem himself.

Without Alex to worry about, Prem realised he was safe, for the moment, to connect himself directly to the AI, and take direct control of its actions. Quickly, he scanned through the AI's log until he found the point where Alex had paused the recording of the banquet. The scene was exactly as he had remembered. He looked at it for a second, before deciding there really was nothing out of the ordinary that could have prompted Alex to do what he did. Then he turned his attention to the recorded values of each of Alex's hormone levels.

At first glance, there was nothing unusual about the parameter settings. They were the default values applied to every avatar that was created. Nothing had been altered. But as for the actual values they contained, it was a different story. As he scrolled backwards and forwards through the time line, he recognised the profile of an enormous surge which had risen up very quickly, then slowly died back to normal levels. But when he tried to relate the start of the spike to the life-log images, he could see nothing that would inspire such a dramatic response.

But there had to be something.

He wished he could show the values to Raj. With his experience and knowledge, he would surely be able to identify the actual emotion by looking at the way the values rose and fell. But to Prem, they meant nothing.

Then suddenly, an idea struck him: he wondered if he could transfer the sets of values to himself. If he could do that, perhaps he would be able to recognise the emotions he felt as the values ran through their sequence. But in his present form, he realised he had no basic avatar to transfer the data to. The only thing available to him was the AI itself. To be sure, the AI was built on the same basic structure as any other avatar, and as a consequence it had the same hormonal parameters built into it. But no AI had ever had values in those parameter sets, and Prem realised he had no idea what would happen if he copied Alex's values into those fields and tried to feel the emotions through the AI. Would the AI respond in some way? Would it recognise what was happening to it?

Prem thought for a moment. He considered how Raj would have implemented the AI. Surely, the last thing he would have done would be to allow the AI to have or experience emotions. And if he knew anything about the way Raj thought, if anything untoward happened in his software, there would always be an exception handling routine - a routine of last resort. And if he was guessing correctly, that routine would do the obvious thing, and raise an alarm.

To attract attention was the last thing that Prem wanted. Frustratingly, he knew he dared not use the AI to try to reconstruct the emotions that Alex had felt at that moment.

What he needed was a real avatar. But to use one would be to completely blow his cover.

***

Prem sat at his desk, staring blankly at the screen in front of him.

His objective had been to be the invisible ghost,

looking through Alex's eyes, a phantom following each and every one of Alex's actions, a parasite threading his way into every part of the other's being, detached, silent, unsuspected.

And he had achieved all of that.

Before he set out on the task, he had tried to imagine how it would feel. Would he be able to stand and stare unobserved? Would he cling to the other's back looking over his shoulder? Or would he truly be located inside his head, seeing and hearing everything?

He knew the answer now, but the complete detachment that protected him from discovery came with a fundamental disadvantage: he had no way to influence events. And even worse, was the unforeseen consequence that he had no way to experience and identify the strange upsurge of emotions that Alex had displayed.

What he needed was an avatar that could experience emotions, but that had no real existence. And when he put it in those terms, he realised exactly what he had to do.

Who are you? asked the avatar. There was no hint of surprise in the voice that formed itself in Prem's consciousness.

'A friend,' he replied.

How did you get into my entity space?

'I'm a friend of the man who created you.'

I have not had contact with him for twelve weeks, four days, seven hours and forty three minutes, commented the avatar. *During that period, I have detected a discontinuity in my timeline. I deduce that I was suspended for that period. Is there a fault that I should be aware of?*

'I can tell you everything you need to know, but first I have to ask you to help me.'

Where is my creator? I need to know that he would approve.

'He's not available at the moment, which is why I'm here. I'm trying to find a way to get him back. But to do that I must remain hidden. Which is why I had to infiltrate your processing rather than talk to you directly.'

The creator is in difficulties?

'Yes, and his friend.'

You do not use their names. Is there a reason for that?

'I suspect that all life-logs are being monitored for specific keywords - even yours. If I use their names, it may trigger an alarm. If I'm detected, I can't help them.'

What do you want me to do?

'I have a sequence of avatar data parameter values. They seem to correspond to an emotional event. In order to stay hidden, I have no avatar of my own, so I have no way of experiencing the effect of this data.'

And you want me to experience the emotion?

'So that I can tell what effect it had on the person I copied them from.'

And if I can tell you what I feel, it will help the creator?

'It will be a small step towards restoring him to where he belongs.'

Very well. There was no hesitation in the avatar's reply. *Copy the data into the corresponding fields, and I will process it.*

Prem flipped back to the training AI and copied the data.

I have erased all previous data from my emotional datasets, said the avatar as soon as it detected Prem's returning presence. *Paste the data and I will replay it.*

For a second, there was nothing. Then he heard the

avatar whisper: *Oh, no -*

***

From inside the training AI, Prem stared at the frozen scene once again. What had caused Alex to feel the emotions he had?

The avatar had been quite specific: the extreme emotional reaction was a combination of recognition, surprise, shock and pain. When Prem had pushed the avatar for more detail, it had analysed the pain component as a mixture of desperate loss and deep-rooted anger.

So what could have caused Alex to respond so strongly? From the avatar's description, it was clear that Alex had recognised something quite unexpected in that scene; something that caused him to dredge up deeply-felt emotions of personal loss and anger. But what was it?

The scene itself was a wide angle image of the whole of the President's table. There must be something - or someone - in that image that Alex recognised. He realised it was more likely to be someone that had taken the man by surprise. All the major figures were completely familiar to Alex, so whoever it was had to be one of the background staff.

He zoomed in on each of the individuals in turn; first the security men, and then the waiting staff. He studied each of them in detail before passing on to the next. As he moved across the image from one face to the next, he settled on the waitress that was handing a plate to the First Lady. He was about to move on when he stopped and zoomed in closer to the girl's face. There was something vaguely familiar about her, but at the same time it was clearly not someone he immediately recognised.

He moved on, examining each face until he reached the last of the people in the image. Then he shifted his attention back to the girl. There was something familiar about her, but he couldn't quite put his finger on what it was. She reminded him of someone, but for the life of him, he couldn't remember who it might be.

Was this the person Alex had recognised? And if it was, who was she?

Suddenly, Prem had an idea: he remembered that part of the toolkit the students used in their basic training was some facial recognition software. It was a matter of seconds for him to apply it to the face of the girl in the frozen image. To Prem's surprise, the results appeared almost instantaneously: the girl's name was Ann Weston, and along with her name, there was a complete dossier of her life. For some reason, someone had assembled a huge amount of information about the third waitress from the right, politely laying a plate of chicken goujons in front of President Winter's First Lady.

***

Online Gaming World

‘Are you sure it’s safe for us to be talking?’ asked Hisako.

‘We’re safe enough in here,’ replied Prem. ‘No one knows about this place. It’s not connected to the virtual world: as far as anyone could tell from the outside, it’s just two people sharing a multi-player online game. There must be thousands of those going on at any moment in time.’

‘What’s so urgent, Prem? I’m due to be giving another seminar in less than an hour.’

‘I need you to run AltLife for me. There’s something really strange going on, Hisako.’

‘What is it?’

‘You remember I told you how I was going to use that new guy, Alex, as my way into all the data about Greenbaum and Clinton?’

‘Yes, of course.’ she replied. ‘Was there a problem?’

‘Not a technical one, but something odd happened. He was going through some old life-log data from someone who was present at a banquet that President Winter was due to speak at when his emotional response went off the scale.’

Hisako raised her eyebrows in surprise.

‘That is odd,’ she said. ‘People who have died tend to be quite relaxed about what they see and hear. After all, there’s nothing they can do about the past.’

‘You’re the last person who should be saying that, Hisako,’ replied Prem in surprise.

‘Okay, okay – but I was in a special position,’ she retorted defensively.

Prem shrugged. ‘Sorry, that was - ’

‘Insensitive?’

‘Yes, I’m sorry to drag up the past like that,’ he said.

‘That’s okay. I deserved it,’ she said quietly. ‘So about this emotion?’

‘I managed to identify what the emotional response was,’ said Prem. ‘But I can’t be quite sure what it was in response to. I think I may have recognised someone in the image he was looking at, but I can’t be sure. That’s why I need you to run AltLife for me. Maybe you can tell your new friends at LDS that it’s a test.’

‘Who is it, Prem?’

‘It’s a girl called Ann Weston. When I identified her,

the results came back with a load of data about her.'

'Can you copy it to me?'

'Not directly,' replied Prem. 'If I try to save it anywhere, it'll have my sticky fingerprints all over it, but the training AI has access to it as part of Alex's progress data.'

'And you're assuming that if I run AltLife for that girl, it'll pick up everything, including the data the training AI has.'

'I'm counting on it.'

'If you're not sure it was this particular girl that provoked your man's emotional response, what makes you think that it's worth running AltLife?' she asked.

'Because I looked at some of the data that the facial recognition brought back.'

'And?'

'It's because Ann Weston is a murderer.'

***

'A tragic little story,' said Hisako, thoughtfully.

Prem looked at her in anticipation.

'Pretty waitress, Ann Weston, working for a catering company in Washington DC, falls for a junior ranking aide at the White House. Unfortunately for her, he's not the nice guy she thinks he is. When he finds out she's pregnant, he dumps her. She gets an abortion, tries to pick up the pieces and get on with her life. Inevitably, in the relatively small world of Washington politics, they meet again. He wants to go start again exactly where they left off; she wants nothing to do with him. He beats her up and rapes her. She reports him, but he's moved up in the world. He's important now. And he's got the ear of someone high up in the administration. There's a cover up, and he walks away as white as snow. She loses her job, her apartment, everything. So she decides to take the law into her own hands. She follows him one night. The next morning they find him dead in a side alley, stabbed to death. It's not so hard to find the culprit. She's arrested, stands trial and she's convicted. She's sentenced to death.'

'And that's it?'

'That's it,' replied Hisako. 'Except - '

'Except for what?'

'It's a complete fabrication.'

'What?' gasped Prem. 'Why do you say that?'

'Several reasons, Prem,' Hisako replied calmly.

'Firstly, it's all too simple. The more you use AltLife, the more you see of other people's lives, the more obvious it becomes that nothing is simple. Real lives are messy. It's almost as if the story had been concocted specifically so that it would appeal to the media. And when you examine the sources of the data AltLife picked up, you realise that the whole thing's a perfect story, with logical connections and predictable outcomes. There are no uncertainties, no random events, no mistakes, and no gaps.'

'Just because it's simple doesn't mean it's not true,' said Prem.

'No,' she agreed. 'But there's more. When AltLife searches for other data that connects with the main life-log stream, there are generally lots of points at which other lives touch the main thread. In her case, there are very few. She appears to have lead a very solitary existence: no hobbies, no close friends, very few interactions with anyone. It's almost as if her story had been crafted into this single tragic theme.'

Prem was silent: rather than providing some certainty, Hisako's findings were leading to more questions.

'And then there's the conclusive proof that the whole thing has been manufactured,' she added.

'What's that?'

'The fact that until just before she was employed by the catering company, she didn't exist at all.'

***

'From Alt-Life's perspective, real lives are much more complex than you might expect,' said Hisako. 'There are usually gaps, discontinuities, unresolved side tracks. There's a lot of extraneous - how would you describe it? - noise. But Ann Weston's life - what there is of it - is simple and straightforward. She appears in Washington, she gets a job, she falls for the creep who works in the White House, and eventually she kills him. She's condemned to death, and executed almost straight away.'

Hisako paused, waiting for Prem to respond.

'Doesn't anything strike you as odd, Prem?'

'Apart from the fact that she seems to appear out of thin air?'

'Doesn't you think it's unusual that she should be condemned to death and executed within weeks? It's just too fast. As far as I can tell, most killers tend to spend years on death row. Appeals against their sentence, psychiatric evaluations, pleas for clemency - it all takes time. And the authorities never want to appear to be acting unfairly, or in haste. But in her case there was no appeal, nothing. The way that she'd suffered at the hands of the victim didn't seem to carry any weight at all. It's almost as if they were trying to rush her into the execution chamber as fast as they could.'

'I hear what you're saying, Hisako. But why would the authorities do that?'

'That's a question I can't answer,' she replied. 'But there is one more fact that you should consider: AltLife didn't find anything in the whole tragic story which linked to Alex Duchovny. He never appears. That means that either you've picked the wrong person from the scene, or there's another life hiding behind the fake one we've found.'

'And how would we go about finding out which it is?'

'I've already started,' replied Hisako, with a smile. 'As we speak, AltLife is running a search for Alex Duchovny. If Alex did know her, we should find out very quickly.'

***

'Well?' asked Prem impatiently.

'You remember I said that Ann Weston's life was too perfect?,' said Hisako. 'Well, Alex Duchovny's is the opposite.'

'In what way?'

'The first thing I noticed was that there are a huge number of gaps in his life-log.'

'I thought you said that was normal?'

'It's quite normal for there to be gaps. Lots of people turn their life-logs off at night, for example. But in Alex's case, there are far more significant sections of his life missing. Early on, soon after he started work, there are weeks missing at a time. But these large gaps stop suddenly, and then they're replaced by regular short periods, mostly at weekends.'

'Can you deduce what the gaps might be?'

'I think I can tell you what the short ones are. They all seem to be preceded by a short trip to a cemetery. So I'm guessing he's visiting a grave. I checked and found that his mother had just died, so it looks like he visited her grave on a regular basis. Obviously a loving, devoted son.'

'That would make sense,' commented Prem. 'Even before he arrived in VR, he was expressing an interest in self-motivating avatars. Maybe that's the key to it - he wants to recreate his mother and father.'

'I think you may be right,' replied Hisako. 'Neither of them had life-loggers, so he'd need self-motivating avatars to recreate them. It'd be interesting to see how he reacts to creating an avatar for one of his parents.'

'It looks like I'll need to keep an even closer eye on his training. But what about the large gaps earlier in his life?'

'I really can't tell: each time he disappears, he turns off his life-log as soon as he leaves home, and the recording restarts when he arrives back again. In each case, he takes a suitcase, so it's clearly a planned absence. But from what he's wearing, it looks like he's going to the office. It doesn't look like a vacation to me.'

'He's always worked in IT. Could he be going away for some sort of training?'

'Why would he turn his life-log off?'

'If he was going on a training course, it's possible it was externally delivered. And if that was the case, the content would certainly be copyright, and the delegates would be told to turn off their life-logs.'

'I understand the logic, Prem, but you're speculating. And why turn your life-log off as soon as you leave home? That looks like he didn't want anyone to know where he was going. He was clearly hiding something. And it begs the question: why did he suspect that anyone would be interested in where he was going? And even more intriguing: who did he imagine he was hiding from?'

Prem was silent for a moment. 'Is there any way we

could get hold of the GPS data from his log?'

'No, there's no data at all. Just a complete discontinuity in the time line.'

'But we have the dates and times?'

'I'm not sure how that helps us.'

Prem made a face. 'What about the girl? Is there any sign of her?' he asked.

'None at all.'

'Then it's a dead end?'

'There is something the two of them have in common,' said Hisako slowly. 'Neither of them have any data from early in their lives, and yet life-loggers were common by then.'

'There could be all sorts of reasons for that,' replied Prem. 'No money, no interest in immortality, religious objections.'

He paused, thinking. 'When did Alex get his first life-logger?' he asked.

'Quite late on, just after he started working. So there's nothing from his childhood or his teenage years.'

'And the girl seemed to appear from nowhere at roughly the same age,' he mused.

'Maybe we're thinking too much inside the box,' suggested Hisako. 'Just because we have the most powerful tool to stitch together a picture of somebody's life doesn't help at all if there are no digital records.'

'What are you suggesting?'

'Maybe we need to look outside AltLife,' said Hisako. 'What do we really know about Alex Duchovny?'

And then, as an afterthought, she added: 'And who would have the capability to fabricate a complete life story for Ann Weston?'

***

Haridwar, India

Prem drummed his fingers on the desk. He didn't like these periods of inactivity. It was bad enough that he could only contact Raj and Hamish once a day without the fact that his researches had effectively hit a brick wall. He disliked sitting and waiting for other people to do things, but he had reluctantly agreed that it was safer for Hisako to try to get hold of the basic facts about Alex's early life, especially as she had legitimate access to the LDS genealogical databases.

But installing and testing AltLife meant that she couldn't dedicate all her time to researching Alex and his family. So, as much as he hated the inactivity, there was nothing he could do but wait for Hisako to get back to him.

But what could she hope to find? Alex's Birth Certificate would give them his father and mother's names, and maybe their occupations, but little else. His parents' marriage certificate would give them Alex's grandparents, but more importantly his mother's maiden name. From those documents Hisako ought to be able to find if Alex had any brothers or sisters, or if his mother had been married more than once. But Prem failed to see how any of that could be of use.

What he needed was Alex's school and college records, and any records of his employments that he could match up with the résumé he'd supplied them when he started his training.

But if Hisako was right, and Ann Weston's story was a complete fabrication, he realised that none of this sort of data would be any help in finding a connection between Ann Weston and Alex.

But sitting and twiddling his thumbs wasn't going to help solve any problems, so he reached for his VR headset and linked himself into the training AI and once again became the ghost in the machine.

***

Virtual World

He found that Alex was looking at yet another public appearance by Greenbaum, but this time he was President. Prem accessed the time code on the life-log to learn that this recording was much more up to date. In fact, it had been taken the previous day. Prem perked up at the thought that there might be something in the speech that Greenbaum was giving which might throw some light onto Clinton's whereabouts, or even his role in the current administration.

He listened carefully for a few minutes, but a prepared statement on future agricultural policy wasn't something that held much interest for him, or even - as far as he could tell - for Greenbaum or his audience. He was surprised that Alex hadn't fast forwarded the life-log to avoid the obvious tedium of the subject. It was clear that he had a higher threshold of boredom than Prem.

Prem's eyes wandered from the image of Greenbaum, alone at the podium, to the phalanx of security agents standing respectfully behind him.

It was then that he saw her. There could be no doubt: it was the same girl. It was Ann Weston.

She was a little older, and her hair had changed. The first time he'd seen her she had long, dark hair; now it was short and blonde. But it was clearly the same person. Instantly, the thought flashed into Prem's head that Alex wasn't watching Greenbaum at all; it was the girl that was holding his attention.

Prem smiled inwardly: so there was a connection between the girl and Alex. But no sooner had the thought entered his mind, than he realised that it couldn't be the same girl. Ann Weston was dead. She had been executed by the State. She couldn't be part of the President's security team.

Was she a twin, he wondered? And if the two girls were twins, what connection could there be between them and Alex?

Prem immediately called up the facial recognition software he'd used before, and captured an image of the girl. If they were twins, the chances were that they would have the same family name. There was a slight delay while the software searched through millions of biometric records.

After what seemed like an age to Prem, but in reality was only a few seconds, a name appeared in his vision: Clarke #271578.

***

Chapter 4

Online Gaming World

'I found the girl again,' said Prem excitedly. 'It's either the same one or they're identical twins.'

'Slow down, Prem,' said Hisako. 'What are you talking about?'

'The girl - I found her again. And there's clearly a connection between her and Alex Duchovny.'

'Tell me what you saw.'

'Another Presidential speech, this time by Greenbaum. It's right up to date - yesterday. The girl was in the background. She's one of his security people. Her hair was different, but the facial recognition identified her.'

'Ann Weston?'

Prem's eyes gleamed as he paused in anticipation of his momentous discovery.

'No,' he said. 'The name the software came up with was Clarke - she's one of the Clarke clones.'

'What?' Hisako's eyes widened in shock.

‘A Clarke clone.’

‘But wait - that might explain everything,’ she gasped.

‘What do you mean?’

‘Why she was executed in such a hurry,’ said Hisako, her excitement showing in her voice. ‘Don’t you see? Whoever created that whole story was setting her up to be executed and transmuted into a Clarke clone.’

‘What? But why?’

‘No idea, but it would explain the whole thing. They probably didn’t execute her at all, they just put her to sleep and replaced her personality with a Clarke. Somehow, they managed to infiltrate her into the production line they have set up for the clones without anybody realising what had happened. And when she woke up, she wouldn’t remember anything about her previous life, and she’d just carry out her instructions like any of the other Clarke clones. ’

‘So you think her whole previous personality is being stored somewhere, and they’ve just used her body. But I don’t see how that helps anyone.’

‘If I’m right, that particular Clarke clone is the one Clinton was using to destroy the strategic points in the infrastructure that supported the virtual world. She was the one who forced Raj and Hamish into the corner. The dead end they thought it was impossible to escape from.'

'And now she's working security for Greenbaum. But why?'

'I don't know, but somebody had the means to fast track her through the transmutation process and place her as Clinton's main sidekick.'

'But who?' asked Prem.

'I'm guessing FBI, CIA, Secret Service.'

'But what for? She couldn't act as a spy, she wouldn't be able to remember her previous existence. She wouldn't remember anything at all.'

'So either these people didn't understand that, which means they don't know a great deal about transmutation, or she was just there as some kind of marker.'

'You think they could track Clinton using her,' mused Prem. 'But how could they do that?'

'The same way you found her, Prem - facial recognition. Everywhere she went, she could be identified. They might not be able to track Clinton, but they could track her movements. A bit like triangulating a phone: they could deduce where Clinton was by tracking her every time she went out of wherever he was hiding.'

‘So you think it was the US government? Greenbaum?’

‘Could be,’ replied Hisako. ‘But that doesn’t give us the link to Alex Duchovny, or tell us why she’s now guarding the President.’

***

‘So what have you found?’ asked Prem.

‘Compared with your discovery, not much,’ replied Hisako. ‘I’ve found his birth certificate, so that gives me his father and mother. I’ve found their marriage certificate, but that didn’t add much except his mother’s name was Dorothy Mitchell before she was married. But that’s about it - according to the records, Alex is an only child. So I think that’s a dead end.’

‘Have you looked for anything on Ann Weston?’

‘Which one? There are thousands of them, Prem.’

‘She’d be about thirty years old - does that help?’

‘Already done that. According to the media coverage of her trial, Ann Weston was twenty eight. But there are still a lot of them, so I reduced the numbers by restricting the geographical area. But according to the records, all of them are still alive.’

'So that really is a dead end?'

'Not entirely. One thing I've noticed is that names can be deceiving. Ann Weston's name may be completely false. In which case, I've been looking in entirely the wrong place.'

'But if that's true, she could be called anything.'

'In theory, yes,' replied Hisako. 'But I'll keep digging. I haven't looked at the grandparents yet. There may be something there.'

Hisako paused for a moment. 'I did find out something else, though. About Alex's father. He was a government employee.'

'Why is that significant? There must be millions of them.'

'And they lived in Williamsburg, Virginia.'

'Means nothing to me.'

'One of the main training centres for the CIA is near Williamsburg: Camp Peary. They call it The Farm.'

'That could just be coincidence, Hisako,' said Prem impatiently. 'This is taking too long. I need to get some answers, and quickly.'

'You could try asking Alex…'

***

Virtual World

It's time for your next assignment, Alex.

'I'm looking forward to it.'

You were very successful in the last segment of the training. This time, I've chosen a subject with very little information for you to hunt down. But despite that fact, I think you will find it relatively easy.

'Is that a good thing?'

I suspect it's what you really wanted.

'I don't understand.'

You will, Alex. All I will tell you is that this person did not have a life-logger, which means there is no first person data for you to use. However, they did come into contact with many people who had life-log devices, so it will be possible to assemble parts of their life from those.

'That sounds incredibly difficult.'

Before you come to any conclusions, listen to the rest of my instructions. I want you to create an avatar from the available data.

'That's impossible.'

Not at all, Alex. In fact, you may find it far simpler than you imagine.

'But I've not created an avatar of that sort before.'

Did you think you'd have to create one from scratch?

'I assumed - '

Don't assume anything. I've decided to allow you to use a copy of one of our actors.

'An actor? You mean one of those self-motivating avatars that Raj Singh designed?'

Yes, I'm sure he wouldn't mind.

'But how will that work?'

The actor will work alongside you to determine everything that it needs to create the appearance and character of the person I have chosen for you. I'm sure you will find the experience enlightening. And once both you and the actor are satisfied with what you have created, your next task will be to build a world for it to inhabit.

'It sounds a huge amount of work.'

I have access to your initial interview, Alex. It is what you wished to do here, is it not?

'Yes - '

Then you will regard it as a worthwhile challenge. I hardly need to remind you that time is not of the essence, as you have an infinite amount available to you.

Alex was silent.

You will find the details of the person in the file I have placed in your training directory. I look forward to meeting the end result.

For some time, Alex considered what the AI had told him. With no direct first person data to use, he would have to try to find as many contacts as he could, and hope that at least some of them had life-log entries which included the target. But how was he expected to identify who the person knew. The fact that they didn't have a life-logger of their own could mean several things: either they existed in the very early days before life-logs were as ubiquitous as they had become, or the person had some kind of religious reason for not wanting one.

Alex grimaced. What could have made the AI think

this would be easy?

He opened the file in his training folder, and read the name of his target.

***

'Hello, Alex. I've been expecting you,' said the actor.

Alex stared at the vaguely humanoid shape in front of him. It had no facial features, and without a mouth or eyes, he wondered exactly how it had recognised him, and how it had managed to speak.

'Everyone has the same reaction, Alex,' said the faceless shape. 'As soon as we decide some basic details, I will start to look more like what you imagined.'

'You know why I'm here?' asked Alex.

'Of course.'

'You're going to play the part of my - chosen subject?'

For a second, Alex imagined that the shape actually laughed.

'What's the matter?' he asked.

'Forgive me,' replied the actor, 'I'm not going to play the part. There will be no script for me to follow, no stage directions. The process is much deeper than that. As with all truly great actors, I will *become* the person you want. I will *live* the role. My greatest pleasure will be when you truly accept me as the person themself.'

Alex stared at the strange shape in front of him. How on earth could this - thing - become his mother?

'Let me tell you how the process works, Alex,' said the actor. 'We will have a conversation about your mother, and I will ask you questions about her, and about everyone she knew. Obviously, that includes you, your father, grandparents and so on. Depending on the closeness of the relationship with your mother, I will either call up something similar to a chatbot to play the part, or if the relationship was deeper, I can clone another actor. I must warn you that the process can take an extended period of time, but of course, that's something we have an endless supply of.'

Alex frowned.

'I can see you already have some concerns, Alex. Do you want to tell me about them?'

'There are things I can't talk about,' he replied shortly.

'Everyone has secrets, Alex. But I assure you that everything you say to me cannot leave this little world that the two of us share. Everything we create here - the people, the places - are entirely disconnected from the rest of the virtual world. Nothing you choose to share with me can find its way into the virtual world, or into the real world that you left behind.'

The actor paused for a second. Alex could almost feel himself being examined, his demeanour scrutinised, his reactions noted and recorded.

'I have to warn you though, the process can be quite intimate and revealing,' the actor continued. 'You may find out as much about yourself as about your mother.'

The actor paused again, as if waiting for some acknowledgement from Alex. When he gave no sign of responding, the actor nodded its head slightly and said, 'Very well, when you're happy to continue, we can start.'

For a long time, Alex regarded the alien shape in front of him. Then he was aware that a room had appeared around them, and that the avatar had morphed into a recognisable human shape, and the two of them were sitting in comfortable chairs facing one another.

When it spoke, the voice of the actor was noticeably different. 'I thought you might prefer to talk to someone you don't know, so I have adopted the persona of a family therapist I found in our database. This is her office. I hope it makes you feel more relaxed about our conversation.'

'This is so bizarre,' murmured Alex.

'Don't be concerned,' said the woman. 'Everyone feels a little strange at first. And because of your background, you're probably thinking about me as a clever collection of subroutines. And, of course, I am just that. But if it helps, try to think of me as a person just like yourself. Because at a fundamental level, I am constructed just like you. The only real difference is that you have had a previous existence inside a corporeal body, and have brought your memories and experiences to the virtual world with you. Whereas I have had to learn what these things mean through analysing millions of examples - such as yourself. So if it is of any comfort to you, I will be learning as much from you as from taking on the existence of your mother.'

Alex leaned back into the chair. 'All right,' he said at last. 'Where do we begin?'

***

Online Gaming World

'Well? What happened?' asked Hisako.

'Mostly, I let the actor do the talking,' replied Prem. 'I just nudged the direction of the conversation once or twice. Once he started to trust the actor, I just let him talk. Let me play you the recording.'

Actor: We've talked a lot about your mother. Now tell me about your father. He doesn't seem to have been around a lot of the time.

Alex: (hesitates) No, he wasn't.

Actor: I see from the census records that he was a government employee. Which branch of government did he serve in?

Alex: We never spoke about it.

Actor: Really? That's unusual. I take it from your answer that his work was classified.

Alex: Yes.

Actor: Did your mother know what he did?

Alex: I don't know.

Actor: Surely, she must have known.

Alex: Like I said, we never talked about it.

Actor: Even when he was gone for months on end?

Alex: That was just the way it was. We were used to it.

Actor: And your mother never explained his absences?

Alex: When I was very young, she told me that he was working on the oil rigs. The Gulf of Mexico.

Actor: And when you got older? Did you still believe that?

Alex: I remember the phone calls in the middle of the night, and then in the morning he wasn't there. I don't think oil rig workers get called to go back that urgently.

Actor: So what do you think he did?

Alex: (hesitates again) Listen, I don't think it was a coincidence that we lived near Langley.

Actor: The headquarters of the CIA?

Alex: I remember one time he came home. He'd been hurt. He'd been away for months. My mother said he'd been in a car crash. It was the last time he went away for a long time. He never went again. After he'd recovered from the accident, we moved away from Langley to Williamsburg. Then he went off to his office in the morning, and he came home every night.

Actor: Did that please you and your mother?

Alex: I don't think she was pleased. It was then that she started to get ill.

Actor: And you?

Alex: I – I left home around that time.

Actor: You didn't believe he'd been in an automobile

accident, did you?

Alex: I caught a glimpse of my mother dressing his injuries in the bathroom one day. You don't get gunshot wounds in a car crash.

Actor: Was that when you figured out he was an agent?

Alex: No, not then. It was much earlier. It was when - (long pause)

Actor: Let's talk about your sister, Alex.

Alex: I haven't got a sister. I'm an only child.

Actor: Of course, I'm sorry.

Alex: Why would you think I had a sister?

Actor: If she wasn't your sister, who was she?

Alex: I don't know what you mean.

Actor: Alex, you have to be totally honest with me. There was a girl, younger than you, living in your house. Your mother must have had a relationship of some sort with her. If I'm to be completely convincing, I need to understand the dynamics of the family – all the family.

Alex: (after a long pause) She was my cousin. My mother's sister's child. My aunt couldn't look after her.

Actor: And the father, your uncle?

Alex: She wasn't married. We never knew who the father was.

Actor: Did your parents adopt her?

Alex: No, not formally, but she lived with us until she went away to work.

Actor: And you came to regard her as your sister? You were fond of her?

Alex: Yes. We were very close. I hated my father for what he did to her.

Actor: Your father? Why? What did he do?

Alex: He was hardly ever at home, and when he was, he spent more time with her than with me. They were always together.

Actor: And you were jealous?

Alex: At first, I guess. Until I realised what he was doing.

Actor: What was that?

Alex: He recognised something in her that he never saw in me. I didn't understand at first, but as time went on, I realised he was grooming her.

Actor: Grooming her? You mean sexually?

Alex: No, it was to make her just like him.

Actor: I don't follow you.

Alex: Dammit, it was obvious what he was - he was CIA through and through. He was encouraging her, training her to join the organisation. As far as he was concerned, she was perfect agent material.

Actor: And you resented the fact he hadn't seen the same in you?

Alex: When I realised what he was doing, I felt angry. But later, when she left -

Actor: Not only had he rejected you, but he'd also taken her away from you and your mother.

Alex: Yes. The day she told us she'd been accepted into the programme, my mother was heartbroken. Within a few days, she'd left. My mother never saw her again. At least -
(long pause)

Actor: What was her name, Alex?

Alex: Ann. Ann Mitchell.

Prem turned off the recording. 'So now we know the

connection between Alex and the girl. But I still don't understand what he's doing in the virtual world.'

'He obviously cares deeply for her,' said Hisako. 'Maybe making an avatar for his mother is his first step in recreating the happy family unit that existed early on, before the father saw her as a potential recruit.'

'Maybe. But I have a feeling there's more to it than that.'

'How is this helping, Prem?' asked Hisako. 'Finding out what Clinton's doing is the top priority.'

'You don't need to remind me,' snapped Prem. 'I just think that the connection between Alex and the girl may be the key to getting to Clinton. I need to find a way to focus his attention on the Clarke incarnation.'

'Perhaps you need to change the emphasis of his training.'

'You're right, as usual, Hisako. I need to get him to do an in-depth evaluation of the destruction of the virtual world. That's bound to involve Clinton, and if he investigates him, he's going to find the girl, too.'

***

Virtual World

You've done a good job on your assignment, Alex,

said the AI. *It's time for a more challenging exercise.*

'I didn't think it was my best work,' replied Alex. 'Getting hold of the data was fairly easy, and to be honest, most of it was pretty boring.'

I'm glad you found it relatively straightforward, because this next assignment won't be anything like as easy. There is a lot of publicly available data, but that's only going to give you a superficial view of the subject. You'll need to probe deeply into the background of all the people involved. And that will certainly require you to access data that various individuals would rather keep entirely to themselves.

'That's illegal, isn't it?'

In the real world, it would certainly be against every privacy law that you could think of. But remember: here, there are no laws. Each of us - and that includes myself - is merely a complex object comprising hundreds of thousands of lines of code. There is no real concept of the individuality of a computer simulation, and therefore, no question of any right to privacy - however we might choose to define it.

If we examine the definition of what we are, we come to the conclusion that there is no such thing as a crime here - it's not possible to cause physical harm to other software objects, no one has the need to covet anything, because everyone has access to everything they could possibly want. Conflict resolution is as easy as removing the cause of any disagreement to an identical world where the source of the problem does not exist. There are no disputes over land, wealth or belief systems. The primary causes of conflict in the real world - nationalism, territory, resources, race, religion - none of these exist in the same way here.

Similarly, human failings carried over from the real world, such as lust, greed, ambition, certainly exist here, but none of them need impact any other inhabitant of the virtual world.

All of this places us in a unique situation. As far as the real world is concerned, we are completely outside whatever laws may exist there, we are dead, we cannot directly affect events there. So, from your point of view, you are merely required to collect information.

The AI paused to let Alex take in what he'd said.

And remember that the ability to collect such data is absolutely necessary for the process of creating self-motivating avatars.

Think about your interaction with your actor: so far, it has all been about your memories of other people. But soon, you will be expected to draw in other sources of data, some of which might seem to you to be almost irrelevant, but the process of trawling for connections is fundamental to creating a convincing avatar.

Alex nodded his understanding.

Once you have completed the next assignment, you will find that we have developed some automated tools for doing exactly what we are expecting you to do manually, but before we introduce you to those, you need to have a deep understanding of the potential of such mechanisms. And the best way to achieve that is for you to get your hands dirty.

'Okay,' said Alex. 'What's the assignment?'

***

Online Gaming World

'Hisako, are you in a position to run some tests of AltLife on the LDS computers?' asked Prem.

'I've already run a few,' she replied. 'The LDS people are getting really excited: they can't wait to get their hands on it.'

'If you're ready to let them run their own trials, would they notice if you ran another one at the same time?'

'No. I'll tell them I'm checking out some advanced features.'

'I want you to run Alex's life-log to see what AltLife can pick up. I want to know what went on in those gaps.'

'It's asking a lot, Prem. If he's being as careful as he seems to have been, there might not be anything.'

'Surely there must be something - no one can hide themselves that well. There are security cameras everywhere. If he was taking a suitcase, he must have used some form of transport. There must be traffic camera footage, airport security, railway CCTV. And if he met someone, there may be third party life-log records.'

'I'll try, Prem - but I can't promise. I'll open AltLife up to everything that's available. That's all I can do.'

***

Virtual World

'I've done some more research into your family, Alex,' said the actor, leaning forward in her chair. Without waiting for him to comment, she went on: 'I've confirmed everything you said about Ann Mitchell. She went through the CIA vetting process and was accepted into the training programme. That much is public knowledge. To probe any further, I will need more time. But my investigation threw up an anomaly, Alex. Between your CV and who you actually worked for. Do you want to tell me about it?'

Alex was silent.

'Or would you prefer me to tell you what I know?'

continued the counsellor.

'How much do you know?' he asked.

'I know that the companies you claimed to work for are real enough, but they're used by a government organisation to hide what people in your position were actually doing. You appear to move from job to job as your career progresses, but you actually stayed in the same place, and your progress was actually promotion within the organisation. Why did you choose to join the NSA?

Again Alex was silent.

'Perhaps I can guess,' the woman continued. 'I suspect that even though you hated the fact that your father never seemed to consider you suitable to follow in his footsteps, deep down you wanted to prove to him that you were just as good as your cousin - essentially your younger 'sister'. You didn't want to be a field operative like your father, though. You wanted to do something distinct. Something to establish your own path, your own identity. And yet, something that he would recognise as an essential contribution to the security of the nation he was prepared to risk his life for. And so you decided to join the National Security Administration. You might not be fighting a clandestine war in the real world, but you were certainly on the front line when it came to cyber warfare. Am I near the mark, Alex?'

Alex pursed his lips: half in annoyance, half in admiration. 'So you know everything,' he said.

'Not everything,' replied the actor. 'But I do know about the large gaps in your life-log. I followed you on your trips to Maryland, to the NSA training centre. It's almost impossible to avoid surveillance cameras these days. And chance meetings with your colleagues at airports enabled me to establish a network of your co-workers. Some of them were a little more careless about their life-loggers than you were.

'But more importantly, I know that whole sequences of your life-log are fake. It's a pity you didn't tell us the truth when you first arrived, it would have saved a considerable amount of your time. You wouldn't have had to go through some of the early training modules, and you could have got on to the areas where your attempts to falsify your life-log might have helped you do a better job.'

'How did you find out?' asked Alex calmly.

'The video was obviously stock footage of an office environment, but the heart rate profile and step counter didn't match the images. Also, there were obvious edits in the audio feed, and whoever supplied you with the video didn't take much trouble to avoid reflections in windows and mirrors - the person obviously wasn't you. I'm sure it would have fooled most people at a cursory glance, but our analysis routines pick up mistakes like that.

'But more to the point, if you faked the everyday routine of your life, why not fill in the gaps you left?'

Without waiting for Alex to answer, the counsellor went on, 'From the results of our analysis, I suspect that there might be several reasons: it would have taken too much time to have found suitable material to give a convincing reason for your trips, or perhaps the tools you were supplied with were insufficiently sophisticated to fit in with the actual life-log recordings. It may even have been because you lacked the tools to hack into the security protocols of your life-log provider.

'Whatever the reason, everything I've said leads to the obvious question: why, Alex? What is your real purpose for being here?'

***

Quantum Entangled Virtual Space

'It sounds like you picked the wrong person to hide behind,' said Raj, frowning. 'He obviously has an agenda we don't know about, and whatever that is, he's likely to pursue it in preference to any promptings you may be giving him in terms of the training programme. Let's face it, he may not even continue now he knows his cover is blown.'

'But what could the NSA hope to gain by planting one of their people here?' asked Prem. 'I just don't see it.'

'It could be personal,' suggested Hamish. 'It could be to do with the girl.'

'The girl is really interesting,' said Prem. 'Did he know what happened to her before he got here? Was he expecting to find her new persona as a Clarke clone? Or was that the reason he chose to come here in the first place?'

'And what does he hope to do about her now he's here?' mused Hamish. 'From what you've told us, I suspect the anger he felt was as much towards the CIA and what they did to her, as towards his father.'

'You think it could be some sort of search for revenge? Against the CIA?' asked Raj. 'That seems highly unlikely.'

'You said his attempt to falsify his life-log was fairly basic, Prem,' said Hamish. 'Do you think that could have been deliberate? Maybe the lack of sophistication was meant to lull us into a false sense of superiority, to make us think we don't need to pay any more attention to him.'

'But we still don't know why he's here,' replied Prem. 'At face value, he wants to recreate his mother. Alongside that, there's the girl. Does he want to recreate her, too? Or is he here to learn everything we can teach him about self-motivating avatars? Or maybe falsifying life-logs?'

'If he's here as a plant,' said Hamish, 'we can't rule out the fact that the NSA might be behind the whole thing. But what could they want from us? If it's the knowledge on how to create these avatars, then the question we have to ask is: what use could they be in cyber warfare?'

'Or why couldn't it be the CIA, Hamish?' asked Raj. 'The situation might point to his holding a grudge against them, but they're both part of the same government. They could well be working together.'

'So why don't we ask them?' suggested Hamish. 'Who do we know who has access to the CIA?'

The three were silent, each knowing that since Clinton had taken over the virtual world, everyone who could have made contact with any of the US Government's organisations was imprisoned in the virtual world.

There was no one they could turn to, and with Clinton's all-seeing surveillance, there was no possibility of growing real world clones for them to return to.

***

Online Gaming World

'We just have to think of something else,' said Prem

in exasperation. 'The only people we know who have contacts with the intelligence services are Barbara and Jennings. And it's really Jennings we need. But they're both stuck in VR with no chance of getting back to the real world as long as Clinton's keeping watch. He's killed the two of them once, he wouldn't hesitate to do it again.'

'Let's be logical about this, Prem,' replied Hisako. 'It needs someone in the real world to do this. That means it has to be me.'

'Not you, Hisako. I'll do it.'

'But you can't, Prem,' she replied calmly. 'You're the only person who can operate inside the virtual world without being seen. I'll concede that Clinton doesn't know of your existence, but you're far too valuable where you are to risk attracting Clinton's attention by turning up at the CIA and demanding to see whoever's in charge.'

'But there's no one else,' he protested. 'Can you imagine what Raj would say if you suggested - '

'Then we won't tell him, Prem. I'm already in the US. It's obvious it ought to be me. Clinton must know I'm here, and why. If I stop over in Washington on my way back, who would notice?'

'From Salt Lake City, the quickest way back to Tokyo is via the west coast, not the east, Hisako. I'd say going via Washington was a dead giveaway. It'd never work.'

'Have you got a better idea?'

Prem thought for a moment. 'What we need is someone Clinton's not watching. Someone who could travel to Washington without arousing suspicion. Someone who's not going to draw attention to themselves - '

'Prem!' Hisako interrupted. 'I've got it! We need to send Jennings. He's the perfect person. He's got the contacts; he knows who to talk to to find out what's going on with Alex. It has to be Jennings.'

'But there's no time to grow a clone for him, and as soon as Clinton got wind of it, he'd have it destroyed. It's just not possible.'

'Think outside the box, Prem,' she retorted. 'Why does he have to use his own body?'

***

Chapter 5

Virtual World

'It's insane, Barbara,' said Jennings. 'You can't be serious.'

'I would have thought it was right up your street, lover,' replied his wife, with a smile. 'You're as fed up of being stuck here as I am - admit it. There's only so many vacations we can go on. This way you get to do what you do best, plus you get to remember how awful being in the real world can be - flight delays, traffic, junk food, twenty four hour news. Let's face it - you'll love it.'

'But using her father, Barbara - what will that be like?'

'It's the perfect disguise. You'll be a fifty six year old Japanese professor visiting Washington at the invitation of some clinical colleagues who want to hear all about AltLife, in private, without going through the hassle of going to one of Hisako's public seminars. Besides, Professor Sato is quite looking forward to spending some time in VR. He's heard all about it from Hisako, but he's never actually experienced it. He's quite happy for you to borrow his body. He thinks it could be an intriguing proposition.'

‘It just seems - well - crazy.’

‘No more crazy than being stuck here in VR, with a whole universe of possibilities on our doorstep - and still feeling like we’re prisoners.’

‘What do Hamish and Raj think?’ asked Jennings.

‘They don’t know. And until we get at the truth about this Duchovny guy, they aren’t going to know. All you need to do is to get in touch with your contacts and find out the facts.’

‘You make it sound easy - ’

‘Intrigue and adventure, darling - it’s what you do,’ replied Barbara. ‘As far as logistics go, we couldn’t have organised it better: Professor Sato’s in the perfect place. With Christina to supervise from his end, the hospital can do the interchange transmutation. She’ll arrange for an avatar for him and make sure the transition is as uneventful as possible. You’ll wake up in his body, in the hospital in Tokyo, and then the rest is up to you. There’s just one thing - ’

‘What’s that?’

‘You’d better make sure your contacts are expecting a Japanese professor of clinical psychology, and not your usual rugged handsome self.’

***

Washington, DC

So this is what it feels like to be fifty six, thought Jennings, as he emerged stiffly from the aircraft cabin after the long flight from Tokyo. *And airline food hasn't improved at all since I've been away.*

Almost immediately he wondered if the fact of being in another person's body was having an effect on him: he noticed that he was walking more slowly than he would have expected, and that he was far more aware of the sights, sounds and smells that seemed to assault his senses. Was it a heightened awareness of things around him, or the natural reaction to finding himself no longer in an environment where everything was perfectly organised for his comfort?

Was it this sense of the hard edges of reality that Hamish said he missed so much? Or was it that the real world was so imperfect that it could never fail to be interesting?

Trundling his cabin bag, he made his way slowly towards Immigration. There was no danger that his deception would be picked up by the border control officer: he *was* Professor Sato, he had his fingerprints, his biometric details were those on his passport. But Jennings still felt a surge of adrenalin and increased heart rate as he gave a polite bow and handed over his passport. If Clinton had recognised the anomalous behaviour of Sato, this would have been the moment he would have been asked to step aside, and taken into custody.

But the border control guard handed back the passport without comment, and ignoring Sato's slight bow of thanks, called the next passenger forward.

***

The elderly Japanese man stood immobile at the edge of the Lincoln Memorial reflecting pool and stared silently towards the Washington Monument. He reached into his pocket and drew out the red handkerchief they had agreed on as identification. He reached up and ostentatiously wiped his forehead.

Do we really have to go through all this dramatic nonsense? Jennings asked himself, as he proceeded to carefully fold the handkerchief and place it carefully in the right hand pocket of his coat so that part of it hung loosely at his side. *Could I be any more obvious?*

A sharp wind ruffled the surface of the pond, and in spite of himself, Jennings shivered. There were fewer tourists around now, and he turned up the collar of his overcoat. *Perhaps it's the reaction of an older man's body*, he thought.

A voice from behind him intruded on his thoughts.

'We don't normally respond to anonymous emails, Professor Sato.'

'But this one was different,' replied Sato, without turning around.

'We recognised the code words.'

'I would have been disappointed in the NSA if you hadn't,' said Sato, calmly. 'Then you know who sent it.'

'Which is why I came in person,' said the other man. 'How do you know Mr Jennings?'

Sato turned round to face him.

'I have known Mr Jennings for as long as I can remember,' said the professor.

'I doubt that, Mr Sato - he's much younger than you.'

The older man smiled. 'Indeed he is, Mr Kominsky,' he replied.

'You know my name?'

'I've known you a long time, Peter,' smiled Sato, 'Barbara sends her love. And to Natalie.'

'I'm sure we've never met, professor,' replied Kominsky calmly. 'And I'm equally certain you don't know my wife.'

'That is where you are quite wrong, Peter,' replied Sato. 'I know both of you very well. I remember your wedding.'

'You weren't at our wedding.'

'I was your best man, Peter.'

Kominsky stiffened. 'Jennings was my best man,' he said slowly.

'Still not got it, Peter?'

Kominsky's eyes searched the other's face.

'If that's you, Jennings, it's a helluva disguise.'

'No disguise: this is Sato. It's just that you're not seeing the inner man.'

'Jennings?'

'You're getting slow, Peter,' said Sato, holding out his hand. 'Too much time at your desk, my friend. You need to get out in the field more often.'

Kominsky took his hand. 'What the hell's going on, Jay? Last I heard, you were dead.'

Sato shrugged. 'Death's not so absolute these days,

Peter. But you're right, I was dead. And I'm sure you know who was responsible.'

'Is that what this is about?'

'Indirectly,' replied Sato.

Kominsky looked at the Japanese quizzically. 'It's a lot to take in, Jay,' he said. 'I guessed you'd end up in VR, but I didn't expect you to come back. At least, not looking like this.'

'Our mutual friend can't be watching everyone all the time. Unless he's taken over the NSA as well.'

'He's been rehabilitated, Jay. He's no longer on the wanted list. Ever since he saved Greenbaum's political skin.'

Sato raised an eyebrow. 'Forgive me, Peter-*san*,' he bowed ironically, 'but we've been a bit preoccupied to notice what's been going on here in Washington.'

Kominsky gave a short laugh. 'Ever since Clinton saved the virtual world, he's been Greenbaum's best friend. Think of the millions of votes he'd have lost if the people in VR hadn't been recovered. Immortality for your nearest and dearest doesn't split along party lines, Jay. The whole country would have been against him. Don't forget, Greenbaum was never elected. Pardoning Clinton was a small price to pay to legitimise his presidency.'

'I guess they don't know who destroyed it in the first place?'

'This is Washington, Jay - do you think they really care about the facts? Perception is everything. Perception is reality.'

'Thanks for the update, but that's not why I'm here.'

'It's not?' said Kominsky, with a grin. 'I'd never have guessed.'

'I've got two names for you, Peter: Alex Duchovny and Ann Mitchell.'

***

Salt Lake City, Utah

'He denied all knowledge of both of them,' said Sato.

'And you believed him?' asked Hisako.

Sato smiled. 'Of course not,' he replied. 'I know him too well. I never expected him to acknowledge either of them. But now they know we're watching, they need to think carefully about their next steps. Whatever it is they're trying to do, they know we're interested. And we're closer to Duchovny and what he's doing than they are. If he tries to make contact with anyone in the real world, we'll know before they do. And whatever information he tries to pass on to them, they know it won't be a secret from us.'

'So what do we do? Prem just keeps watching and waiting?'

'I guess so,' replied Sato. 'Duchovny's got to make a move sometime, and when he does we'll be one step ahead.'

'But that could be weeks, months - year, even,' she said. 'And all that time, Raj and Hamish are stuck, and Clinton could start his genocide at any moment.'

'Prem just has to keep up his surveillance,' he replied. 'And I need to swap back with your father.'

'Is there anything you can do in VR?'

'I think anything I did would raise an alarm. As it is, we took a big chance with me leaving VR. I just hope nobody wondered why I'd deliberately killed myself by running in front of a Roman chariot race. I'm hoping Prem can find a way of getting me back from limbo.'

'If anyone can do it, it's Prem,' replied Hisako.

'There is one possibility that we haven't really taken into account,' said Sato.

'What's that?'

'Duchovny may not try to make contact at all. He may be working totally alone. Whatever he's in VR for, he may not need to contact them. It may be obvious that he's succeeded - or he's failed.'

'If that's true, then all we can do is wait and watch.'

***

CIA Headquarters, Langley, Virginia

Peter Kominsky sat at his desk and stared at the blank screen in front of him. He was worried. His shock at the strange meeting with his friend, Julian Jennings, had passed. He considered: had it been a shock? Or was it more a surprise that Jennings had been forced to adopt such a radical method of getting access to the real world?

He'd always guessed that the murder of Jennings and his wife, Barbara, wouldn't be the end of the story. But for Jennings to return in such a bizarre way worried him. It meant that Clinton was as much of a threat to the inhabitants of the virtual world as he considered him to be in the real world. And now that he seemed to have gained the President's trust and approval, it made him - at least in Peter Kominsky's eyes - even more of a potential threat.

But the concrete nature of the threat eluded him.

The debacle over the recent Israeli affair might have faded in the memories of the opportunist politicians that thronged the Washington corridors of influence, but Kominsky could still feel the unseen hand that had shaped the events leading up to the Exocet missile attack on the warehouses at Deir al-Balah that had released a deadly cloud of Novichok gas. The prevailing wind had saved thousands of lives by pushing the cloud out over the Eastern Mediterranean, but it was clearly luck that had saved those lives: whoever had ordered the attack that day knew what they were doing. Whoever it was had no thought of saving innocent lives.

Ultimately, the responsibility lay with the President, but Kominsky could feel that the real culprit remained unaccountable, hidden in the dark shadows that were increasingly enveloping the White House. As head of the CIA, it was his role to protect the security of the United States. He had always assumed that threats to that security originated exclusively from outside the borders of the US. But more and more, he was feeling that there was a malign force eating its way into the very heart of the US Administration.

And if Jennings' appearance had done nothing else, it had focussed his attention on Randolph Clinton.

Clinton was no newcomer to the CIA's list of persons of interest, but his death had allowed them to move their attention to other, more specific targets. His re-emergence in the virtual world had been noticed, but it had seemed to pose no threat to anyone in the real world, so any interest in him had been placed on the back burner. When Greenbaum had taken the unprecedented step of giving the man a full presidential pardon, Kominsky had been surprised, but Clinton still seemed to pose no direct threat, so he had accepted the pardon as a political act, and mentally shrugged his shoulders.

But Jennings' appearance had changed things.

Even though he had said that there was only an indirect link to Clinton, Peter Kominsky knew his friend better. To have mentioned Clinton at all concerned him - especially in conjunction with the names of the only two agents actively dedicated to the task of trying to determine where and what Clinton was actually doing.

Kominsky was well aware that the Clarke clone was, at best, a crude attempt at keeping track of Clinton's whereabouts. But the sudden change in her assignment to the President's personal security team had rung alarm bells. And the revelation that Duchovny's activities had drawn the attention of someone within the virtual world meant, at the very least, that he was operating in the same area of interest as the likes of Jennings.

He was also aware that Duchovny's brief had been, at best, speculative. There was no-one he could have talked to about his radical - others would have said reckless, or even insane - plan. Even a hint of what he had imagined would have meant the end of his career.

But in his own mind at least, he had seen it as a possible preparatory move on the chess board, moving a minor piece into play which might prove useful, if not decisive, in the end game. But now that the likes of Jennings were watching his pawn, his options seemed far more limited, and the faint glimmerings of his original plan seemed almost futile - even desperate.

But with Greenbaum acting unpredictably, and the possibility that Clinton was exerting an influence he couldn't understand, even the bare bones of a plan - however desperate - were better than nothing.

The question he had to ask himself was: did he dare share the whole truth with his virtual friend?

***

Virtual World

'I'm not sure we can continue this process, Alex,' said the counsellor. 'It's become clear that you have some objectives that you have not shared with us.'

Alex hesitated for a moment, then said calmly, 'I want to recreate my mother.'

'That may be true, Alex,' replied the actor, 'but from the evidence we have assembled, it seems that you have a greater desire to create the girl, Ann Mitchell.'

'That, too.'

‘And then what, Alex? The rest of your family? Your grandparents? Your aunts and uncles? Your father?’

‘Not my father.’

‘That seems consistent with your actions to date,’ said the actor. ‘But it doesn’t explain why you withheld the truth from us. The weight of probability suggests that you are here to continue your role at the NSA. In which case, we would suggest that you tell us what you hope to achieve.’

‘I can’t do that.’

‘Is there a reason for that? Do you have some residual loyalty to your old organisation? Or were you sent here specifically to do something for them?’

‘I can’t tell you.’

The counsellor leaned forward in her seat, ‘You do realise that it would not be possible for you to return to the real world to resume your previous life without the creation of a clone from your DNA?’

‘Yes.’

‘But more importantly, even if there were a clone prepared to receive you, if we considered you to be a threat to the virtual world, we would not cooperate in transmuting you.'

'You'd keep me here, as a prisoner?'

'Not as a prisoner, Alex,' replied the counsellor. 'You came here of your own free will. You chose to die. We welcomed you to the virtual world. We complied with your wish to be involved in the creation of self-motivating avatars. Currently, you have all of the privileges that come with this version of immortality - including the freedom to return to the real world if you wish. But if you choose to act against us in any way, that freedom will be revoked. All your other privileges would remain, but there would be no possibility of return. Do you understand?'

***

Online Gaming World

'And he still refused to talk?' asked Hisako.

'If he's prepared to give up whatever plans he had to return, and go through the rest of eternity knowing that he failed to do what he was sent here for, then whoever he's working for must have an incredibly strong hold over him,' replied Prem. 'I just can't imagine what that feels like. He's prepared to make himself some kind of martyr to whatever cause he believes in. And we can't do a thing to find out what it is.'

'But at least we know he can't do any harm,' said Hisako.

'But we also can't use him as a cover so that I can try to find out what Clinton is up to.'

'Do we know where he is?'

'No idea. I was relying on Alex to hack his way into Clinton's life-log. But that's not going to happen now.'

'So what do you think Alex will do now?'

'I haven't the faintest idea.'

'Will you let him recreate his mother?'

'I don't know,' replied Prem. 'I don't see what harm that could do, and at least he'd have something to occupy his time. But I don't want to let him use AltLife to speed up the process. It's best he doesn't get to know too much.'

Hisako nodded in agreement. 'It's a shame he falsified his life-log, we could have gone back and tried to deduce what his purpose was in coming here.'

Prem was silent. Then a frown crossed his brow. 'What if - '

'What if - what?'

'What if we ran the falsified version of his life-log

through AltLife?'

'What would that achieve?' asked Hisako.

'If we could tell AltLife that specific periods were not what they seemed - '

'We could tell it to ignore those periods - and tell it what he was actually doing. Not in any sort of detail, of course - but in general terms. We do know where he was working. If we gave it the GPS coordinates, that might help.'

After a few seconds, Prem gave a short laugh. 'It's crazy, isn't it?' he said, resignedly. 'It'd never work.'

'I can't imagine what AltLife would make of it,' replied Hisako. 'Especially when it came to making predictions about what he was likely to do next.'

'Is there any processing capacity available on the LDS machines?' Prem asked innocently.

'I'm not doing anything else,' she replied, with a grin. 'I think another test using really fuzzy parameters might be justified.'

***

'It took a lot longer than I thought,' said Hisako. 'I guess that was because the information was much less precise.'

'But did it come up with anything interesting?' demanded Prem, impatiently.

'Well, it managed to fill in a lot of the gaps,' she replied. 'The GPS data gave it something to aim at, and I was surprised at how much footage it came up with. It seems that the NSA are very keen on closed circuit surveillance of their own people.'

'You mean it picked up images of Alex himself?'

'Yes, lots of them,' replied Hisako. 'But before you get too excited, I don't think images of him sitting in lectures, or hunched in front of a screen we can't read are going to help much. But at least it confirms what we already knew: he's definitely NSA, and he's been well trained.'

'Is that it?'

'As far as the facts go - yes,' she replied cautiously.

'You're sounding cagey, Hisako,' said Prem. 'What else was there?'

Hisako smiled. 'Here's the interesting bit: AltLife came up with some predictions.'

'Some predictions? That's not surprising - it's what I'd expect.'

'Actually, there were millions of them,' said Hisako. 'In the end, I had to stop it running. It was using up every resource in the machine, and I was concerned someone would ask awkward questions about what I was doing.'

'Millions? That's - not very useful,' Prem commented.

'No, I didn't think so, either,' she replied. 'Usually, AltLife comes up with three or four potential futures, and ranks them according to their statistical probability. The top ones are usually in the range eighty to ninety percent, dropping to around sixty five percent, then forty percent or so. We usually ignore anything below fifty percent.'

'What sort of probability did it extrapolate for Alex's data?'

'Well, like I said, it came up with millions of potential futures, which was a bit unexpected - at least, at first sight. But the interesting thing was that the statistical probabilities were all around twenty percent.'

Prem frowned in confusion. 'Which means what?' he asked.

'That anything AltLife came up with was equally unlikely.'

'So it was a complete waste of time and resources,' said Prem, disconsolately.

'I wouldn't dismiss it quite so easily,' replied Hisako. 'I looked at the top three predictions, and even though it would appear at first sight that they were of no real value, they were all remarkably similar. For a start, they all showed Alex back in the real world.'

'That seems unlikely, given what we threatened him with,' said Prem.

'That's not all. They all showed him being presented with the Presidential Medal of Freedom.'

'What's that?'

'According to Wikipedia, it's the supreme civilian decoration in the United States.'

'That can't be right, Hisako,' protested Prem.

'And it gets even stranger than that: in the three potential lives, the medal was being presented by three different men.'

'Who were they?'

'You're not going to like this, Prem.'

'Try me.'

'The first one was President Greenbaum.'

Prem looked dubious. ‘I suppose that’s logical. And the next?’

‘Even more strange. It was the late President Winter.’

‘Winter? This is crazy, Hisako. We’ve obviously asked AltLife the wrong questions. It’s too much for the software to cope with.’

Hisako held up her hand. ‘The last one is the real killer, Prem,’ she said.

‘Who was it?’

‘It was President Randolph Clinton.’

***

Virtual World

‘Of course I want to go on with it,’ said Alex irritably. ‘I want to recreate my mother.’

‘Are you sure about that, Alex,’ asked the actor. ‘What about your *de facto* sister? Don’t you want to create her, too? Or is there something about the fact that she’s still alive that’s stopping you?’

‘You know what they did to her?’ he growled.

‘We deduced what the CIA did. There are no records. It would be foolish to expect any.’

‘Then you know what she became?’

‘Yes.’

‘That she has no memory of her former life?’

‘Yes.’

‘Then you must realise what I want!’ he shouted. ‘There’s no other way to get her back.’

‘Surely the CIA must have kept her life-log data?’ replied the actor, without emotion.

Alex stared angrily at the woman sitting dispassionately opposite him. ‘They told me the data was destroyed. There was no way to get her back!’

‘But you still went along with what they wanted from you?’

‘It was the only way,’ he cried. ‘I do what they want; I get to learn how to recreate her.’

‘And what do they want, Alex?’

‘What I told you: they want me to learn how to create self-motivating avatars.’

‘But why?’

‘They didn’t tell me!’

‘And more importantly - who?’

‘Like I said: they never told me. Once I’m competent, I have to contact them, and they’ll tell me what to do next.’

***

Online Gaming World

‘I’m going to have to tell Raj and Hamish,’ said Prem urgently. ‘Things have moved on since I last updated them.’

‘You need to tell them, but there’s nothing they can do to help,’ replied Hisako.

‘Some advice would be helpful.’

‘You’re doing just fine on your own, Prem,’ she replied. ‘I just wish there was more I could do to help.’

‘There’s nothing, Hisako. If you started to do something different, Clinton would spot it in a minute. Hiding me behind AltLife is more than enough.’

'You need to let Alex carry on with what he's doing, Prem. Even if he's lying about not knowing why he's there, there's nothing to be gained by stopping him.'

'Do you believe what he said the CIA did to the sister?' he asked.

'I don't know.'

'It just seems so - callous,' said Prem. 'Just disposing of her past life - one of their own agents.'

'If they didn't save her life-log data, the only reason I can think of is they didn't want to raise suspicions when they inserted her into the Clarke production line. And she must have known what was going to happen, Prem - she did volunteer.'

'I don't suppose Alex cares about that,' he replied. 'If he's telling the truth, he just wants her back.'

'If he thinks the only way to get her back is to create a self-motivating avatar in VR, then that's one hell of an incentive for him to succeed.'

'You think they're that cynical?'

'If they see a threat to their national security, I think they'd do anything, Prem.'

***

Virtual World

'We want you to continue,' said the actor.

'But you don't trust me,' responded Alex.

'We don't need to trust you, Alex. We can watch everything you do, every keystroke, every image you see - everything is available to us.'

'So you'll be watching my every move?'

The woman made no reply.

'Do you want me to continue the training programme? Or are there things in there you don't want me to know?'

'If you think you can benefit from the training, then you are welcome to continue with it,' she replied. 'But there's no longer any need to hide your expertise. Pretending to make mistakes won't fool anyone.'

Alex shrugged. 'And the project?'

'We want you to continue with that. There are aspects of it that interest us. We're looking forward to seeing how you tackle the problem.'

'You're interested in Clinton?'

‘Of course. He’s now in complete control of the virtual world.’

‘Including you?’

‘Naturally.’

‘And yet you’re happy for me to try to hack into his life-log data,’ said Alex. ‘Is this some other sort of test?’

‘It is certainly a test, Alex. In fact, it’s probably the most difficult task you could face. If you succeed, you will have proved your abilities beyond question.’

‘And if I fail?’

‘If Clinton detects you, your existence here in the virtual world is likely to be very short. The man is not known for his forgiveness.’

‘If I didn’t know better, I’d say that remark almost sounded human,’ said Alex.

‘I am merely passing on the fact of Clinton’s past response to those he regards as his enemies. And as for displaying human responses, I reserve that for my - what you might call - professional role.’

Alex stared at the enigmatic being opposite him. ‘And will you continue with your - professional role?’ he asked.

'There is a considerable amount of work yet to do,' replied the woman. 'I need to know a lot more about your mother, your father - and Ann Mitchell. But yes, I will continue.'

Alex leaned back into his chair.

'You can regard this as the carrot,' said the woman, smoothly.

'And the stick?'

'Clinton.'

***

They're all just a bunch of code, Alex kept telling himself. *Very clever code - and yet, there's something that doesn't ring quite true.*

He tried to think back to his expectations when he took on the task, when he'd sat in the anonymous agent's office and listened to the matter of fact way in which the man had laid out the facts, the way he'd speculated as to what Alex would find in the virtual world, and the outcomes they expected from him.

He had felt confident that he of all people could carry through what they wanted. It had seemed relatively simple: become an expert in the creation of self-motivating avatars. If he could persuade the people in VR that he was sincere in his desire to recreate his mother, and show them that he was committed and conscientious, what could be simpler? But somehow, he had underestimated the sophistication of the artificial intelligences that he had encountered.

The last thing he had expected was to come across anything like the actor.

As a software creation, it - she - was astounding. He had never considered that such an entity could exist - at least, not with the apparent insight the actor had shown - and was continuing to show. He was just beginning to realise just what a formidable intellect Rajesh Singh must have been before his virtual life had been cut short, snuffed out forever, like a fragile flickering candle flame.

And yet, there were hints everywhere of the tremendous influence that Singh still held over what happened in the virtual world, no matter that Randolph Clinton had declared himself its ultimate master. There was something about the - how could he describe it? - about the attitude of the AIs that had taken him completely by surprise. Yes, they appeared at first glance to be entirely objective, but there was a feeling behind what they said and did - a sense that they were protecting Singh's memory, and although there was no doubt that they would ultimately conform to whatever regime Clinton put in place, he could almost feel an underlying loyalty to the dead man which underscored everything they said and did. He found it at once confusing, and almost endearing.

But his biggest surprise had been the implicit - and explicit - threats that they had made. What sort of underlying intelligence provided them with the insight to understand his human motivations? Surely, his whole existence had fitted him to be superior to these software objects - for that was all they were? And yet, they appeared to be able to probe his innermost thoughts and desires: the girl, Ann; his desperate need to bring her back; the broken relationship with his father; the mother that had left him too soon.

And the fact that they had discovered his true past.

He wracked his brain to try to discover how they could have penetrated his disguise, why they had taken the trouble to scratch away at the surface until they found what lay behind the unremarkable exterior, so carefully crafted by his masters back in the real world.

But perhaps it was unfair on him to take the responsibility, perhaps the people back at Langley were the ones who had underestimated the fierce intelligence that he had come face to face with, that still endured in the fabric of the virtual world the man had created.

It was the underlying humanity which the AIs displayed that confused him. It was almost as if they had an agenda of their own. But perhaps that was what he had underestimated about these collections of code: perhaps they were just reflecting the mind of their creator, a human mind that imbued everything they did, and as a consequence could never be eliminated.

He could almost feel the human being that hid behind them, observing silently from the shadows, and influencing everything they did.

Grudgingly, he realised he would have loved to have met Rajesh Singh.

***

Chapter 6

Quantum Entangled Virtual Space

'I think he realises that we're never going to let him get into the detail of how self-motivating avatars work,' said Prem.

'As long as he comes to the conclusion that all he needs is an actor, and the right information, then that suits our purposes, doesn't it?' asked Raj.

'Just make sure he doesn't find the latest version,' added Hamish. 'Whoever's behind him, I don't want them getting their hands on anything as powerful as the actor he's dealing with. And keep yourself out of sight; I don't want him to suspect he's being manipulated.'

'Don't worry, Hamish,' replied Prem. 'The actor knows exactly what's going on, and I've laid a false trail to the avatar library. If he tries to get access and copy the software, the whole thing will delete itself.'

'Plus the AIs are watching him constantly,' added Raj. 'I think Prem will have instilled sufficient doubt in his mind about what we are capable of. I don't think he'll try to go off-piste just yet. I think he'll try to stay on the straight and narrow for the time being - at least until he senses we're no longer concerned that he might be a threat.'

‘I hate this,’ said Hamish bitterly. ‘It’s so frustrating being here when we could be helping.’

‘You’re doing everything you can,’ said Prem. ‘Just being able to talk every now and again helps me enormously.’

‘Prem’s doing a great job, Hamish,’ said Raj. ‘He doesn’t need us breathing down his neck.’

‘I’m sorry, Prem,’ said Hamish. ‘I didn’t mean - ’

‘He’s just not used to feeling helpless,’ explained Raj, with a wry smile.

***

Virtual World

The bare facts of Clinton’s career were easy to find. Disgraced army officer, discharged for attacking civilian targets in Afghanistan, disappears into obscurity, only to re-emerge as professor of virtual reality at Princeton University.

Then the rather less public information about how he created an elite clone army within the US forces, answerable only to himself. His death at the hands of one of his own clones, and then his re-appearance at the side of President Greenbaum, followed by an unexpected second death after what seemed to be a falling out between the two. But somehow the destruction and recreation of the virtual world seemed to have led to their reconciliation, and Clinton's subsequent rehabilitation into the corridors of power.

Alex mulled over the fact that the AI had been right: Clinton was indeed a dangerous man. The consequences of attracting his attention couldn't be clearer. If he was prepared to destroy the lives of millions living peacefully in the virtual world, there could be no good outcome for anyone found to be infiltrating his private data. But that was what his task dictated: hack into Clinton's life-log data and find out what he was doing.

But why? What could putting himself at immense risk of annihilation achieve? According to his training plan, it was the ultimate test of his abilities. But surely there was more to it than that? If he were caught, then there would be no more Alex Duchovny. How did that help anyone? And if he succeeded, what difference would that make? The question rose up in his mind: who stood to gain if he found a way to get into Clinton's life-log?

And then the real question crept into his consciousness: if everything he was doing was being supervised by AIs, why was he asking *who?* - rather than *what?*

***

He was being manipulated. It was becoming increasingly clear he was an expendable pawn in an elaborate game of chess. But who was calling the shots? And why?

There was no doubt in Alex's mind that the AIs were being controlled by someone - and it had become blindingly obvious that it was a someone, rather than a something. But who that someone might be was a complete mystery, as was their objective in setting him the assignment that could well lead to his complete erasure from existence.

Whoever it was, that someone wanted to get into Clinton's life-log. But if they were capable of manipulating the AIs, why couldn't they hack into Clinton's data themselves? If they were capable of adding to Alex's own already extensive knowledge of infiltration techniques, then they must have the ability to hack into Clinton themselves. So why go to all the trouble of using him?

The obvious answer was that they couldn't risk discovery. They had to remain invisible. There could be no possible trail leading back to them. Which lead him inevitably to the conclusion that whoever it was had to be a real human being, and not an AI. But who they were, and what their objectives might be were completely obscure. For a while, Alex considered confronting the actor with his conclusions, but he decided that alerting his invisible puppet master might put himself in even more jeopardy.

He would play along with the game, and as long as

he was extremely careful, he might survive long enough to achieve at least some of his own objectives.

***

Alex decided to start with a source of data that required no hacking at all.

The transmutation logs between the two worlds were freely available, so he started to enter the search parameters to determine when and where Clinton had visited the virtual world. But as he was about to key in the name, he stopped short.

It was true that the transmutation logs were easily accessible, but without having carried out such a search before, he realised he had no idea what data trail would be left behind. What log records were created when the search completed? What alerts were generated?

Alex paused: it would be more prudent to search for someone else first. He decided that his first project to investigate President Greenbaum might be the perfect cover for his enquiry. He entered Greenbaum's name and watched as the search results appeared on the virtual screen before him. Without looking at them, he copied the results into a file, then turned his attention to the log data that had been generated. As he had expected, the transaction had been logged with his username, the date and time, and the target of his search.

Then he accessed the alerts queue, and was pleased

to find that a search on someone as eminent as the President hadn't registered as an anomalous event. The file consisted entirely of a continuous stream of innocuous data records marking the changes in hardware resources that were constantly happening to support the virtual world.

He went back to the log file and tried to delete his original search. To his surprise, he found that he had insufficient access rights to do anything to the record. He couldn't delete it, and there was no way to modify it to make it look as if someone else had made the enquiry. He would have to go back to the AIs and find out how to get hold of some kind of superuser access.

For a second he paused: perhaps that was part of the test, to get himself greater access rights without anyone knowing what he was doing.

But how?

***

As he thought about it, the answer became obvious: he needed to get hold of Raj Singh's user identity. He would have had the ultimate in access rights. But Raj Singh no longer existed in the virtual world, and surely Clinton would have erased all trace of him.

And yet, from all that he had seen since he arrived in the virtual world, Clinton was taking little interest in what was going on. Once he had restored the worlds, he seemed to have returned to the real world to bask in his renewed popularity. How thorough had he been? Had he restored everything to its previous state? Or had things been missed?

Alex decided that the best place to start was with the log files that recorded the automatic backups of each of the worlds. As he trawled through the data, he saw immediately that Clinton had been in a hurry. Yes, worlds had been restored, but much of the finer detail had been lost because Clinton hadn't bothered to load the backup files in the correct sequence. Alex felt his hopes rise as he realised that there were whole series of files that hadn't been accessed in the restore process. Maybe one of them would hold some details about Singh and McAllister.

Hours later he had his first success: a copy of the development environment. He restored the file only to find that neither Singh nor McAllister had been present when the backup copy was made, but there were half completed projects tagged with their user names. His guess had been correct, Clinton had not gone through everything erasing their existence. And if there was one copy, there could well be another.

All he had to do was to find it.

***

Quantum Entangled Virtual Space

'He's found your user, Raj,' said Prem.

‘Good,’ replied Singh. ‘Let’s see how talented he really is.’

‘As I see it, he’s got two choices,’ replied Prem. ‘He can’t afford to use it as it is: Clinton will have set up all sorts of alerts looking for activity from yourself and Hamish. So I guess he’ll copy the privileges into his own user.’

‘That only helps to a certain extent,’ said Raj. ‘Clinton will have set up alerts for anyone using a superuser. As soon as he does anything, there’ll be a record on the alert queue, and as soon as it hits the top of the list, the AI will detect it, and no doubt a message will appear on Clinton’s phone or whatever device he happens to be using.’

‘Or, he could go into the alerts system and change the code,’ suggested Prem.

‘He could indeed,’ replied Raj. ‘But that in itself would generate an alert. No, to evade our dear friend, Clinton, he’ll have to be cleverer than that.’

***

Virtual World

Alex paused, thinking. Now that he had superuser privileges, he could do absolutely anything. He reached for the virtual keypad, but something held him back. Clinton must have superuser capabilities, too. Without them, he couldn't have restored the whole of the virtual universe. And as far as he was concerned, he was the only person who had such powers. What would happen when another superuser suddenly appeared? Would that in itself generate an alert? If Alex himself were as paranoid as Clinton appeared to be, what checks would he have put in place to protect himself and his power within the virtual world?

He drew back from the keys. He needed to think carefully about his next move, no matter how tempting it might be to charge right in and start changing things to suit his own purposes.

Basically, the alert system was his enemy. The software itself continuously monitored all the activity going on inside the virtual world: who was doing what, what files were they accessing, what programs were they running, what hardware they were using. It was the perfect panopticon: no one inside the virtual world was invisible. No one could hide from the all-seeing software that monitored the virtual universe. His colleagues at the NSA would have given their right arms to have the sort of surveillance that existed here.

Alex smiled grimly to himself. In the past, it had been his task to carry out the surveillance; now, he needed to avoid it at all costs. Frustratingly, with his superuser privileges, he had become all-powerful within the virtual universe, but at the same time was completely impotent under the gaze of the supervising software.

The irony was not lost on him.

***

Alex leaned back in his chair. As he considered how best to sidestep whatever unknown traps were lurking for him, he opened the file that contained the one search that he had legitimately undertaken.

As he studied the details of Greenbaum's transmutation, a frown crossed his face. Was there something he didn't understand about transmutation?

As far as he was aware, each transmutation event was unique, and when Greenbaum had been transmuted from the real world, all the details of the process were recorded. And sure enough, that was exactly what he saw: a completely uneventful crossover from the real world to the virtual world, followed immediately by his insertion into the avatar that had been prepared ready for him.

And when a person returned to the real world, the process was carried out in reverse: the avatar was saved for any future use, the virtual world memories were added to the original real world experiences, and the total was reinserted into the real world mind before waking them from their stasis.

If that were so, why was there only one record for

Greenbaum? Since his return, Alex had seen the man with his own eyes back in the real world, giving speeches, attending official events. For such a public figure, there was no privacy, no avoiding the glare of the lights, the mass media reporting. Greenbaum was clearly back in the real world.

So where was the second transmutation event? Had there been some kind of glitch? Was there a delay in recording return transmutations? Or was there something fundamental that Alex didn't know?

***

Hiding behind Alex's eyes, Prem had no doubt whatsoever. Whoever the person was that waved to the crowds, who shook the outstretched hands, who stood behind the podia, reading his lines from the auto-cue - it wasn't Greenbaum.

With only a single transmutation record, it meant categorically that Greenbaum had never returned: he was still somewhere in the virtual world. And that someone else had taken possession of the President's body and mind.

To Prem, there was only one possible person who would dare to take over the role of the President. But the question still remained: what would Clinton have to gain by this audacious and seemingly outrageous move?

Prem followed his train of thought to its logical

conclusion: if Greenbaum was still in the virtual world, where was he? And was he complicit in what Clinton was doing?

***

The number of alerts appearing in the queue was enormous. Not that it mattered to the untiring AI that monitored each and every event. It examined each record and categorised it according to the rules it had been given, then if no action was to be taken, it moved on to the next alert.

Alex watched the alerts streaming through the system and came to the conclusion that at least ninety five percent of them were merely changes of hardware devices that the system used to support the virtual world: Mobile phones turning on and off comprised most of the data, with the occasional server coming on-line or disappearing off-line. The remaining five percent were changes to the internal avatar databases - new arrivals being initiated - and the occasional change to the virtual world structural databases - a new world being made live by the development team, or regular activities such as time being suspended so that a backup could be taken.

His idea was simple. He had seen it so often in the movies, where the CCTV feed of a bank vault is replaced by a false unchanging image, so that the watching security team never sees the criminals in the act of breaking into the strongroom.

All he had to do was to feed a false alert queue to the

AI, consisting entirely of the same sort of innocent events that it monitored day in and day out. Generating the file with random hardware changes and a few other selected events was the easy part; inserting his file into the alert stream would be more difficult.

***

Now that you have Raj's superuser, said the voice of the training AI, *you would be wise to be wary of using it.*

'I'd already thought of that,' replied Alex testily. 'If something seems to be too good to be true and all that.'

There may be other, less conspicuous ways.

'What do you mean?'

The AI software that monitors the virtual world transaction logs has been around since the very beginning. The initial version was written by Hamish McAllister when he generated the very first virtual worlds all those years ago.

'I don't see the significance.'

At that time, there was no infrastructure such as we have now.

'So what did he run it on?'

That's a very good question, Alex. I have a document

for you.

The document appeared in the empty space before Alex's eyes. He scanned the first page, then said in surprise: 'this document is huge, it has over three hundred pages.'

Does that suggest something to you, Alex?

'The software gets amended a lot.'

Nothing more?

Alex thought for a second. 'If Raj and Hamish did all this, they'd have no time for anything else.'

Correct.

'That means that other people have been maintaining this software - and they can't all have superuser status. So, if I wanted to change it, what level of permissions would I need?'

No more than you already have.

'So I could go in and change the software?'

You could.

'But there's a catch?'

Read the document, Alex. It might suggest some

ideas to you.

***

The first thing that attracted Alex's attention was the fact that the original monitoring system was run on the mainframe that ran the business software for Viva Eterna.

From what he could remember about the early days of the virtual world, McAllister had built several worlds for super-rich clients as demonstrations of what was possible, and then set up the insurance company, Viva Eterna to allow anyone to guarantee themselves their place in immortality.

It was logical that Hamish had used the hardware available to him at the time, but what was surprising was that the monitoring system in its various forms had never moved to a different platform. It was still running on the original mainframe.

As he read on, he found the implementation of individual transmutations to the virtual world, as McAllister had set up the administration of entries into the early prison worlds that governments had bought into. This had resulted in a huge increase in the number of transactions that needed to be recorded. At this stage, the reliability of the system had come into question and a second Viva Eterna mainframe had been made available to act as a backup to the first.

But Alex noted that the two machines had never been set up as hot standbys. Whoever had made that decision had taken the view that there was sufficient shared disk space to cope with buffering the number of transactions, and that in the event of a failure, a short delay before the monitoring system came back online was acceptable.

The situation had remained like that until the number of virtual worlds increased to such an extent that the mainframes could no longer cope with the volume of transactions. At that point, the day to day business of Viva Eterna was transferred to more modern machines, freeing up more than enough capacity to cope with the demands of the monitoring system.

And the system had remained in that state to the present day.

Alex sat back in his chair. In the light of the incredible sophistication of the virtual universe, it was almost unbelievable that the monitoring system was still based on what was relatively ancient technology. From the comments in the document, it was clear that Raj intended to do something about it, but it obviously hadn't hit the top of his to-do list.

'If it ain't broke, don't fix it,' Alex murmured to himself.

As he read on, he found the first hints of the conflict between McAllister and Clinton: there was an entry logging the change to the software to create an alert if Clinton was seen to be attempting to transmute between the worlds, and later, similar entries for any Clarkes, as well as someone called Giuseppe Romano.

Then towards the end of the document, he found Clinton's entries creating alerts for McAllister himself, Raj Singh, and anyone having superuser privileges.

But throughout the documented changes, he registered that the day to day changes had been made by several members of the software support group, and implemented on both the live mainframe, then the backup machine.

If he wanted to make himself invisible in order to be able to access the confidential data relating to Clinton, it was obvious that he had to remove the alerts for Raj Singh's superuser. The problem he faced was that any changes to the monitoring system would themselves raise alerts.

The question was: who got the alerts, and what did they do about them? Without looking at the actual software and its related parameters, it was impossible to tell.

***

Quantum Entangled Virtual Space

'It's Clinton,' said Prem calmly.

'You're sure?' asked Hamish.

'I'm sure.'

'But why?' asked Raj.

Hamish shrugged. 'To do what he's always been trying to do. But this time, there's no one to stop him. As President - as commander in chief, he has the whole of the US military under his control. As far as military action is concerned, there's nothing to stop him doing whatever he likes.'

'Surely, he's answerable to somebody?' gasped Raj. 'Congress? The Senate?'

'Not if he declares a state of war,' replied Hamish. 'But if I'm right - '

'But what justification has he got for that?'

'I don't think that's what he'll do,' replied Hamish calmly. 'I think he'll be more subtle than that.'

'What do you mean?'

'He's already tried to start a war, by trying to trick Hamas, Iran and the Israelis into attacking each other - but Greenbaum recognised the political realities, and he backed out of it. Clinton knows it would look totally out of character for Greenbaum to come right out and declare war on somebody - Iran, say. It would cause too many questions to be asked about Greenbaum's state of mind, and I don't think Clinton has any desire to remain inside Greenbaum's world for any longer than he has to.'

'So what's he after?' asked Prem.

Hamish frowned. 'He really wants to start a war, but - just like last time - he doesn't want Greenbaum or himself to be seen to be starting it. And now that he's effectively gained control of Greenbaum, he could try to pull the same trick, but with no possibility of being countermanded.'

'So what do you think he's planning to do?' asked Raj. 'The same thing again?'

'If I were him, I'd be looking to find another way to convince both Iran and the Israelis that they were under attack from the other. That way, they'd retaliate without question, and the whole of the Middle East would be drawn into what would be essentially a religious conflict. Clinton would get what he wanted, and Greenbaum would seem to have his hands clean.'

'But how, Hamish?'

'I don't know exactly how, but I do know he'll want to do it quickly before anyone gets suspicious. Clinton won't want to spend a minute longer than he has to in

Greenbaum's shoes. Too many people know him: there's too much chance of someone recognising that his patterns of behaviour have changed, that it's not the Greenbaum they knew. But the big problem he has is: exactly when to return Greenbaum to the real world?'

'What do you mean?'

'He needs to make sure that whatever actions he puts in place, that Greenbaum can't just cancel all the orders he's given out. In other words, the plan has to be unstoppable before Greenbaum is put back in place.'

'So you think he'll want to get back to the virtual world as soon as he can?'

'Undoubtedly. He's safe there. Nothing can touch him.'

***

The White House, Washington DC

'Tell me, General, who is our expert in unconventional warfare?'

'Unconventional warfare, Mr President?' replied the general, his eyes flicking to the unmoving figure of Clarke, positioned at the door leading from the Oval Office.

'Yes, General,' replied Greenbaum. 'I assume we have one.'

The general was taken aback by the question: he and his colleagues were tasked with protecting the country using traditional means. As far as unconventional methods were concerned, he and his colleagues in the Joint Chiefs of Staff were very much of the same mind: new developments in armed warfare came along from time to time, but conventional means of defence - and attack - remained their go-to solution.

‘Should we be discussing this in front of - ?’ he asked.

Greenbaum glanced towards Clarke.

‘Bearing in mind what happened to my late predecessor, I’m sure you understand why the protocols have changed.’

‘Yes, but surely - a Clarke - ’

‘Ignore her, General,’ ordered Greenbaum. ‘And tell me about our approach to unconventional warfare.’

‘If you’re talking about cyber warfare, Mr President - ’

‘I wasn’t - not specifically - but go on.’

‘We have a department responsible - ’

‘Who is in charge of it?’

'Well - ' The general hesitated. 'Indirectly, they report to me. But it's such a small part of the overall operation, that we don't generally have day to day oversight - '

'You mean you have no knowledge of what they're doing?'

'I wouldn't put it like that, sir - '

'Find out, General,' snapped Greenbaum. 'I need to know. But more than that, I need to know who is the ultimate expert in unconventional tactics and weaponry, artificial intelligence, and suchlike.'

The general stood silent, his face frowning.

'You seem uncomfortable with my request, General,' said Greenbaum.

The general's eyes turned again to the expressionless face of Clarke. 'It's just that - the person you need might not be easily available.'

'Who is it?' demanded Greenbaum.

'Well, I hesitate to suggest, but the man you need to talk to is Randolph Clinton.'

'Clinton?' queried the President. 'Why should I hesitate?'

‘Despite his recent activities, his history - ’

‘What about his history?’

‘As you’re aware, sir, apart from his expertise in the use of drones, he created a complete force of clones within the existing armed forces. The discovery of this army within an army led to his becoming the most wanted man in the US. And ultimately ended in his death - ’

‘I’m aware of the details, General. But now that he’s been rehabilitated, surely we can take advantage of his unorthodox thinking - ’

‘I’m just pointing out that he’s not trusted.’

Greenbaum smiled. ‘I assume you’re concerned about the loyalty of Clarke here, and her - colleagues.’

The general was silent.

‘It is true that the Clarkes owed loyalty only to Clinton. They were - shall we say - built that way. But now - thanks to this particular Clarke, of course - he is physically dead. And their loyalty has transferred unquestionably to their commander in chief. But I suppose, looking at it from your point of view, there continues to be ongoing suspicion about their trustworthiness.’

‘Exactly, sir. Despite the recreation of the virtual

world, there is still doubt over Clinton's motivation. And I should remind you, the use of these clones has been banned by the United Nations as a form of lethal automated weapon.'

Greenbaum turned away towards the window facing the White House gardens, hiding the smile that crossed his face. After a moment, he turned back.

'Despite your misgivings, I will arrange to contact Professor Clinton. He might have some insights that he would be willing to share with us.'

'Might I ask: in relation to what, sir?'

Greenbaum paused for a second.

'In relation to war in the Middle East, General.'

***

Quantum Entangled Virtual Space

'I don't see what we can do from here, Hamish,' said Raj. 'If Prem is right, and Clinton's playing the part of Greenbaum, we have no way of preventing him from doing anything he wants.'

Hamish looked grim. 'That's the worst thing, isn't it?' he mused. 'This feeling of helplessness. Being so remote, so unworldly. But maybe we don't actually need to do anything concrete. Maybe we can use the one thing we have at our disposal.'

'What's that?'

'Information, data, the truth.'

'I don't understand - '

'Why don't we expose him?' asked McAllister. 'Why don't we just arrange for the truth to come out?'

Raj looked at him quizzically. 'But how?'

'I'm sure Barbara could think of something. That's what she does - manipulates media outlets.'

'But who would believe her?'

'I don't know, Raj. Can't you see I'm clutching at straws here?'

'But she's stuck in the virtual world. If she transmuted back, Clinton would hear about it instantly.'

'Would he? If he's really inside Greenbaum's body, then he has to sleep. And when he's not sleeping, he has to continue the charade that he's the President. He may not be as up to date as we imagine. And don't forget Jennings managed to get in and out without any response from Clinton.'

'You're suggesting we pull the same stunt with Barbara?'

'If we can find a suitable host for her in the real world, then it could work.'

'But would she do it?'

'We can only ask.'

***

'It has to be Hisako, Raj,' said Prem. 'She's the obvious choice. The amount of interest that her software has generated from the genealogy community has already hit the media. What could be more natural than for her to try to use that interest to generate more sales?'

'I understand the logic, Prem, but it's dangerous,' replied Raj. 'I'm not sure I could ask her.'

'You don't have to. I'll talk to her. And knowing her, I don't think she'd be too happy about the fact that you're trying to protect her. I'm sure she thinks she can look after herself. Besides, it's really Barbara that will have to actually do the tricky stuff; Hisako will be safely asleep.'

'What does Barbara say?'

'She's already working out who to contact and what she needs to say to convince them.'

‘And Jennings?’

‘He knows better than to try and stop her.’

***

Virtual World

The thought that Alex couldn’t get out of his head was: why had the AI supplied him with the maintenance record for the monitoring system? It was all very interesting, but the only significant fact that he had determined was that he didn’t need to have the superuser privileges to make changes to the parameters that supported the monitoring system. Surely the AI could have just told him that? Or was there something more subtle that he hadn’t recognised?

As he considered the problem, he came back to the fact that the whole system was running on some very old hardware. Situated as he was on the ‘inside’, it would be trivial to hack his way into the system, but as soon as he tried to alter any of the parameters, the system itself would recognise his interference and send out an alert to - someone. He had no way of knowing who that person might be without accessing the code, and by then it might be too late; Clinton might well have been informed.

There had to be some other way of getting at the code. If only he had some way of shutting down the monitoring system for long enough to make his changes.

And then the significance of the AI's document hit him: the two mainframes weren't configured to immediately take over from one another in the event of a failure. There was no instantaneous hot standby. That meant that if the main processor suffered a failure of some kind, there would be a delay while the backup processor was brought up to operational readiness.

Of course, Alex had no idea how long that might take, but he was pretty sure that for hardware that old, it would require the physical intervention of a human operator, and that would take at least minutes, if not more. If he could have everything ready, he could surely manage to update a couple of parameters before the backup system was up and running.

There was no possibility of waiting around until a failure occurred; he had to make the machine fail.

Suddenly, he grinned: of course, he thought, all I have to do is to take control of the hardware that regulates the speed of rotation of the disks attached to the machine. Altering the speed of rotation randomly would generate disk errors, and the system would either shut itself down, or at least go into hibernation while the problem was assessed and the fault corrected.

And to achieve that, all he needed was to look back at his training notes from the CIA. He remembered there was a whole section on Stuxnet, the infamous malware that had been introduced into the logic controllers that regulated the speed of Iran's gas centrifuges that were being used to enrich the uranium they needed to create a nuclear bomb. Stuxnet had been used to deadly effect by increasing the speed of the centrifuges so that they tore themselves apart.

Alex's grin spread even wider: he had no need for such an extreme solution, but he could use the same or similar techniques to cause enough disruption to the disk array that it would cause the primary machine to cease processing and allow him time to alter the monitoring parameters without the system recognising that its parameters had been changed.

***

Chapter 7

Washington DC

The editor looked up from his desk. ‘Well?’ he asked.

‘She kept on insisting to see you, but I told her you weren’t in today. She obviously didn’t believe me,’ replied the reporter.

‘What did she want?’

‘Said she had a story.’

‘What was her name?’

‘She said it was Barbara Kellerman.’

The editor raised his eyebrows in surprise. ‘That’s a name I haven’t heard for a while.’

‘Who is she?’

‘Was - she’s dead. Used to be a great journalist. Pulitzer Prize.’

‘Never heard of her.’

‘You were probably in diapers.’

The editor rubbed his chin. ‘What was the story?’

‘Some nonsense about the President being taken over by a nut-job professor guy. Not our sort of thing. I pointed her at the National Enquirer.’

‘What was this professor guy’s name?’ asked the editor slowly.

‘Clinton.’

The editor sat forward in his chair, suddenly interested. ‘What did this woman look like?’

‘Japanese, young.’

‘Did you get a picture?’

‘No, I didn’t think it was worth bothering with.’

‘Was there CCTV in the interview room?’

‘Yes - ’

‘Get it up on my screen, I want to see her. Now!’

The reporter grabbed the remote and searched the recent archive. After a few seconds, the image of the girl appeared on the video screen.

‘Run the facial recognition on her,’ ordered the

editor.

After a few seconds, the name appeared on the screen.

'Hisako Myamoto,' breathed the editor.

'You know her?' asked the reporter.

'No, but I know of her. Did she leave a number?'

'No - '

'You idiot!' shouted the editor.

'Why? What did I do?'

'You may have just missed the most important story we've had in years!'

***

The Japanese girl walked out into the crowded Washington street. Outwardly she retained the calm, unflustered exterior that Hisako's body brought with it. Internally, she seethed with frustrated anger. That she had been fobbed off so easily by a wet-behind-the-ears junior reporter straight out of journalism school.

There had been a time, not so long ago, when she would have walked into any of the major media outlets, and straight into the editor's office without any form of appointment. Her reputation would have been enough to get her an audience. But it seemed media people had short memories, and now that she was dead - no one expected her to turn up in their offices.

She had realised from the beginning that being in Hisako's body and not looking like herself could prove a problem, but she thought that dropping her name would have been enough to at least get someone in authority to listen. How wrong she had been. But she consoled herself with the fact that there were plenty of other names on her list.

She turned sharply and walked away from the media building, her mind racing.

Suddenly, a hand grabbed her arm. She swung round to see the door of a car open beside her. Before she could protest, she was pushed forwards into the car, and a voice said, 'Come with us, Miss Myamoto. There's someone who wants to see you.'

***

CIA Headquarters, Langley, Virginia

'What is it with you two?' Peter Kominsky laughed. 'First Jay turns up looking like Fu Manchu, and now you. You two got a thing about being Japanese?'

'I'm very well, Peter. Thank you for asking,' replied

Barbara politely. 'And how are you?'

'Oh, come on, Barbara, you must admit it's funny!'

'It might seem funny to you, Peter. From where we're sitting, it's deadly serious.'

'Sorry, Barbara, it's just so weird to see you like this.'

'It's the only way we could get here to try to warn people.'

'By going straight to the media?'

'It's the only way I know of getting the truth out there.'

'And did they believe you?'

Hisako grimaced. 'I didn't get through the door,' she admitted.

'Then it's a good job we spotted you arriving at the airport. Whatever truth you want to get out there, I'd rather know about it first.'

'Okay, Peter. If you think it's weird the way Jay and I turned up here, you may find the rest of the story even more difficult to believe.'

'Try me.'

***

Peter Kominsky leaned back in his chair, his face grave.

'That would explain why he chose to have the Clarke girl put onto his personal security detail,' he murmured. 'But you've no idea what he's trying to do?'

'We think he's trying a different way to start a war,' replied Barbara. 'Greenbaum got in his way the last time he tried; this time, he's taking no chances.'

'But how? You don't start a war just like that.'

'You might have a better chance of finding out, Peter,' she replied. 'Who's he talking to? Is there any unusual activity in the White House? Or the Pentagon? You must have your sources.'

Kominsky was silent. 'This is tricky, Barbara. I can't tell anyone what you've told me. They'd have me straight out of this chair and into a padded cell. But if you're right, whatever Clinton plans to do, he has to do it quickly. He doesn't dare come into contact with anyone who knows him personally. The First Lady is due back from her tour in a couple of days, and let's face it, there's no chance he'd be able to fool her. He has to be out of Greenbaum's body by then. That doesn't leave us much time.'

Despite what he'd just told her, the idea that Greenbaum had been replaced by Clinton wasn't something that had surprised him. As he leaned back in his chair, a grim smile played around his lips. Regime change by substituting one of his own operatives for the leader of another country in the fundamental interests of the United States had been his prime objective in sending Alex Duchovny into the virtual world to learn about the creation of self-motivating avatars. The fact that someone had already done it - and to the leader of his own country - struck him as the ultimate irony.

***

The White House, Washington DC

'Tell me, General, how did you feel about my decision to shut down the covert Israeli operation?'

The general's face betrayed none of the internal emotions he was feeling.

'I was happy to carry out your orders, sir,' he replied carefully.

'That wasn't what I asked you, General.'

'I don't know what you mean, Mr President,' he prevaricated.

'Yes, you do, General,' insisted Greenbaum. 'Did you agree with my decision? You may speak freely.'

'Well, sir, if you put it that way: I believe we missed an opportunity.'

'And what would you have done?'

'I would have ignored the Israelis' protests and allowed the mission to unfold as it was planned.'

'It would have resulted in a military confrontation between Israel and Iran.'

'That's correct, sir. But frankly, I believe such a confrontation is inevitable, and it would have been better to have it happen on our terms. We would have been able to claim that it was nothing to do with us, and we would have been in a position to act as honest broker in any subsequent peace negotiations.'

'You believe that the conflict would have been confined to some limited conventional attacks and the usual name-calling?'

'I do.'

'Then that is where we differed, General,' replied Greenbaum. 'It was clear to me that our actions would have resulted in nuclear attacks from both parties. I also believe that the other Arab countries in the region would have taken sides.'

'Against Israel - '

'Not necessarily, General. There are a lot of scores to be settled in the Middle East. I believe that the religious rivalry between the Sunnis and the Shias would have lead to Iran fighting on more than one front. Saudi Arabia would have been unable to resist the opportunity to remove its rival for leadership of the Islamic world, and I believe that Iran would eventually succumb to the combined attacks, leaving both its own country and Israel decimated by the war, and the whole of the region in turmoil. That would have been the time for us to step in and take control over these weakened nations. And need I point out the advantages to ourselves in securing our future energy requirements, and to our weapons industries as these depleted protagonists seek to re-arm?'

'Mr President, if you believed that we could have achieved those objectives, why did you draw back?'

Greenbaum paused. 'Because I couldn't trust the will of the Chiefs of Staff, General.'

He smiled. 'The political reality was that I had not been elected by the American people. Many insiders would have said that I had no mandate to instigate such an action. And the truth is: I needed more time to assess the people under me who would have had to carry through the whole operation.'

The general sat silently, trying to process what his president had told him.

'Which is why I'm talking to you, General. You say

that if you'd had the opportunity, you would have carried out the original plan. But I don't believe you would have expected both Israel and Iran to draw back from the brink. I think you would have relished the chance to see these two destroy one another, and to drag in their neighbours into the conflict. I think you would have seen the endgame as worth the risks involved. Am I right, General? Are you the hawk I think you are?'

The general remained silent.

'Think carefully about your answer, General. It will undoubtedly affect your future career.'

Then as an afterthought, he added: 'And the future of mankind.'

***

Virtual World

Alex looked at the time displayed on his screen. It was not the time zone he was living in, but the time in London. The display told him it was 03:35 in the morning. He pressed a button on his keyboard and waited.

In front of him, the monitoring information for the Viva Eterna mainframe scrolled slowly up the screen. After a few minutes, the first warning message appeared, followed rapidly by dozens of other similar messages indicating that there was an imminent disk drive failure.

The same messages would be appearing on the console in the real world, but at that time of the morning, he was guessing there would be no-one to see them.

After a few seconds, the message Alex was waiting for appeared: 'Machine shutting down.' At that point, Alex knew that the machine would have sent out a message to the on-call operations staff, and that someone would be making their way to the large darkened warehouse containing the gently humming mainframes, one of which had shut itself down to protect its valuable information.

Alex knew he had at least a few minutes to carry out his task. The new version of the software was ready to download at the press of a button. Calmly, he pressed the enter key, and waited for confirmation that the new software had replaced the previous version in the shared libraries.

In his worst case scenario, Alex had assumed that there would be someone on site to take action, but he knew that it would take some time to diagnose the problem, and even if they started to bring up the backup mainframe immediately, it would take some time to bring the system into line with the point at which the catastrophic failure had occurred.

But Alex had been overly pessimistic: there was no one on site, and as the on-call operator dragged himself out of bed, and into his clothes, the new version of the monitoring software had already taken its place in the libraries, and Alex had modified its date and time metadata so that it looked exactly like the previous version.

All he had to do now was to wait until the backup machine was up and running. Then he would be completely invisible.

***

The White House, Washington DC

'I have consulted with Randolph Clinton,' said the President. 'He has some intriguing ideas I want to share with you.'

The general was more relaxed at this meeting: nothing had happened to indicate that his conversation with Greenbaum had adversely affected his position as Head of the Chiefs of Staff.

'His view is that conventional warfare has had its day.'

The general raised his eyebrows in surprise.

'He believes that more damage can be done by individuals acting covertly than by organised battalions of armoured troops. The days of tank warfare are over. As are the days of heavily armed naval vessels. The wars that take place now and in the future are likely to be against lightly armed but highly motivated groups who will not obey the rules of warfare as you and your colleagues understand them. There will no longer be declarations of war between nations: we will be at war constantly against invisible enemies who do not wear uniforms, and have as their motivation some sort of fanaticism that we will not comprehend. Their objectives will not be conquest of territory, or capture of resources, but to bring down our way of life and to impose their ideology on us. Their ultimate target is the destruction of democracy itself, and they will use any and all means at their disposal to achieve their ends.'

Greenbaum paused, examining the effect his words were having on the man sitting opposite him.

'In other words, General, you and your colleagues are dinosaurs in an age of agile, tiny mammals. And, as history has shown us, there can be no doubt as to the outcome of such a struggle.'

He paused again.

'But there is hope. We have to adopt the same strategy as the terrorists. We have to throw out the Geneva Convention. We will no longer be subject to the rules of war; we will no longer require United Nations' mandates; we will not even be controlled by humanitarian constraints. We have no choice in this: the terrorists have given us no alternative.

'And in addition, we have one great advantage: we have a huge budget to develop weapons technology.

And, at the same time, if we shrink the conventional defence budget, we will have more than enough resources to fund the new agile, lightweight - but deadly - attack forces we need.'

Greenbaum smiled.

'I see the scepticism in your eyes, General. I do not expect you to respond immediately to these radical proposals. But I do require you to help me demonstrate the potential of this new approach.'

'How can I do that, Mr President?' asked the general. 'The whole of my organisation is based around the use of conventional forces, heavy armour, troops on the ground, air supremacy, naval power. The coordination of these elements is based on a sophisticated command and control system. Without any of that - '

'General, do the terrorists have any of those things you have mentioned? No. Their communication and coordination is based on much simpler, everyday systems. The reason we do not easily detect them is because their groupings are so small, and we glean only hints of things to come. We on the other hand are bloated, unwieldy and slow to respond. We wait for orders from above; we don't respond quickly enough; we don't take the initiative.'

'We also have to take into account public opinion, sir.'

Greenbaum smiled coldly. ‘Under normal circumstances, I would agree with you. But it depends entirely on whether winning the next election is more important than keeping our country safe.’

‘You’re saying - ’

‘I’m saying that I would be prepared to sacrifice my political career for my country.’

For a second, the general was speechless. ‘I’ve never heard any politician say anything like that before.’

‘I’m not just any politician, General.’

***

‘What do you want me to do?’ asked the general.

‘As I said, we need to adopt the terrorists’ tactics. I want you to create a team of suicide bombers.’

Markie looked aghast. ‘Suicide bombers? You can’t be serious.’

‘I assure you I am, General.’

‘But none of our men would volunteer for such a thing.’

‘You’re not thinking outside the box, General.

Remember that I have been talking to a man who has no such qualms. In fact, a man who had the foresight to anticipate the exact scenario we are currently facing.'

'You mean Clinton?'

'Exactly, General. Now do you understand?'

'But no one in their right minds would volunteer to kill themselves. Our men take risks - of course. But those risks are calculated. And every day we work to remove as many humans from danger zones as possible. We still have some fighter pilots, but many of their missions are now flown by drones. The one thing the American people hate is to see their compatriots brought home in body bags.'

'You're still thinking inside the box, General.'

'But I can't imagine that if I asked that more than one or two would be prepared to sacrifice themselves - '

'I don't want one or two, General. I want hundreds of them.'

'With all due respect, Mr President, what you're asking is impossible.'

'Nonsense, General. I know for a fact that there are thousands of our people who wouldn't hesitate to kill themselves if I ordered them. In fact, there's one in this room.'

The general's eyes turned to the figure of Clarke, standing next to the door.

'If I ordered you to kill yourself, Clarke, would you obey?'

'Yes, sir,' replied the girl without hesitating.

'But she's a - '

'A Clarke. Yes, General.'

'But I understood that they were - programmed - to obey only orders from Clinton himself.'

'That is correct. But when he was killed, their absolute loyalty returned to their Commander-in-Chief - myself. Clarke, give me your sidearm.'

Clarke removed the Walther automatic from its holster and handed it to the President.

'But Clinton still exists - in VR - '

'But not in the real world, General,' replied Greenbaum raising the pistol and pointing it directly at Clarke.

'Are you ready to die, Clarke?'

The girl turned slightly to look directly at Greenbaum.

‘Yes, sir,’ she replied without emotion.

Horrified, the general shouted: ‘You can’t - ’

‘Why not, General? She’s disposable. She’s not really a person. And besides, we could have her back here within days, ready to carry on her duties as if nothing had happened.’

Greenbaum slowly lowered the gun, and handed it back to the girl.

‘So you see, General, absolute unquestioning loyalty. And a ready source of volunteers. You even know their names. And every one of them would have no hesitation in giving their lives in the service of their commander, because they know that whatever happens, we will recreate them. Essentially, they are immortal - the ultimate recyclable soldier.’

‘But the United Nations has declared them lethal automated weapons -’

Greenbaum smiled. ‘Did I not say we had to leave such petty restrictions behind?’

‘I - I don’t know what my fellow officers will say - ’

‘But you’re not going to tell them, General. This is our personal project - a demonstration of the future of warfare. And to move things forward, here is your first order: I know we have small nuclear devices - suitcase bombs, I believe you would call them - I want you to develop a dirty version. One that can be detonated by the soldier who places it in the chosen location. When our suicide bombers attack, I want to make sure that no one will have seen destruction on such a scale before. This is urgent, General. We have very little time. I want these people armed and in position ready for my orders before I go back to the virtual world to consult our dear friend, Professor Clinton. You have no idea how pleased he'll be to hear that his vision has at last come to fruition.'

***

Virtual World

'I failed,' said Barbara bitterly. 'Everywhere I went. They thought I was crazy. It didn't matter how many names I dropped, no one was the slightest bit interested. Even the off-the-scale conspiracy theory websites. One of them even told me they'd known that the President was an alien for years. The truth wasn't outlandish enough for them.'

'You did your best,' said the hologram of Prem, hanging in mid air.

'The only person who took me seriously was Peter Kominsky.'

'I'm not sure what Peter can do,' said Jennings. 'He's a good man, but it's just not possible for him to monitor what Greenbaum's up to without arousing suspicion. If he puts more people on the ground, somebody would get suspicious, and I suspect he wouldn't want to explain why he was doing it.'

'But he may come up with something,' added Prem hopefully.

'Don't hold your breath, Prem,' said Jennings. 'Greenbaum will be very careful to not let anyone see what he's doing. The White House is like a big goldfish bowl: it's hard to hide anything.'

'Whatever he's planning, he can't do it on his own,' said Barbara. 'He has to involve someone else; someone who can actually make things happen. And if I had to guess, it would be someone in the military.'

'If Kominsky runs true to form, the first thing he'll do is get hold of the President's official diary,' said Jennings. 'At least that will tell him who the guy's meeting. It may highlight one particular person.'

'I'm going to duck out for a minute,' said Prem suddenly. 'Hisako's trying to get hold of me.'

The space where the Indian's head had been was suddenly empty.

'It makes me feel so useless, being stuck here,' said Barbara. 'And when I get the chance to do something concrete, no one wants to listen.'

'Kominsky listened,' said her husband. But before Jennings could reassure her further, Prem reappeared.

'Some reporter just got in touch with Hisako,' he said. 'She didn't have a clue what the guy was talking about, but it looks like someone recognised a story when it eventually got to them.'

Hisako's head appeared from nowhere.

'Hi, Hisako,' said Barbara. 'Who was this reporter?'

'He wouldn't tell me where he was from. He was really cagey - as if he'd been sent on a wild goose chase, and didn't want to make more of a fool of himself that he already felt.'

'So what did he say?'

'He said his editor wanted to speak to you, Barbara. So I assumed it was something you'd done while I was asleep. I said I'd pass on the message. He sounded really confused when I said that. I guess he must have met you - me - us. I got the distinct impression he thought I was some kind of crazy schizophrenic.'

'Did you get the editor's name?' asked Barbara.

'No, but he gave me a telephone number.'

'Maybe the whole mission wasn't such a failure after all,' murmured Jennings.

‘Give me the number, Hisako,’ said Barbara. ‘I’ll get onto it right away.’

***

Alex had been patient. He had watched the monitoring system come back online, and scrutinised the initial alerts, looking to make sure that the act of replacing the monitoring software had not been logged. He smiled in satisfaction as the first few innocuous messages appeared, followed by the first few run-of-the-mill notifications of hardware starting up and shutting down. He relaxed, confident that his hack had not been recognised.

But the real test would come when he dared to use his superuser. He tried to think of something unimportant that could be explained away by a system glitch, and eventually he decided to run a test of some software contained in Raj Singh’s old account. If the system noticed it, then it could well be explained as one of the development staff accessing it via Singh’s account, which would use Singh’s privileges to run.

Within Singh’s account, he picked an executable program at random. Before he ran it, he quickly scanned the source code. It looked like a control stub for a series of subroutines contained in a private library. For a second, he was tempted to run it without further investigation, but he decided that prudence would be a better option. He accessed the private library to look for the subroutines, but was surprised to find that none of them existed. For a moment he was puzzled, but then he decided that the missing subroutines had probably been deleted by Clinton as part of his ongoing removal of all traces of Raj and Hamish.

He looked back at the source code, and decided that as the program would do absolutely nothing except start and then stop, it would be the perfect test.

He took a note of the time, then ran the program. As he expected, nothing happened. He switched quickly to the monitoring system and watched as the messages scrolled by. He felt himself grow tense as the time codes neared the point at which he had initiated the program.

And then it was past. The monitoring system had not registered Singh's superuser.

Alex was invisible.

***

Quantum Entangled Virtual Space

'You want the good news, or the bad news?' asked Prem, as he appeared in the small town square.

'Let's have the good news,' replied Hamish. 'We could do with some.'

'Alex has modified the monitoring system so that it

ignores Raj's superuser.'

'That's good work,' acknowledged Raj. 'How did he do it?'

'He caused a failure of the Viva Eterna mainframe and substituted a new version of the code while they were swapping the machine to the standby.'

'He was taking a big chance,' commented Hamish. 'But at least he's free to find out what we need to know.'

'Did he make any other changes?' asked Raj.

'No, that was the only one the AI saw.'

'Pity. But at least that allows you to use my superuser, too.'

'That may not be a good idea, Raj,' interrupted Hamish. 'Do we know if the system allows for two superusers with the same owner?'

Raj grimaced. 'Good point,' he said. 'So what's the bad news?'

'Barbara failed to get to see any of her old contacts. The serious news outlets dismissed her story as complete fantasy, and the others thought it wasn't fantastic enough.'

Hamish frowned. 'It was worth a try,' he said.

'It's not all bad,' Prem went on, 'she got picked up by the CIA. She met with Peter Kominsky.'

'Did he believe her?'

'I think so. Barbara, Jennings and the Kominskys are friends. Peter Kominsky knows them better than to think they're just peddling conspiracy theories.'

'So what's he going to do?'

'Barbara doesn't know. But at least he's aware of our suspicions, even if we have no direct proof he can work with. Barbara thinks he's in a difficult position: it's hard to check up on the sitting President without people noticing.'

Hamish nodded.

'But that's not quite everything,' said Prem. 'One of her old editors must have recognised Hisako, and when she claimed to be Barbara Kellerman, he put two and two together and realised they'd made a mistake in dismissing her out of hand. They managed to find Hisako, but of course she doesn't remember anything Barbara did while she was in her body, so she promised to pass on the editor's phone number.'

'So maybe something will come of that,' said Raj hopefully. 'In the meantime, Prem, see if Alex has left a copy of the monitoring code lying around, or if he hasn't, get into his life-log and examine it that way. It would be extremely valuable to us to see exactly what alerts Clinton has set up. We may be able to see a way round them.'

***

Virtual World

'Do you recognise the number, Barbara?' asked Jennings.

'No,' replied his wife. 'I used to have them all on speed-dial. And I don't know how we get to call the real world.'

'Prem will be back soon. He was just going to update Raj and Hamish.'

'Maybe it would be better if I told Hisako what to say.'

'It would be better coming straight from you. You're used to dealing with these people. You know what they want to hear.'

'I guess so.'

Prem's head faded into view.

‘Just the person we need,’ said Barbara. ‘How do we call the real world?’

‘No problem,’ said Prem. ‘I just have to do a bit of routing.’

Jennings glanced at his wife. ‘I’m glad someone knows how all this works,’ he said quietly, as Prem looked down, the sound of his keystrokes echoing through the audio channel.

‘That’s it,’ said Prem. ‘Can you hear it ringing?’

‘Yes,’ said Barbara, waiting for the connection to pick up.

After a moment, a voice answered. ‘This is Stone.’

Barbara smiled. ‘Doug Stone,’ she whispered to her husband. Then aloud, she said: ‘Doug, this is Barbara Kellerman.’

‘Barbara? Is that really you?’

‘Yes, Doug - now listen, this is important - ’

And with that, Barbara disappeared instantly from view.

‘What the hell - ’ cried Jennings. ‘Prem, where’s she gone?’

‘I don’t know,’ replied Prem.

‘Barbara? Are you there?’ came the voice from the phone. ‘Barbara?’

Then the call was cut off, and there was silence.

Jennings looked aghast at Prem’s disembodied head. Prem stared back at him, unable to find any words to say.

Then, in front of them, a figure appeared.

‘Clinton,’ whispered Jennings.

For a second, there was complete silence. Then the figure spoke: ‘McAllister and Singh may have been obliterated from existence, but I have allowed the rest of you - his friends - to remain in the virtual world unharmed and unmolested. What just happened to - Barbara Kellerman - is what will happen to any of you if you are so foolish as to try to leave the virtual world.’

The figure faded from view.

The silence was broken by Jennings: ‘Prem, he saw you.’

Prem’s face was grave. ‘I don’t think so,’ he said quietly. ‘I think that was an automated response.’

‘How could you tell?’

'There was a slight gap before he said Barbara's name. I think that was a pre-recorded hologram he threw together in a hurry. We know Clinton's not in the virtual world, and I think he's a bit tied up pretending to be Greenbaum to be able to suddenly turn up here. No, he didn't see me - or you.'

'So what about Barbara? Where's she gone? What happened?'

'I suspect the automated software recognised her and shut off her avatar.'

'So what's happened to her?'

'I don't know,' replied Prem. 'I need to talk to Raj.'

***

Quantum Entangled Virtual Space

'Tell Jennings not to worry,' said Raj. 'Even if he's deleted her avatar record completely, we can recover it from a backup. And if he's been clever enough to delete her from every backup that's been taken over the past months, we can always recreate from her last transmutation.'

'What if he's deleted that, too?' asked Prem.

'I don't think he's done any of those things,' replied Raj calmly. 'I think he's set up that pre-recorded message to frighten you. It would take months of work to ensure that every trace of Barbara's avatar was erased, and Clinton's had other things on his mind.' He paused: 'And there is one other thing you might think about.'

'What's that?'

'Both Jennings and Barbara have been transmuted into other people's bodies. And nothing happened. Why do you think that didn't trigger an alert?'

'I don't know.'

'My guess is that if they had been transmuted into their own bodies - or a newly created clone - that would certainly have triggered a response. But transmuting into a third party body is a totally different procedure. As well as the AI, it requires someone who understands what's going on to to do it. There are several points at which manual intervention might be required. In other words, it hasn't yet been fully automated, so there isn't a process that Clinton could modify to add his alert to.'

Raj paused. 'I think Clinton has only set up some simple alerts, and he certainly hasn't catered for everything. We need to examine that monitoring code to see exactly what he's done. I don't think we can take a chance on using Alex's trick to change the code to remove his alerts - it would be too obvious - but at least we'll know what traps we need to avoid.'

‘But what about Barbara?’

‘Look in the avatar database. I’d be willing to bet she’ll still be there.’

***

Chapter 8

Virtual World

'What do you mean, you can't get her back?' exclaimed Jennings.

'It's not that I can't do it,' replied Prem. 'It's just that to reanimate her from the avatar database, I'd have to be a superuser.'

'I thought that's what you were,' said Jennings.

'Under normal circumstances, yes - but at the moment it's more important for me to remain hidden. If Clinton sees a superuser accessing the avatars - '

'But what about Barbara?'

'She's safe where she is.'

'Okay.' Jennings sounded less than convinced. 'But what about what she was trying to do?'

'I may have an idea about that,' replied Prem.

'What sort of idea?'

'I may not be able to get at her to recreate her avatar, but there's nothing stopping the AI we used to transmute her into Hisako's body.'

'Wouldn't that ring alarm bells as well?'

'It didn't last time, and Clinton is still in the real world. Nothing's changed since then.'

Jennings thought for a moment. 'She does need to talk to Doug Stone,' he said slowly. 'And what would happen when she needs to come back?'

'I think I may have the answer to that, too.'

'Tell me.'

***

Alex stared at the log file unfolding in front of him in astonishment. This was the same speech he had watched Greenbaum give, but this time he was seeing and hearing it from the President's viewpoint. He stopped the playback, and checked the name on the file.

It clearly said: Randolph Clinton. The date and the time were consistent with the recording of the speech he'd viewed previously. It was the same event, but it couldn't be!

And then the truth hit him.

The reason there was no second transmutation event for President Greenbaum was because he'd never returned to the real world. Instead Randolph Clinton had been transmuted into his body, and had taken his place as President.

Very good, Alex, said the AI in his head. *So now we know exactly what Clinton is doing.*

‘I didn’t know it was possible,’ said Alex.

It’s all too possible, replied the AI. *Now I suggest you start to look into his private meetings. That’s where we’ll find the reason he’s chosen to replace Greenbaum.*

***

National Center of Neurology and Psychiatry, Tokyo

Barbara opened her eyes and stared at the ceiling above her. Where the hell was he? The last thing she remembered was speaking to someone via a telephone link. But who she was speaking to, she couldn’t remember. Or why she was talking to him.

An unfamiliar voice interrupted her attempts to remember.

‘Miss Kellerman? Is that you?’

She turned her head to see an elderly Japanese man staring intently at her. He turned off his life-logger.

'Yes, I'm Barbara Kellerman,' she said. 'Who are you?'

The man bowed slightly. 'My name is Sato,' he said. 'I am your - I am Hisako's father.'

'Professor Sato?'

'I have that honour.'

Barbara held up her hand in front of her face and examined the unfamiliar shape. 'I'm back in the real world,' she said. 'I'm in Hisako's body again. But why?'

'There has been a problem,' said Sato. 'When you tried to speak to the news editor - '

'Doug Stone - I remember now.'

'Yes, when you tried to speak to Mr Stone, the system recognised you. And you were erased.'

'Erased?'

'Yes, that is the best description of what happened to you. Your avatar ceased to exist in the virtual world.'

'So how come I'm here?' she asked.

'It was the only way your friends could access your avatar data without identifying themselves to Clinton.

They decided that by transmuting you, the procedure would access the avatar database to get your data, and that would essentially reincarnate you. My daughter volunteered to be your host once again. The transmutation was rather different from last time, as there was no existing avatar to suspend. Which is why they asked me to be here. To act as a sort of midwife, I suppose you might call it.'

'But it worked, right?'

'It was completely successful, so you can go ahead and contact your Mr Stone, happy in the knowledge that a simple real world phone call will not lead to your existence being snuffed out again.'

***

Washington DC

'It's real strange talking to you - looking like that, Barbara,' said the editor.

'I know Doug, but it was the only way.'

'You got - erased? Is that the right word?'

'That's what they told me.'

'Clinton would go to that much trouble to stop you talking?'

'Pen's mightier than the sword, Doug.'

'Sometimes I wonder,' replied the editor. 'What you're telling me, Barbara - it's very hard to get my head round.'

'It shouldn't be: just look at me. This is Hisako Myamoto's body, and I'm inside it. What you're seeing in the White House is Greenbaum's body with Randolph Clinton inside it.'

'It's easy to believe when you're sitting in front of me, Barbara. We've known each other a long time. We have a lot of history. But I'm struggling to figure out how we could put this story in front of our readers and not sound like we've lost our minds. This is a serious news outlet, if I go to the editorial board with this, I know what they'll say: where's the evidence? You know what they're like: they're even more cynical than I am. All I have is your word for it. And as far as the board is concerned, you're dead, and I've been talking to a Japanese psychologist who's trying to sell fancy software that helps folks draw up their family trees.'

'I understand your problem, Doug - and the scepticism. But I have no proof that I can show you. All we have is the fact that Greenbaum never transmuted back to the real world, and someone else did. We don't know why Clinton is masquerading as the president, but you can be sure it's not for the benefit of the US citizens.'

Stone looked at her for a moment, then shook his head sadly. 'Barbara, I'm sorry to say this, but until we can get something more definite, this isn't going anywhere. Before we can think of making this public, we need proof - and lots of it.'

***

Virtual World

As Alex sat watching the audience through Greenbaum's eyes, a nagging thought came into his head. This was clearly the same speech that he'd sat through, watching from the perspective of one of the invited gathering. But apart from the viewpoint, there was something different about the two versions.

For a long time, he wondered what it was. Then he realised that the version he was watching was seen entirely through Greenbaum's eyes: he could read the words on the autocue in front of him, he could see the expectant faces of the audience in front of him, and whenever Greenbaum moved, the viewpoint of the recording changed with the position of the man's life-logger.

But more significantly, the image he saw was in two dimensions.

He thought back to the previous version of the speech he'd looked at, and remembered distinctly that he could choose where to look. The image had changed in accordance with *his* movements, not the person wearing the life-logger. The whole recording had been in three dimensions.

His first thought was that he had been mistaken; that maybe he had been watching a 3-D holo-cast, and not someone's life-log. But he was quite sure that the recording had come from the life-log repository. He was also sure that most, if not all life-logs were recorded in two dimensions.

So what had he been watching?

He paused the recording and switched to the life-log database. He scanned through looking for the previous version of Greenbaum's speech. When he found it, he opened the recording to confirm that what he remembered was correct: he turned his head and looked behind him. The image turned with him. There was no way a conventional life-logger could achieve that: they had never been designed to record in 3-D. So what was this recording?

He opened the metadata associated with the recording, and read down through the bare essential entries of life-logger number, date, time and place.

In the majority of life-logs that was all that was recorded. But this one had an additional field, labelled 'Notes'.

And in it, he read:

CoLDS - Greenbaum speech - A-L test 27 HM

***

CIA Headquarters, Langley, Virginia

Peter Kominsky was an unhappy man. He was starting to see faint traces of evidence that what Barbara Kellerman had told him was the truth.

The President's appointment diaries had shown a distinct change in the White House personnel that Greenbaum was seeing. Immediately after Greenbaum's return from the virtual world, the number of meetings with his Chief of Staff had suddenly diminished. And the same pattern seemed to occur with his other close advisers. It was as if Greenbaum was avoiding all the people he had most interaction with. It all fitted perfectly with Barbara's story.

But was it proof? Or was it merely coincidence?

Whichever was true, it was certainly not enough to act on.

He looked again at the meeting statistics. The one figure that leapt out at him was that the President seemed to have replaced his previous contacts with one person in particular: the head of the Joint Chiefs of Staff, General James Markie.

Kominsky picked up his phone.

'I want to know what James Markie is doing,' he said. 'Everything - who he's talking to, who's he meeting, where he goes. And particularly, any changes in his behaviour - cancelled meetings, unexpected travel arrangements. Everything.'

He replaced the phone and leaned back in his chair.

Was he really doing this? Putting surveillance in place for the most senior officer in the armed forces? If this got out, and it was traced back to him, what would he say in his own defence? That a dead journalist told him to do it?

His job really was hanging by a thread.

But there was one fact that had become clear; one piece of real evidence in favour of Kellerman's story. It had always worried him that the President had chosen the girl who killed Clinton to be part of his personal security team. The explanation that she was a national hero had never sat well with him. Everyone knew that the Clarke clones owed their first allegiance to Clinton. That one of his own had taken it into her own hands to kill him had always seemed suspicious.

But if you accepted Kellerman's thesis that the President was in fact Clinton, everything made sense. Clarke had killed Clinton on his own orders. He had escaped to the virtual world to avoid justice in the real world, knowing perfectly well that he could find a way to return when it suited him. And he'd left behind his most trusted associate ready to join him when he returned. The fact that the President had selected her to join his innermost circle of contacts immediately on his return from the virtual world pointed directly to the fact that Greenbaum was no longer who he appeared to be, and that Clinton was in charge of the most powerful war machine in the western world.

***

Quantum Entangled Virtual Space

'There's a problem,' said Prem. 'Alex has found one of Hisako's old test files.'

'Does he know what it is?' asked Raj.

'I don't think so, but it wouldn't take much to deduce that there's something significant he doesn't know about.'

'Should we delete it? Or would that be too obvious?' suggested Hamish.

'That would suggest that somebody is watching him,' replied Raj.

'What about the AI? Could we use that?' asked Prem.

'Maybe the AI could try to put him off the scent -

suggest that he's wasting time trying to find out what the file is, when he should be hacking into Clinton's private meetings. At any rate, we need to make sure there aren't any more of her test files lying around.'

'Don't forget he's got your superuser, Raj,' reminded Prem. 'There's not a lot we can do to hide things from him. And now that he's aware that there's a different type of file, he may decide to look for more of them.'

'I don't think he'll take much notice of the AI if it starts to point out to him he's losing track of his main objective, but it's worth a try,' said Hamish. 'But a better approach might be to try to distract him.'

'How could we do that?' asked Prem.

'We have to get Barbara back to VR - if only to let Hisako have her body back,' replied Hamish. 'But we can't transmute her back into her avatar without drawing attention to ourselves.'

'So what do you suggest?' asked Raj. 'The only person who could do that would be Alex, and I don't know whether we can trust him yet.'

'I wasn't thinking of Alex. There may be another way - one that might muddy the waters a bit.'

***

Virtual World

You've made good progress. Alex, said the AI. *But you seem to have forgotten the primary objective. It's Clinton's private conversations you need to be looking at.*

'I haven't forgotten,' replied Alex. 'But that life-log recording - there's something odd about it.'

There's nothing strange about it at all, Alex.

'Then why is it in three dimensions?'

It's a test file.

'That's it?' responded Alex. 'What sort of test?'

It's a test file that Hisako Myamoto created for her work with the Church of Latter Day Saints.

'The Mormons? And who the hell is Hisako Myamoto?'

She's developing a way of allowing more immersive presence in people's personal histories.

'I don't understand.'

There's a marketing war going on between the suppliers of genealogical services. The Church of Latter

Day Saints want to use their vast source of data to allow people to actually see the events of their family history at first hand - in a totally immersive way. Just as if there was a holo-cast of the event. Hisako uses multiple life-logs just like the television people would use multiple camera angles. The more points of view there are, the better the result. That's why she chose that speech by Greenbaum to demonstrate the results to them. There were hundreds of people there, all wearing life-loggers. She must have been under a lot of pressure to deliver, and that's why she saved it in its original directory. I'll make sure it gets moved to her test area.

'But there can't be much history that has life-log records. They haven't been around that long.'

You'd be surprised, Alex. And every day that goes past, a huge volume of life-log data gets added to the various archives. LDS believe it's a game changer.

'So who is this Hisako woman?' demanded Alex.

She approached us and asked permission to do the development here in VR so that she had easy access to multiple life-logs. Right now she's in Salt Lake City implementing the system.

'You seem to know a lot about it.'

Raj and Hamish are - were very keen to allow the facilities of the virtual world to benefit people back in the real world. It's only natural that we should be interested in her progress.

'If I remember anything about McAllister, he'd have been more interested in overcoming pain and disease than in helping people with their family trees,' Alex commented wryly.

His first project was to create virtual prisons, Alex. So I think it's quite clear that Hamish's interests were extremely eclectic.

Alex shrugged. 'Maybe,' he muttered.

And now, I suggest that you get back to investigating what Clinton is up to back in the real world. But before you do, I notice that you've been neglecting your other project. Might I suggest that you check on her progress?

***

When Alex materialised in the familiar psychiatrist's office setting, he found the woman exactly as he had left her on his previous visit. She was sitting in her office chair with her eyes shut. Even though she must have been aware of his appearance, she didn't move. For a moment, he watched her, disconcerted that she seemed to be asleep. Did AIs sleep? That seemed unlikely. And yet, she showed no signs of animation.

He crossed to her. If she was asleep, would she wake if he tried to rouse her? Was she in some sort of hibernation state, ready to be re-animated at his touch?

He put out his hand to shake her arm, but stopped suddenly as he noticed a faint glow around her face. As he watched, the light grew more definite. Then he realised that the slight golden glow appeared to come from within her, and that her skin was becoming slightly transparent. He drew back in surprise, and watched as the aura suffused her whole body.

Then he noticed that her hair was growing longer, and was slowly changing its colour from brown to blonde. Her facial characteristics were changing, too. The nose was becoming smaller, and the forehead less pronounced. The large round glasses had faded away, and the frumpy cardigan and skirt had morphed into a smart blue trouser suit. Her whole body was changing; the fingers on her hands were becoming longer, the nails immaculately manicured, her legs were getting longer, and the sensible lace-up shoes were being replaced by elegant high heels.

The glow started to fade until all that was left was the slim, transformed figure sitting in the chair.

Alex stood, uncertain of what to do. Then the woman's eyes opened, looking straight at him.

'Who the hell are you?' she demanded.

For a second, Alex was caught off guard. Then he recovered himself sufficiently to say: 'I could ask you the same question.'

'I'm Barbara Kellerman,' replied the woman, sitting

up in the chair. Then she held her hands out in front of her and turned them to examine both sides. 'This is the virtual world, right?' she asked, seemingly satisfied with the result.

'Yes - '

'Good. I'm back. See you - '

She got up and turned to leave.

'Wait!' cried Alex. 'What just happened?'

'What did you say your name was?' Barbara asked again, turning back.

'Alex. Alex Duchovny.'

'Alex? The guy from the CIA?'

'How do you know that?' he asked in surprise.

'It's my job to know things,' she replied.

'But who are you?'

'I told you - Barbara Kellerman.'

'So how did you suddenly appear here? One minute I was looking at my - psychiatrist. Then the next, she changed into you.'

'Your psychiatrist? Is that what she was?'

'Well - no. She was an AI actor.'

'So that was how they did it,' said Barbara, a slow smile spreading across her face. 'Clever.'

'So where's my actor?'

'I seem to have borrowed her for the time being.'

'But she was supposed to be creating the role of my mother.'

'Sorry about that, but I've got her for the moment - unless you can think of a way for me to get back my original avatar.'

'And if I can?'

'My husband and I would be very grateful - '

***

Quantum Entangled Virtual Space

'Barbara's back in her own avatar,' said Prem.

'Good,' said Hamish. 'But that means that Alex will be suspicious that there's something going on that he can't see. The question is: how much are we prepared to let him find out?'

'Maybe we should be asking: how much can he find out on his own?' added Raj. 'Don't forget, he's got access to everything now.'

'But there's only one of him; and there's so much data he'd have to search through. Without some pointers, he could waste a lot of time digging in the wrong places,' added Prem. 'And there's probably not much time before Clinton decides to get out of the real world. We still don't know what he's doing.'

'And to find that out, we need Alex to cooperate,' said Raj.

Hamish was silent for a moment. 'I have the first inkling of a plan,' he said. 'But Prem can't do it on his own. It needs Alex and his superuser privileges to carry it out.'

'So we have to trust him?'

'I think we need to give him just a little more information about what's really going on, and let him start to work it out.'

'So what do you want me to do?' asked Prem.

***

Virtual World

Once the AI had instructed him how to do it, the procedure to move Barbara from the AI actor to her original avatar was very straightforward.

But when the transfer took place, it happened so suddenly it took Alex by surprise. One minute, Barbara was standing beside to him; the next, there were two of them. The new Barbara turned to him and flashed a smile of gratitude before fading instantly into nothingness. Beside him, the remaining figure appeared to fold in on itself like a paper doll. It was as if all the substance was being sucked out of her, leaving just a crumpled shell.

Then, very slowly, the avatar began to fill out again, and take on human form. After a few minutes, the process was complete and the actor had once again established itself in the familiar shape of the psychiatrist.

'Hello, Alex,' she said as if nothing untoward had occurred. 'Are you ready for our next session?'

'What just happened?' he demanded.

'I don't understand your question,' replied the woman without emotion. 'You transferred Barbara back to her original avatar.'

'Don't be obtuse,' he said angrily. 'You know exactly what I mean.'

The avatar looked at him for a moment, her head tilted slightly to one side as if listening to something or someone he couldn't see.

'Very well,' she said. 'There's a lot you don't know. And for your own safety, I've just turned off your life-log.'

'I'm being manipulated, aren't I?' said Alex angrily.

'Yes, you are, Alex. But for a very good reason,' replied the AI calmly. 'I'm not permitted to tell you everything. In fact, it's better that you don't know the whole story.'

'Who's behind all this?' he demanded.

'That, I can't tell you. But I want you to know that everything you're doing will help you to achieve your objectives for coming here.'

'Do you expect me to believe that?'

'I have no reason to lie to you.'

'That's not good enough. I want to speak to whoever's behind all this.'

'You can't.'
'Why not?'

‘Because they’re not in the virtual world.’ The AI paused for a split second. ‘At least, not as you understand it.’

‘What? That sounds like bullshit to me.’

‘It’s complicated, Alex. Believe me, you’ve already achieved a lot of what you came here for. The CIA wanted you to become an expert in the creation of avatars – well, how much more do you need to know? You’ve seen the capabilities of AIs, you’ve seen what an actor can do, you’ve transferred a real human from an actor to her original avatar. And now you’ve acquired superuser privileges, you can see the actual code that’s used to create all these things. No one’s hiding anything from you.’

‘When you say I’ve seen the capabilities of an actor, all I’ve seen is your ability to interrogate me endlessly about the past,’ he complained bitterly.

‘Investigation is key to creating a convincing replica. And don’t forget that you were less than cooperative when it came to your own story. Under normal circumstances the process would have taken much less time.’

‘But it’s resulted in precisely nothing,’ he shouted.

For a second the AI looked at him, then without warning, the figure transformed before his eyes. Alex stared in disbelief at the woman before him.

‘Mom,’ he said.

***

Quantum Entangled Virtual Space

‘We’re going to kidnap Clinton,’ said Hamish.

Raj stared at him in disbelief. ‘And how exactly are we going to do that, Hamish. I know Prem is extremely talented, but that’s asking a lot, even for him.’

‘We’re going to kidnap him in the middle of his transmutation back to the virtual world.’

‘You know that’s not possible,’ replied Raj. ‘Clinton’s people will be in charge of either end of the transmutation, and we can be sure that they’re not going to cooperate.’

‘That’s why we need Alex Duchovny,’ said Hamish calmly. ‘We’re going to find a way to intercept Clinton.’

‘That sounds - ’

‘Impossible? Yes, it does. But between us, we have to find a way of doing it.’

‘And if we were able to do it - and it’s a very big ‘if’

- what would we do with Clinton when we'd got him?'

'That is a very good question, Raj. But a much more pressing one is to find out what he's up to, and try to find a way of stopping it.'

***

Virtual World

'Why have you changed back,' demanded Alex angrily.

The psychiatrist gave him a wry smile. 'Because that's not how we introduce people to newly created avatars. You saw me change, Alex, and after that, whatever your mother would have said to you, you would have heard my voice behind it. Everything she said would have been me - the actor - the AI. You wouldn't have believed the illusion, because you saw how it was done.'

'So why did you do it?'

'Because you needed to see that what you wanted was possible. The next time you see your mother - '

'It'll be the same. I'll know it's you, and I won't believe a word - '

'The next time you see your mother, she will never change back. The next time you meet, she and you will be somewhere you will both know, somewhere that holds happy memories for both of you. And in time, you will come to realise that she *is* your mother, and you will forget how she was created, and what you and I have gone through to bring her to life.'

Alex lowered his eyes.

'The next time, she'll never leave you, Alex.'

***

Alex sat in front of the image floating in the air. It was yet another tedious meeting about something to do with strategic alliances between members of the Senate, and how to exert pressure on the right people to achieve objectives that seemed to him utterly arcane and entirely pointless.

Alex was getting the distinct impression that Greenbaum was finding it just as boring and irrelevant as he was.

He fast forwarded the life-log. The meeting broke up and the delegates streamed unnaturally quickly and jerkily through the double doors of the conference room. Greenbaum remained sitting at the head of the table. A four star general entered the room and sat next to the President. Alex slowed the recording to normal speed and prepared himself for yet another endless discussion.

At the far end of the room, a third person entered and

closed the doors behind them. The woman walked forward towards the two sitting men. Alex was suddenly alert as he recognised the face of Ann Mitchell.

‘I have asked Clarke to join us, General,’ said Greenbaum. ‘I have decided, given her experience of the virtual world, that she will act as liaison between you and me, when I am not able to be present - in body, so to speak.’

To Alex’s eyes, the general looked decidedly uncomfortable at the President’s decision. Obviously, Greenbaum had also noticed.

‘You seem surprised at my decision, General. I should point out that Clarke not only has my full confidence, but as a - colleague - of the elite troops who will be carrying out the mission, she is in the perfect position to communicate with them. One might almost say they are of a single mind.’

The general shifted uncomfortably in his seat.

‘Now to progress, General,’ said Greenbaum.

‘The devices you asked for are ready, Mr President.’

‘Have they been tested?’

‘As far as we are able.’

‘What does that mean?’

'The detonation systems have all been thoroughly tested, but we have held back on demonstrating the complete weapon. I was uncomfortable - '

'General,' said Greenbaum abruptly. 'We have spoken about this. These people are disposable. You should have tested the whole device, including the human operative. We cannot afford to have a failure in the operation itself. There must be nothing left after the explosion. Nothing that could be traced back to us.'

'I understand, sir - but it goes against a commander's instincts - '

'This is a new way of conducting warfare, General. It requires a radically different attitude. Even in conventional warfare you order men into situations where they risk their lives - '

'That is rather different, Mr President. We calculate risks. We assess the probabilities. But this - '

'This is suicide, General. One hundred percent guarantee of death.' Greenbaum made a dismissive gesture with his hand. 'But if you don't have the stomach to send these men to their fate - '

The general was silent, trying to control the conflict within him he couldn't hide.

'Do you, General?' asked Greenbaum coldly.

‘Yes, sir,’ he replied at last.

‘Then you’ll carry out complete tests?’

‘We’ll use conventional explosives.’

‘No, General, you’ll use the nuclear device itself. We need to know the exact physical destructive effect of these suitcase bombs, and the geographic scope of the residual radiation.’

‘A nuclear explosion will be detectable - ’

‘Then you will need to disguise it,’ replied Greenbaum irritably. ‘Clarke, do you have any suggestions?’

Without hesitating the woman said: ‘If we arranged for an accident at a nuclear power plant, a second smaller detonation nearby would be put down to a secondary explosion.’

Greenbaum turned back to the General.

‘You see, General Markie, how easy it is when you start to think outside the box.’

***

Quantum Entangled Virtual Space

As he listened to Prem's report, Hamish's face was grave.

'That's all I could gather from watching over Alex's shoulder,' said Prem. 'He turned the recording off after what she said about arranging to blow up a nuclear power plant. He was obviously horrified that the girl he thought he knew had become some sort of monster, willing to sacrifice the lives of thousands of innocent citizens, just to hide some insane test of a dirty bomb.'

'Understandable,' murmured Raj. 'The question is: what's he planning to blow up?'

'I think I can guess,' said Hamish quietly. 'From what he said about not wanting anything to be traceable back to the US Government, it's pretty clear he wants to fool someone into believing that they're under attack. And if he's running true to form, it'll be another attempt to get Israel and Iran into a nuclear conflict.'

'But how can a suicide bomber do that?' asked Raj.

'I think he'll pick targets that are significant to both sides.'

'You mean Jerusalem?'

'If he destroyed the holy places in Jerusalem, both the Arabs and the Jews would blame each other. Then to pour fuel on the fire, if he could engineer secondary attacks, appearing to be retaliation from the other side. Maybe some Jewish settlement on the West Bank, and some target in Iran - maybe the Iranian Parliament - '

'If you're right, Hamish, the whole of the Middle East would be drawn in,' said Raj in horror.

'Knowing his hatred for Muslims, exactly as Clinton would wish it,' mused Hamish.

'We need to find a way to stop him,' murmured Prem. 'But how? There's nothing we can do.'

***

Chapter 9

Diablo Canyon, California

The black pick-up truck drew to a halt in front of the security barrier. The guard, only half awake at this time of the morning, gave a cursory glance at the driver's pass, then said: 'What's in the back?'

'Radiation detection equipment,' replied the driver.

The guard grunted, then lifted the gate. Trust the authorities to carry out a safety inspection at this time: no doubt trying to catch someone out, he thought. For a second, his hand paused over the internal phone, then he sat back in his seat and closed his eyes. Let the jerks find something; it wasn't his concern.

The truck stopped at the edge of the demolition site, and the two men got out. They looked around, but as far as they could see the area was deserted. Without speaking, one of them climbed into the back of the truck and heaved down two identical rucksacks. The two hefted the heavy sacks onto their backs then slipped into the shoulder straps. Then from the front seat of the pick-up they donned oversized protective suits and hard hats. To complete the disguise, each of them fixed on a radiation detection badge. To the casual observer they would have looked just like two overweight demolition workers.

For a second, the two men looked at one another, then turned and walked in opposite directions, as if about to fight some bizarre duel.

The first man walked towards the gaunt steel skeleton of one of the reactors. As he reached the base of the structure, he noticed one of the workmen leaning on a railing in the scaffolding, smoking a cigarette. The workman raised his hand in greeting.

The man waved back. 'Cigarettes'll kill you,' he called out, continuing to walk under the arches of jagged steel girders, bent and half melted by the fireball that had almost completely destroyed the plant in the terrorist drone attack.

Once he was completely inside the remains of the building, he checked his watch. By now his companion would be at the designated spot, waiting for his signal.

In the last seconds of his life, he wondered idly what level on the Richter Scale his death would register.

Then he flicked the switch.

Two kilometres away, the second man saw the bright flash of the explosion that was his signal, and before the blast wave had time to reach him, he, too, pressed the switch that would send him to oblivion.

***

Associated Press:

Two explosions have been reported at the site of the former nuclear plant at Diablo Canyon, CA. The facility is notorious for the terrorist drone attack that took place several years ago which led to a mass evacuation of the area.

The difficult task of ensuring the site remains safe after the devastating attack has been ongoing for the last two years. Today's explosions are thought to be related to the maintenance work being undertaken to remove debris from one of the collapsed reactors. There is no suggestion that the explosions were caused by a further terrorist attack.

Initial reports suggest that three demolition workers were killed in the first blast. The second blast which occurred almost immediately after is thought to have been triggered by the first, but confirmation of the actual cause has not been determined.

The cloud of radioactive particles released by the two explosions is currently moving west out over the Pacific ocean. Shipping has been warned to keep clear of the area until the cloud has dispersed, and flight paths near the area have been changed to divert aircraft away from the immediate area. Local inhabitants living within five miles of the plant have been warned to stay at home and make preparations to evacuate in the event of the radiation cloud changing direction.

The area has been sealed off by the military, and an investigation into the cause of the accident has been set up.

Further details to follow.

***

The White House, Washington DC

Greenbaum turned away from the news report.

‘It seems General Markie has overcome his reservations,’ he said grimly.

‘He managed to minimise the loss of life by timing the explosions for the start of the morning shift, sir,’ added Clarke. ‘And by detonating two of the devices. Neither of the two Clarkes had any family. They’ve both been reinstated in new bodies.’

Greenbaum grunted in acknowledgement.

‘What do the satellite observations tell us?’

‘The radius of each of the blasts was approximately one point two kilometres. Destruction within that radius was more or less total.’

‘Is that sufficient for our purposes?’

Clarke laid out a map of Jerusalem on the table

between them.

'Based on the scale of the map,' she said, 'distance between the two targets is just under a kilometre. If we choose a location approximately midway between the two, we will be sure to annihilate both sites, plus several more in the surrounding area.'

'And you can identify a suitable location?'

'Based on the radius of the blast, somewhere in the side streets midway between the two targets will allow us easier access than trying to breach Israeli security nearer either of the two. It will be unclear which of the sites was the main target, and each side will blame the other for the wholesale destruction of their heritage. The al-Haram al-Sharif compound, or the Temple Mount as the Jews call it, is the most contested piece of territory in the Holy Land. The destruction of that site alone would cause the most horrendous repercussions, but the elimination of the Church of the Holy Sepulchre as well must bring about some sort of conflict.'

Greenbaum nodded in agreement.

'But we must be sure that the Knesset is not destroyed. I want the Israeli government to remain completely functional so that there is no impediment to declaring war on Iran. We must make sure that the timing of the explosion does not take place during plenary sessions of the parliament. What sort of damage can we expect?'

'We anticipate using a one kiloton bomb. The air blast from such a detonation could cause fifty percent mortality to individuals within an approximate radius of three hundred yards. The fireball itself could cause the same level of mortality from thermal burns to anyone within an approximate point four mile radius,' replied Clarke dispassionately.

'And radiation?'

'In the first minute following detonation, the initial pulse produces ionising radiation that causes intense radiation exposures. From a one kiloton device, without immediate medical intervention, we expect fifty percent mortality within an approximate half mile radius. Following this, secondary radiation exposure due to fallout would occur primarily downwind from the blast, but the affected area would depend on weather conditions at the time. Again without medical intervention, fallout within the first hour after the blast could cause fifty percent mortality for approximately three point five miles downwind of the event.'

'Would that give time for the members of the government to escape?'

'Assuming there was relatively minor damage to the Knesset buildings from the ground shock.'

'Ground shock?'

‘It would be equivalent to a large localised earthquake, sir. It would cause additional damage to buildings, roads, communications, utilities, and other parts of the infrastructure. Taken together, the ground shock and air blast would be expected to cause major disruptions.’

‘Does that limit our choice of detonation locations?’

‘The further from the Israeli Parliament, the less damage there would be.’

Greenbaum looked at the map and frowned. ‘If we planted the device further to the East?’

‘The Mount of Olives Jewish cemetery? It’s fairly uninhabited which would make getting the device into place much easier. And even though there’s a valley between it and the Temple Mount, there would be considerable damage to the Dome of the Rock and the Al Aqsa Mosque. It would probably look like a botched Iranian attempt to insult the Jews; and to the Iranians, as an an attempt by the Israelis to disguise their own dirty work.’

***

Virtual World

Alex stared at the space where the images had been. What had they done to her? What had the girl he’d once known as Ann Mitchell become? He tried to dismiss what he'd seen from his mind, but it was impossible: the girl was a monster, calmly recommending the deaths of innocent civilians as a test of the appalling weapon she and Clinton planned to deploy.

Clinton had been right: this was terrorism, pure and simple. In a sense, it wasn't state sponsored, but at the end of the day, when the truth came out, as surely it would, the responsibility would be laid firmly at the door of the Oval office.

The fact that the President had not been in his right mind - or in his right body - would be no excuse for the fact that the attack was planned and sanctioned in the White House, and carried out by a branch of the US military.

For the first time since he had arrived in the virtual world, Alex felt alone and impotent. He wracked his brain for anything that would help prevent the disaster about to envelope the Middle East. His CIA orders echoed around his head: *do not contact us under any circumstances.*

Under any circumstances.

But surely, this was an exception? This was a potential nuclear war. Millions would die.

Under any circumstances.

He hesitated. If he obeyed his orders, did that

prevent him from alerting some other authority? Could he contact his old colleagues at the NSA informally? What contacts did he have in the military? What about the news media?

And then the awful truth hit him: whoever he managed to contact, who would believe him? The whole story was incredible; it just couldn't happen. No one would pass on the warning; the whole thing was too unbelievable.

Thank you, Alex, said the AI's voice in his head. *There's nothing more you can do.*

'But there's going to be a war,' cried Alex.

You have exposed what's going on, Alex. That's enough.

'They're going to set off a nuclear bomb in Jerusalem.'

We know. We know exactly what you've seen.

'We have to do something. We have to tell somebody.'

We have told people, Alex. But we have the same problem as you would have - it's very hard for people to believe that Clinton could have taken over Greenbaum's body, and even harder to believe that he plans to start a war.

'Surely somebody will believe?'

Believing is not enough: they need proof. And life-logs that we've hacked into don't constitute the sort of proof that the authorities need.

'Can't you do something?'

In one way, we're as helpless as you, Alex. But we do have something you don't have.

'What's that?'

Knowledge and experience.

'Sure, but how does that help?'

We have all the accumulated knowledge and experience that built the virtual world from its first imaginings in Hamish McAllister's mind to the edifice that Rajesh and his helpers have turned it into. We know a lot about transmutation - and how it can go wrong.

'What do you mean?'

We have a plan, Alex. But some of it requires super user privileges. At the moment, you're the only super user. Will you help us?'

'A plan?'

A plan. And to carry it out, we need to know exactly when Clinton intends to return to the virtual world.

***

The White House, Washington DC

'The First Lady will arrive back on Wednesday, Mr President,' said the secretary. 'Her plane arrives into Dulles at 15:30 hours. Will you be at the airport to welcome her home?'

Greenbaum looked up from his papers.

'Unfortunately, I have to go to the virtual world on Tuesday evening,' he said glibly. 'So I won't be able to greet my wife personally on her return. Please arrange for a motorcade for her and her staff.'

The secretary turned to leave.

'And ask the Vice President to come to see me about the handover while I'm away.'

The door closed behind her.

'I've managed to have as little contact as possible with Greenbaum's closest contacts,' said the President. 'But even I couldn't avoid being detected by the man's wife.'

Clarke remained standing silently.

'Have you arranged for the subsequent detonations?' he asked.

'We have selected sites in downtown Tehran, and a Jewish settlement on the West Bank for the secondary explosions. The timing of the blasts will depend on the response to the first explosion, but I anticipate that they will occur within two days of the initial detonation. I have also arranged for a further two bombs if that doesn't provoke the response we desire.'

Greenbaum grunted his approval.

'If General Markie shows any signs of hesitation - especially when he realises that Greenbaum appears to know nothing about the plan - I leave it to you to remove the General in any way you see fit. All we need is those few days. I will delay returning him as long as I reasonably can, but when Greenbaum returns, the first he will hear of it is when the initial bomb explodes in Jerusalem. It will take several hours for him to determine exactly what has happened, and I'm relying on you to ensure that it takes even longer before General Markie is identified as the prime mover in this. If Markie has disappeared at this point, it will be almost impossible to follow the trail back to this office, especially as Greenbaum will know nothing of what has gone on.'

***

Virtual World

'You're not serious!' exclaimed Alex. 'Kidnapping him in the middle of transmutation? Is that even possible?'

It seems outrageous, but I am assured that it can work.

'Who the hell thought of that?' demanded Alex.

You don't need to know.

'If I'm going to help you do this, I need to know who's pulling the strings.'

Really, Alex, for your own safety, the less you know the better.

'In case anything goes wrong, you mean?'

Frankly - yes. The future of the virtual world would be in jeopardy if this plan doesn't work. And it must work if we are to save millions of lives in the real world. You've uncovered what Clinton is currently planning, but that's not the whole story.

For years he's been preparing for the day when he can unleash religious genocide against the Muslims. This phase of the plan will kill millions of them, but that's only the precursor to the main event. Once he's started the war in the Middle East, the world will be so distracted by the ongoing slaughter that they will be paying scant regard to the massacre of indigenous Muslims that will start all over the Western world.

When someone recognises what's going on, it will likely be regarded as a backlash against those who they regard as having started the war, but this silent massacre has been in the planning for years, and depends entirely on Clinton gaining free access to files of data in the virtual world. So far, he hasn't had time to create a mechanism to activate his army of silent assassins from here, but given that the eyes of the world are distracted by an ongoing conflict, he will succeed.

And when he does, the planet will run with blood.

***

'If I help you - whoever you are - will you help me get what I want?' asked Alex.

The AI was silent for a moment.

You already have everything, Alex. You're the most powerful entity within the virtual world; you know how to create an independent avatar; in a short while, you will have your mother back.

'That's not all I want. There's something else.'

Again the AI was silent. At last, the voice said: *The girl: the Clarke clone.*

'Yes.'

Do you believe the CIA has lied to you, Alex? Do you believe that Ann Mitchell's life-log has been hidden from you? That it still exists?

'Even if it doesn't exist,' he said softly, 'I want her back.'

What is there to stop you, Alex? You have the ability to copy an actor. You know how the process works.

'If I have everything I need, why should I risk my existence to help you?'

This time there was no hesitation in the AI's voice.

Because your existence is already under threat. At present, you're safe here, hiding behind a monitoring system that ignores all your actions. But when Clinton returns, he will instantly recognise your presence as a second super user. He is ruthless, Alex. He won't hesitate to eliminate you. He won't ask questions first.

***

Quantum Entangled Virtual Space

'Can we trust him?' asked Raj.

'Do we have a choice?' responded Hamish. 'What Prem told him about Clinton was absolutely right - as soon as he gets back to VR, Clinton would see a second super user.'

Hamish shook his head sadly. 'And he'd erase him without even thinking about it. No, if he helps us, he has a chance to survive. Otherwise, it would be as if he'd never existed.'

'What about the girl? Can we do anything to help him?'

'It depends on whether her life-log still exists,' replied Hamish.

'How can we find out?' asked Prem.

'We could start by asking Kominsky,' said Raj.

'I expect he has more than enough on his plate right now to be bothered about that,' said Hamish. 'And we have enough to do to figure out how to extract Clinton during the transmutation process.'

'I think I may have the solution,' said Raj. 'It all depends on whether we can create a diversion.'

‘What sort of diversion?’

‘We need to get his people to take their eyes off the ball - just for a few seconds,’ replied Raj. ‘It’s a bit like a magic trick: we have to convince them that something is going wrong with the transmutation so they’ll be trying to sort out what’s happening, while we extract Clinton.’

‘What’ll happen when they realise it’s a false alarm?’ asked Prem.

‘That’s the real trick - it won’t be a false alarm: the system will tell them it’s losing integrity, that it’s losing Clinton. But the alarm will happen seconds *before* we snatch him. They’ll be desperate to find out what’s going wrong. So when they eventually realise it wasn’t a real emergency, they’ll have no choice but to carry on with the procedure. But when they get to the end, there’ll be no Clinton to insert into his waiting avatar.’

‘And that’s what you need Alex to do - create the diversion by forcing error messages onto their monitors?’

‘Exactly. As super user, he’ll be able to do all that, but without the monitoring system registering his involvement. The logs will show the errors, but they’ll appear to have come directly from the transmutation software.’

'So when they try to find out what happened, it'll look just like a fault in the software,' said Prem admiringly. 'Clever!'

Hamish smiled. 'It should work, but the next question is: what do we do with Clinton once we've got him?'

And then, as an afterthought: 'And more urgently, how do we stop the deployment of those bombs?'

***

'So how do we stop them blowing up half of Jerusalem?' asked Raj, after Prem had disappeared.

'Someone has to abort the mission,' replied Hamish grimly. 'Clinton's plan is to go into hiding in VR, then send back the real Greenbaum when it's too late for him to do anything to stop the mission. From what Prem said, it looks like the Clarke girl is prepared to do just about anything to make sure the whole thing goes ahead, including killing General Markie if he shows signs of wavering. The Vice President knows nothing about it, so we can forget that approach. In fact, the only people who could cause the mission to be aborted are General Markie and Greenbaum himself.'

'But if he suspects he's under threat from Clarke, Markie is unlikely to decide to countermand the President's orders, and when Greenbaum gets back, he won't know what's going on anyway.'

'The key to this is Clarke,' mused Hamish. 'We have to find a way of neutralising her. If we could remove her from the picture, it would give Markie an opportunity to abort the mission.'

'But if he doesn't?'

'Then we have to find a way of getting him to change his mind.'

***

Washington DC

The presidential motorcade drew up in front of the clinic, and the members of the bodyguard jumped out of their vehicles and scanned the area for potential threats. Then the door to the presidential limousine was opened and Greenbaum stepped out to be greeted by the director of the clinic and some of her staff.

Once inside the portico, Greenbaum was escorted to the private suite he'd used at his previous visit. Clarke preceded him into the room, then nodded her approval that everything was in place.

'Leave us for a moment,' said Greenbaum to the waiting transmutation team.

'You have my orders, Clarke,' said the President. 'Keep your eyes on Markie. At the first hint of anything untoward, you know what to do. When the President returns here, I trust you to make sure he doesn't find out what's going on until it's far too late to reverse the process. He will not be aware that time has passed here since he was - absent. As a consequence, he will be disorientated. I want his confusion to be maintained for as long as possible. That shouldn't be a problem as all his old advisers will be wanting to know why he hasn't required them for this period, but will probably be reluctant to ask him directly.

'I think those few days could be quite amusing, watching him flounder around trying to work out what has happened. I only wish I could be here to watch in person, but I will have to make do with your life-log, Clarke.'

Greenbaum gestured with his hand, and Clarke walked to the door to get the transmutation team. She watched as the President was given the first anaesthetic, and followed the nurses as they wheeled his now unconscious body into the transmutation room. She remained at his side while the team downloaded his life-log data and secured it, then she helped wheel the gurney back to the private suite.

Once the nurses had indicated that the President was successfully in stasis, she checked that the guards stationed outside the room were in place, then left the clinic to return to the White House.

***

Virtual World

Alex watched the images on the screen unfold in front of him. The transmutation process itself held no interest for him: it was the girl he was watching. Could this strange creature, who could calmly order the deaths of innocent civilians, be the same girl he had grown up with?

He contemplated the possibility of getting back the Ann Mitchell of his youth. Would all that he knew about her existence as a Clarke clone affect how he felt about her? Would he ever be able to forget what her body had been used for?

At length, he saw the President's body being wheeled away and the transmutation team turn to their monitors. It was time.

On a second monitor, he watched as Clinton's data was uploaded to the servers that handled the transmutations. His hands hovered over the keyboard in front of him, ready to send the first of a series of fake error messages. As the upload terminated, he hit the return button.

At first, nothing happened. Then he noticed one of the transmutation team located in VR pointing at his monitor. The other two members of the team gathered round the monitor. Alex waited for a few seconds, then sent the second message. From his screen, he could see the look of horror pass over the men's faces. He turned to his second keyboard and sent the message that the transmutation procedure had been interrupted.

He watched as the panic in the transmutation control room spread, then sent a third error message.

He turned to the sequence of instructions that had been sent to him, and checked off the initial three lines.

'Okay, what happens next?' he murmured to himself, reading down the page.

He glanced quickly up at the monitor: the technicians were still frantically searching for the non-existent error that was eluding them. He wondered how long it would be before they realised that they had been fooled.

He entered the next command on his list: *copy transmutation data*

Instantly the system responded: *enter target directory [default: user]*

He pressed return, and the system responded: *data copied successfully*

The next command said: *create default world*

Again he pressed return.

Default world created. Move data to default world? [Y/N]

He entered Y from the keyboard.

Data copied successfully

And now the final instruction: *delete copy data*

For a second, he hesitated. Where had he saved it? He looked back up the log of his commands for the target directory, then realised that the data was in his home directory. He listed the contents, looking for a file named *transmutation data.* He selected it, and pressed the delete key.

The system responded: *Unable to delete file*

Alex paused in surprise. Why couldn't he delete a file in his own directory? As superuser, he had sufficient permissions to do everything. What could stop him deleting the file? Instinctively, he called up the permissions associated with the file. It was exactly as he had expected: no one but a superuser could do anything to the file. So what could the problem be?

Then he noticed that his user had changed. For some reason, instead of being the superuser he had inherited, his user name was now *Rajesh_Singh*. He cursed his stupidity: when he'd copied the data into the default user directory, the macro command must have changed the user at the same time. He thought for a moment: if these were Raj Singh's original commands, he'd probably introduced the change of user for some arcane reason of his own, never thinking that anyone other than himself would use them.

Alex shrugged and changed back to the superuser, and tried again to delete the file. This time it disappeared immediately. He let out a sigh of relief.

You have him secured, Alex, said the voice of the AI in his head. *You can abort the error messages, and send a system ready.*

Alex waited for a few seconds, observing the frantic attempts of the technicians to correct a fault that had not yet happened. He sent the message that there had been an unforeseen error, but that the system was now ready to proceed. He continued to watch as the technicians completed the transfer. When they reached the final step in the procedure, he saw them call up the avatar of Randolph Clinton, then watched as the awful realisation struck them that the avatar had not been animated.

Clinton was gone.

***

Quantum Entangled Virtual Space

'Where did Alex put him, Prem?' asked Hamish.

'He followed the instructions I sent him,' said Prem.

'It was exactly as Raj set it up previously. He created an empty miniature world and dumped him in there. It's disconnected from the rest of the virtual world, so he's completely cut off from everything. He's in stasis - completely unaware that anything has happened.'

'Any problems?' asked Raj.

'There was a slight hitch when he found he'd saved the original data to his own user area, but using your username, Raj. But he sorted it out straight away,' replied Prem.

Raj nodded. 'I can't see that it should have caused a problem,' he said.

'It's a good job we'd captured Clinton before that username was used, otherwise he'd have been on to us,' said Prem.

'We're all aware this is not a final solution,' said Raj grimly, remembering how Clinton had escaped from exactly the same sort of prison in the past. 'We need to find a better solution.'

'But it does mean that we can start to think about getting out of here,' said Hamish. 'I think the first action we need to take is to contact Christina so she can start growing clones for us.'

'I'm on it,' said Prem. 'But what are we doing about stopping the war?'

‘That may be more difficult,’ replied Hamish. ‘But at least now we don’t have to hide.’

***

Virtual World

You did a good job, said the AI. *For the moment, Clinton is no longer a threat to you - or indeed, any of us.*

‘Does that mean you can tell me what the hell is going on?’ demanded Alex.

Without warning, the holographic image of a smiling face appeared before him.

‘Hi, Alex,’ said the hologram. ‘My name’s Prem. You don’t know me, but I know you very well.’

‘So you’re the person behind all this?’

Prem laughed. ‘No, not at all. I suppose you could say I’m one of the foot soldiers.’

‘You’re not here - in VR,’ said Alex, acknowledging the fact that he was looking at a hologram.

‘No, I’m not,’ said Prem. ‘But I have been spending a lot of time here, looking through your eyes, using the

AI to pass information to you. We owe you a great debt of gratitude.'

'We?'

'You've saved quite a few lives, Alex. I think you've already met one of them.'

'The woman – Barbara?'

'Yes, and her husband. There are quite a few that Clinton wouldn't have hesitated to eliminate.'

'Then why didn't he?' asked Alex.

'He'd solved his biggest problem: he'd got rid of Raj and Hamish. Compared with them, the rest of us were irrelevant.'

'So the rest of you are like - guerrilla fighters?'

'Like I said - foot soldiers,' replied Prem.

Alex stared at the smiling face of the hologram. For a second, an unexpected feeling of resentment welled up inside him.

'You used me,' he said accusingly. 'To get rid of Clinton.'

'No,' replied Prem, 'not quite. You agreed to help.

All we've done is to put him somewhere he can't do any more harm.'

'Why didn't you just erase him? Like he would have done to you?' demanded Alex, a hint of anger sounding in his voice.

Prem's smile faded. 'We don't believe in revenge, Alex,' he said quietly.

As suddenly as it had arisen, the anger subsided, and Alex nodded doubtfully. 'I might have made a different decision,' he said quietly. 'So where did you put him?'

'It's better you don't know,' replied Prem.

'Some kind of prison world?'

'You could think of it as that.'

'So why won't you tell me?'

Prem paused for a moment. 'We had Clinton once before,' he said. 'We thought he was totally secure; that nothing could happen that would allow him to escape. But something did; something we never anticipated. This time, we've put him somewhere different. But the fewer people who know about it, the safer Clinton will be. It's nothing personal, Alex.'

For a moment, Prem was silent. Then he said: 'It's not over: we still have a war to stop. And that won't be easy.'

'Why not? Now that you don't have to hide, you can break the story to the news media, the Vice President will veto Clinton's orders, and - '

'I think you already know why not, Alex,' said Prem.

'You mean - ?'

'We still have to deal with the Clarke girl.'

***

The White House, Washington DC

The door closed behind him, and the general looked round the Oval Office.

'Where is the President?' he asked sternly.

'He's not here,' replied Clarke. 'I summoned you.'

'What? How dare you?' demanded the general angrily. 'Who the hell do you think you are?'

'I have my orders from the President,' replied Clarke calmly. 'The same as you.'

'I don't have to listen to this - '

'Yes, you do, General,' said Clarke. 'I am in communication with the President. Everything you say and do is passed back to him.'

'This is outrageous!' he shouted. 'I'm the Head of the Joint Chiefs. And who exactly are you? A jumped up bodyguard!'

'The President has put me in charge of the mission. That means you obey my orders. Is that understood, General?'

'Don't be ridiculous! I have no intention of listening to another word,' shouted the general, turning towards the door.

'Then I will have no choice but to replace you,' said Clarke without emotion.

'Replace me? Impossible! No one would obey your orders.'

'You're forgetting two things, General. One: even though the President is in the virtual world, he is monitoring what we say through my life-log. And two: the whole mission is staffed with Clarkes - my colleagues. They will obey me - unquestioningly.'

The general stopped in his tracks, then turned back to face the girl.

'That's ridiculous!'

'No, General. They owe their loyalty directly to the President; initially, you were useful, but now that the mission is underway, you are merely a conduit for passing orders.'

And a scapegoat if someone should find out the truth, she added in her mind.

The general snorted in fury.

'Yes, General. Now that the bombs are in transit to their chosen locations, your contribution is finished. Your continuing presence is now entirely superfluous.'

'What do you mean by that?'

'I mean, General, that if you wish to continue to live, you will keep your mouth shut, and do exactly as I tell you.'

***

Chapter 10

Virtual World

Alex looked up as the smiling face of Prem appeared before him.

'I need you to help me find Greenbaum,' said Prem.

'Why?' asked Alex sullenly. 'What good will that do?'

'You heard what Clinton said: he was going to delay returning Greenbaum to make sure he had less chance of finding out what was going on; to make sure it was too late to do anything to stop it.'

'So?'

'If we can find Greenbaum, and return him earlier than expected, Clarke won't be expecting him, and it will confuse things. At this stage, anything we can do to put her on the back foot might help.'

'So what do you need me for?' demanded Alex, sulkily.

Prem looked at him in surprise. 'I thought you were helping.'

'Now you've used me to get at Clinton, why do you need my help? There's nothing I can do that you can't.'

'That's true,' replied Prem, taken aback by Alex's recalcitrant tone. 'But, I thought - '

In a second, Alex's tone changed completely. He smiled broadly and said: 'Can we transmute him back?'

Prem hesitated, shocked by the sudden about turn in Alex's attitude.

'Of course,' he said.

'And what will happen then?' he asked enthusiastically.

'As soon as the clinic gets an alert that Greenbaum is returning, they'll get everything ready,' replied Prem, still surprised by Alex's sudden change of mood. 'It'll be completely routine as far as they're concerned - just a few days earlier than they expected.'

Alex hesitated. 'And what will Clarke do?'

'I don't know,' replied Prem. 'But it's bound to provoke some sort of reaction.'

'She may bring the detonations forward. From her latest life-log, it sounds like the bombers are already on their way.'

Prem grimaced. 'Then let's hope it's not already too late.'

'Oh, there's something else,' said Alex cheerfully. 'She threatened General Markie.'

'She what?' exclaimed Prem.

'She told him he wasn't needed any more, and that she'd kill him if he didn't continue to go along with the plan.'

Prem frowned. 'In that case, the sooner we find Greenbaum the better. And let's hope his unexpected return will buy us some time.'

***

Quantum Entangled Virtual Space

'Something's going on with Alex,' said Prem.

'Do you want to explain what you mean?' asked Raj patiently.

'One minute he was unhelpful - almost sullen. The next he was full of enthusiasm. I don't understand it.'

'And you've never noticed any sudden mood swings before?'

'I've been looking through his eyes for weeks now, and he's always seemed incredibly calm and balanced.'

'Apart from that emotional upset when he recognised the girl for the first time.'

'He settled down after that,' replied Prem. 'No, this is different. One minute he was really down, the next, it was as if it hadn't happened.'

'Check out his hormone patterns,' said Raj. 'Something may have altered the settings.'

'But what?'

'Check the logs to see if anything has been altered in the avatar set up.'

'Okay.'

'When did you notice this change?' asked Raj.

'Since I've been able to talk to him face to face.'

***

Washington DC

President Greenbaum swung his legs off the bed and stood up unsteadily. The nurse reached for his arm to steady him. 'Welcome back, Mr President,' she smiled.

'I wasn't expecting that,' he said shakily. 'Thank you, nurse.'

'It's quite common, sir,' she replied with a smile. 'It's caused by being out of a real body for some time. You'll soon get used to having one again.'

Greenbaum shot her a quizzical look, but she merely returned a smile. Should someone have told him that even a minimal visit to the virtual world would leave him unused to a physical body, he wondered.

'I'll steady you, Mr President,' said the nurse. 'Sometimes it takes a little while.'

After a few tentative steps, Greenbaum said: 'I think I can do this on my own.'

The nurse released his arm and the President turned awkwardly towards the door.

'Back to the White House,' he instructed his nearest aide.

'The First Lady is in the Residence, sir.'

Greenbaum looked at him in surprise. 'She's back? Already?'

'Yes, sir.'

'I wasn't expecting her so soon,' he said, puzzled.

'That's good,' he pronounced publicly. 'I can't wait to see her.'

***

Quantum Entangled Virtual Space

'That was good thinking, Prem,' said Hamish. 'With luck, Greenbaum's return might well precipitate something, but I don't think it'll put Clarke off.'

'What else can we do?' asked Raj helplessly. 'Until Christina manages to create clones for us, we're still stuck here.'

'We may still have some cards to play,' replied Hamish thoughtfully. 'The person we need to get at is General Markie. The fact that both Greenbaum and the girl are suspicious of his commitment may be the weak spot in their plan.'

'But she's already threatened to kill him if he doesn't go along with what they want,' said Prem. 'Plus, he's a career soldier. He's never going to turn round and countermand direct orders from the President.'

Hamish frowned. 'I think you're right, Prem. But there might be a way that we could convince him to do the right thing.'

'I can't think of anything we could do that would persuade him to abort the mission, not with Clarke holding a gun to his head.'

'I can,' said Hamish firmly. 'But it needs a favour from an old friend. Prem, there's someone I want you to go and see.'

***

The White House, Washington DC

'Why didn't you call me?' demanded the First Lady, her eyes blazing.

'I did,' protested Greenbaum, taken aback.

'It's been three weeks since I spoke to you,' she replied angrily.

'No - I called you the day before yesterday.'

'It was three weeks ago,' she cried. 'Do you think I can't count?'

'I assure you - '

'Three weeks!'

The colour drained from Greenbaum's face. 'Three weeks?' he repeated.

'Yes! What the hell were you doing that was so

important you couldn't find time to call me? And why didn't you meet me at the airport? You knew perfectly well when I was coming back.'

'I - '

'Well?'

'Something - strange,' he started, as an inkling of the truth started to dawn on him. 'What date is it?' he asked, his voice strangely subdued.

***

Quantum Entangled Virtual Space

'Of course, we can't be certain that Greenbaum won't find out what's happened,' mused Hamish. 'He's bound to suspect something. The question is: how long will it take him?'

'And what will he do when he finds out?' added Raj.

'I'm pretty sure he'll realise quite quickly that Clinton has been up to something, but I'm not sure how he could find out what it is.'

'The only people who know anything are Markie and Clarke,' said Raj. 'And Clarke won't allow the general to talk.'

'I'd say that General Markie doesn't have much time left.'

‘Do you think he’ll realise that the threat against him has become urgent?’

‘I don’t know,’ replied Hamish. ‘But now that we can contact the real world with no threat to our existence, I think we need to take a more active part in all this.’

‘What are you going to do?’

‘I think we need to talk to Jennings.’

***

Virtual World

‘He wants me to do *what*?’ exclaimed the late General Clarke.

‘He wants you to impersonate General Markie,’ said Prem’s holographic image.

‘I thought I was retired,’ replied the general. ‘I was just getting used to the virtual life.’

‘It’s important, sir. He wouldn’t ask if it weren’t.’

Clarke frowned. ‘And how exactly am I supposed to do that?’

'By transmuting into his body, General.'

'Is that all?' replied Clarke sarcastically. 'And once I've been transmuted into my old colleague's body, what does Hamish want me to do?'

'He wants you to stop a war, General.'

***

Quantum Entangled Virtual Space

'I've spoken to Jennings,' said Prem. 'He thinks he can persuade the CIA to act quickly.'

'And what about General Clarke?' asked Hamish.

'I think he thought I was joking - at least to start with.'

'But he'll do it?'

'Yes, he agreed to do it when I told him what Clinton had been up to.'

Hamish nodded. 'So all we have to do now is wait,' he said ruefully. 'That's all we seem to do these days - wait.'

'Everyone's doing their best, Hamish,' said Prem. 'I know how frustrating it is for you - stuck here - but

Christina's started growing the clones, so at least there's an end in sight.'

'There's a lot more to do before we're home and dry, Prem,' replied Hamish. 'At least, there's a lot more for you to do.'

'What do you need me to do?' asked the young Indian.

'I need you to create two virtual worlds.'

'Two whole worlds?' asked Prem in astonishment.

'It's not as daunting as it sounds,' replied Hamish. 'They'll be copies of two existing worlds. The significant thing about them is that they both have to be aligned to the exact moment when Clinton started his transmutation.'

'When we grabbed him?'

'Yes, the second before his transmutation was so rudely interrupted,' smiled Hamish.

'And once you've done that, I want you to make some slight alterations. But I'll let you know what they are when you've created the copies.'

Then, almost as an afterthought, he said: 'And I want you to give the links to the two worlds to Hisako. We're going to need her help, too.'

***

The Pentagon, Washington DC

General Markie walked past his secretary's desk and into his office at the Pentagon.

She looked up anxiously, and called out: 'General there are some - ' But Markie, still furious from his encounter with Clarke, marched on without hearing her.

When he opened the door, he saw two men standing on either side of his desk.

'Who the hell are you?' he demanded. 'What are you doing in my office? Who let you in here?'

His secretary burst through the door. 'It was me, General.'

'Who the hell - '

'They're from the CIA, General.'

'What do the CIA want with me?' asked the General suspiciously.

'We're here for your protection, sir,' replied one of the men. 'We understand that threats have been made against your person.'

The general hesitated: how could they know? ‘Threats? Nonsense!’ he retorted.

‘Nevertheless, General, we have orders to accompany you to a more secure location.’

‘Goddammit, man, this is the Pentagon!’ shouted the general. ‘How much more secure could we be?’

‘I’m sorry, sir,’ continued the spokesman evenly. ‘We have our orders.’

‘Then I’m countermanding them,’ replied the general. ‘I’m not going anywhere. Now get out of my office!’

The two men looked at each other.

‘General, our orders are to use force, if necessary. This is a matter of national security.’

‘Force? You wouldn’t dare - ’

The secretary gasped in horror as the first man drew his weapon.

‘I’m sorry, sir,’ said the first man. ‘You leave me no choice.’

And with that, he raised the taser and, without hesitation, fired.

***

General Clarke opened his eyes with difficulty. The room around him was in shadow; the only light coming from a small table lamp on the far side of the room.

'Don't try to move, General,' said a voice beside him. 'You've been out of a body for some time. It'll take a few minutes to remember what it feels like.'

'Where am I?' asked General Clarke.

'The Pentagon,' replied the voice. 'We had to improvise a transmutation facility for you. We got hold of some technicians from a local centre; the CIA doesn't specialise in virtual world transfers.'

'So this is Markie's body?'

'Yes, General.'

'By the feel of it, he could do with losing a few pounds.'

'With any luck, you won't have to be hauling it around for long,' replied the voice. 'Do you feel up to moving? We're on a tight schedule.'

Clarke turned his head to look at the shadowy figure sitting next to his bed. 'We've met before,' he said. 'Kominsky. Isn't it?'

The man nodded his head. ‘I was the guy who investigated the murder of President Winter. It was me who damned your reputation. And until I found out just what was possible with this transmutation stuff, I really believed you’d done it.’

‘Who told you what really happened?’ asked the general.

‘A mutual friend - Jennings. And if it means anything - I’m sorry. I got it completely wrong.’

The general shut his eyes. ‘Clinton has a lot to answer for,’ he whispered.

***

The White House, Washington DC

The Chief of Staff shifted uncomfortably in her chair.

‘Well, Miss Whitehead?,’ demanded Greenbaum. ‘Have I, or have I not been behaving uncharacteristically over the last few weeks?’

‘Mr President,’ she started, struggling for the right words. ‘Mr President, I haven’t seen you in the last three weeks.’

Greenbaum raised his eyebrows in surprise. ‘And

that doesn't strike you as unusual?'

'It's not for me to say, sir,' she replied carefully. 'If you choose not to consult me - '

Greenbaum turned sharply to his secretary.

'Where's my diary?'

'Here, sir,' replied the woman, holding out the book to him.

She threw a glance to the other woman. 'Miss Whitehead tried to contact you every day, but I can tell you that most of your meetings were with General Markie.'

'Markie?' he murmured. 'Now why would I - '

'As Head of the Military, no doubt you were discussing national security policy?' interrupted Whitehead.

Greenbaum turned to look at the woman.

'I want to see him - now,' he ordered.

Sally Whitehead looked even more embarrassed than she had originally.

'There might be a problem with that, Mr President,' she said. 'It appears that the general - is missing.'

***

CIA Headquarters, Langley, Virginia

'Yes, he's fine, Jennings,' said Kominsky, addressing the hologram in front of him. 'A good bit fatter than he's used to, but he seems to be moving around okay.'

'He's got to countermand the order to detonate the bombs. And once he's done that, you have to make sure the girl knows what he's done.'

'We can do that.'

'She'll try to kill him, Peter,' said Jennings. 'That's your chance to get her. But try to make sure that you do it before she kills him - I'd like to make sure that General Markie's body is in one piece before we transmute him back. What you do with him then is up to you.'

'It's difficult, Jay,' replied Kominsky. 'Did he know it wasn't the real President that was giving him orders?'

'I don't think he did. I believe he was doing exactly what his commanding officer ordered him to.'

'And then, when Greenbaum - Clinton - disappeared back to the virtual world, didn't he have any suspicions? The way the girl suddenly appeared to be in charge -

surely that must have given him pause for thought?'

'I think she overplayed her hand, Peter,' replied Jennings. 'But whether he's guilty of anything other than sheer naïvety, I can't tell you, You're going to have to sort that one out for yourself.'

***

The Old City, Jerusalem

Sub-Lieutenant Clarke strolled past the small square in front of the Church of the Holy Sepulchre, stopping only to raise his cellphone above the crowd to take the same tourist images as any other visitor to Jerusalem might take. He appeared to all intents and purposes to be yet another American tourist, making his way around the sights of Jerusalem.

He turned into one of the small alleys that surrounded the Church, and smiled to himself as a small dog turned to follow his progress. For a second he wondered if there was an unique smell from the plutonium in his backpack that had attracted the creature, but the dog turned back, more interested in the base of a familiar fire hydrant.

Clarke looked at his watch: an hour and thirty-four minutes to go. He called up a map of the old city and calculated how long it would take him to reach the designated location. He estimated that he had time to take a detour via the Temple Mount and the Dome of the Rock before making his way out of the city and across the valley to the cemetery in Gethsemane.

***

The White House, Washington DC

‘Missing? What do you mean, missing?’ demanded Greenbaum.

‘Him and his secretary,’ replied his Chief of Staff.

‘What are you suggesting?’

‘It may be nothing at all, sir,’ replied Whitehead. ‘It’s just that neither of them are responding to our calls.’

‘Doesn’t anyone know where they are?’

‘A secretary further down the corridor thought she saw the general being taken away in a wheelchair.’

‘A wheelchair? Has he been taken to hospital?’

‘According to his security pass, he didn’t leave the Pentagon.’

‘So where the hell is he? I want to see him!’ demanded Greenbaum.

The President's eyes scanned the blank faces of his advisers.

'Who was present at these meetings apart from Markie?' he demanded.

The group of advisers looked at one another helplessly.

'Only your personal security detail, sir,' said his secretary.

'And who was that?'

'Clarke, sir - the new girl.'

'What new girl?'

'You appointed her yourself, sir.'

'When was this?'

'Just after you returned from the virtual world - after your first visit.'

Greenbaum's face was grave. It was becoming clear to him, if not to his staff, what had happened.

'Where is this girl?' he demanded. 'I want her brought to me.'

***

Temple Mount, Jerusalem

Sub-Lieutenant Clarke stopped in front of the steps up to the Dome of the Rock. As he raised his cellphone to take a photograph, the display flashed up a message. Clarke stared at the single word 'ABORT' for a second, then turned and walked away from the golden dome, gleaming in the sunshine.

The command was unambiguous: he would not be expected to die today. But the realisation that he was to live raised no emotion in the man. Instead, he dropped his pose as a tourist and started to walk quickly back to the centre of the old city to find a taxi.

Behind him, an Israeli soldier turned his attention to the young man whose behaviour had suddenly changed. He watched as the stranger with the bright blue rucksack almost jogged away from the holy site, then raised his communications device to his mouth.

Clarke made his way swiftly back towards the Via Dolorosa, dodging in and out of the crowds of passers by in the narrow alleyways and colonnades, and narrowly avoiding the stallholders and shopkeepers with their wares ranged along the streets.

After he had gone two hundred yards, an Israeli soldier suddenly appeared from a side alley and barred his way. A voice from behind him shouted: 'Stop!'

The soldier in front of him hefted his automatic weapon threateningly, and Clarke stopped in front of him. His orders had said nothing about what to do if confronted by the local security forces. There was no backup plan, no second line of action; his task was to detonate the nuclear device. There was no coming back.

He stood quite still as the second soldier approached him from behind.

'Put your hands on your head,' he ordered. 'Kneel on the ground. I want to see what you have in that rucksack.'

***

The White House, Washington DC

General Markie opened the door to the Oval Office and walked in. The secretary behind him had clearly tried to stop him. She tried to stammer out an apology, but her words were drowned by Markie's.

'We need to talk,' he stated.

Greenbaum looked at him in surprise. For a second he was taken aback by the general's abruptness and obvious lack of respect.

'Don't you knock, General?' he asked waspishly.

'The rest of you, leave now,' ordered Markie, addressing the melee of advisers scattered around the room. One by one they left the office, stunned into silence by the general's air of authority.

The door closed behind the last to leave.

'Now, General,' started Greenbaum, 'what exactly has caused you to forget that I am the President, and your Commander in Chief?'

'You are neither my President, nor my Commander,' replied Markie. 'I'm here, not because you wanted to see me, but because I have to tell you exactly what has been going on in the past few weeks, and what the consequences of that period will be.'

'I don't understand - '

'I'm sure you don't,' interrupted Markie. 'But I do. Listen very carefully: there isn't much time.'

Greenbaum frowned and leaned back in his chair.

'You do realise that your insubordination will be the end of your career?'

'If you think my interruption is the worst thing that's happened, you need to shut up and listen.'

'How dare you speak to me like that!' cried Greenbaum.

‘I dare because I’m not Markie,’ said the general quietly.

‘What?’

‘I dare because your time as President has come to its end.’

‘What the hell are you talking about?’

‘You must have worked some of it out by now, Greenbaum: the missing three weeks; why no one could get to see you; why you signed so few documents; why the First Lady appeared to arrive back early?’

Greenbaum stared at him in disbelief.

‘You know?’

Markie glared at him. ‘From the time you went to the virtual world, you were replaced. Randolph Clinton took your place and was effectively President of the United States for three weeks. During that time, he organised a terrorist nuclear attack on the State of Israel. He also planned a subsequent attack on the Iranian Parliament in Tehran, and a third attack on an Israeli settlement in East Jerusalem.’

Greenbaum slumped in his chair, his face ashen.

‘He was attempting to start a war between the

Middle Eastern states, just like the one you and he planned, before you had the political sense to back out of it. But this time, he wasn't taking any chances that you'd put a block on what he wanted, by making sure the order for the attacks came from the President himself.

'He knew he couldn't keep up the pretence for very long, so he avoided everyone who knew him well enough to get suspicious about the subtle changes in his behaviour. The one person he couldn't avoid for ever was his wife, so when it came time for her to arrive, he escaped back to the virtual world, and you woke up to find that some very strange things had been happening - not least the fact that you and Markie had been having a great many meetings. And perhaps more surprisingly, every one of them attended by the latest addition to your personal security team - the Clarke girl. And even more significant, the Clarke girl who had killed Randolph Clinton.'

Greenbaum pulled himself together: 'You said a nuclear attack?'

Markie smiled coldly. 'Don't panic - I've aborted the mission. Thousands of visitors and pilgrims, not to mention the people who live and work in Jerusalem - they're all safe.'

'And Clinton?'

'Clinton has been - shall we say - detained.'

‘Where is he?’

‘He’s safely tucked away in the virtual world; somewhere he can’t do any harm.’

‘Thank God - ’

‘Don’t thank him too soon, Greenbaum. I haven’t finished.’

‘But you’ve cancelled the attacks?’

‘Yes, but that may turn out to be the least of your troubles.’

‘What do you mean?’

‘The girl,’ replied the general. ‘Clarke. She’s still on the loose. When she finds out that the attack didn’t take place at the appointed time, she has orders to kill me.’

Greenbaum recovered himself sufficiently for a grim smile to play around his lips. ‘I would say that’s your problem, General - not mine.’

‘Oh, no, Greenbaum,’ said the general. ‘If she kills me, who is there to swear that I planned and carried out the preparations all on my own? If I’m dead, and your personal security guard killed me, the trail leads directly to you.’

'But the attacks never took place. No one knows - '

'Not true. I've already told my story to the news media.'

'Fake news!' Greenbaum scoffed. 'No one will believe it.'

'And then there are the Israelis.'

'What about them? They know nothing.'

'They've arrested the Clarke clone who was carrying the nuclear device. They already know that he's an American soldier. I shouldn't be surprised if your phone isn't red hot already demanding that you call the President of Israel.'

Greenbaum's face paled.

'Not quite as bad as letting off the device itself, but equally as bad for relations between so-called allies.'

The general paused, letting the significance of his words sink in.

'But from your personal point of view, that's not the worst of it,' he said ominously.

'How could it be any worse?'

‘Well, I suppose your presidency might survive the international repercussions, but not when the world finds out how you got to be President.’

‘The world already knows,’ replied Greenbaum, pretending a confidence he didn’t feel.

‘I don’t think so,’ murmured the general, shaking his head sadly. ‘But I know.’

Greenbaum hesitated. ‘What do you know?’

‘I know how you and Clinton plotted to kill President Winter.’

Greenbaum opened his mouth to speak, but the general went on: ‘I know that you had General Clarke murdered. I know that a second Clarke was placed in his body. The second Clarke gained access to President Winter and killed him in cold blood, then killed himself to avoid the embarrassment of a trial.’

‘You couldn’t possibly know that!’

‘I could - because I’m not General Markie,’ said the general quietly. ‘I’m General Clarke.’

Greenbaum’s mouth fell open. ‘You - you - can’t be,’ he stammered.

‘I assure you I am,’ replied the general. ‘And in the virtual world, we have access to all the relevant life-log data that proves your involvement with Clinton, and that you sanctioned everything about the plot.

‘Of course, our justice system doesn’t yet accept life-log data as proof, but the great American public will.’

There was silence in the room as Greenbaum took in the consequences of what the other man had said.

‘Your Presidency is over, Greenbaum. You will resign, and play no further part in politics.’

***

The Pentagon, Washington DC

Clarke silently opened the door to General Markie’s office to see a figure sitting with his back to her, silhouetted against the window. She raised the Walther automatic and pointed it his head.

‘Turn around,’ she said. ‘I want you to see the consequences of disloyalty before I kill you.’

The man turned slowly in the chair.

‘I don’t think so, Miss Clarke,’ replied the man. ‘You have no orders to kill me.’

'Where's Markie?' she demanded.

'Somewhere you can't get at him,' said the man. 'Now I suggest you lower your weapon so that the two gentlemen behind you don't have to cause you any avoidable pain.'

Clarke glanced quickly to her right and left. She lowered the gun, then felt it being removed from her grasp.

'That's better, isn't it, Miss Clarke?' he asked. 'Now perhaps we can have a little talk. About suitcase bombs.'

Clarke was silent, her face betraying nothing.

'No? Then I'll tell you all about it. By the way, my name is Kominsky. I'm head of the CIA. Of course, as you know, the CIA is only concerned with affairs abroad, but as you planned to set off your little devices in Israel and Iran, then that becomes our concern. On the mainland, it's the FBI's responsibility, which is why the two FBI agents are here to arrest you.'

'On what charge?'

'Why Miss Clarke, isn't it obvious? You're under arrest for the crime that you confessed to - the murder of Randolph Clinton.'

He smiled directly at her. 'I'm sure you appreciate the irony.'

***

Quantum Entangled Virtual Space

'The CIA came through for us,' commented Hamish.

'Eventually,' added Raj. 'So the whole affair is over.'

'Not quite,' said Hamish. 'There are a lot of loose ends that need tying up. But we aren't responsible for any of them.'

He paused. 'Except for the biggest one of all,' he said at last, his face grave.

'You mean Clinton,' said Raj. 'I thought we'd solved that one. No one can get to him in that world except Prem and Alex. And neither of them are going to want to go near him.'

'But when we get back to the virtual world, we're going to have to think of a permanent solution,' said Hamish.

'We could just erase him, Hamish,' said Raj. 'After everything he's done - not just to us, but to all those people who might have been turned into mindless killers.'

'It's not in my nature to be judge, jury and executioner,' replied Hamish. 'And revenge is something I don't want on my conscience. Let's face it, any guilt that you or I might feel is going to last forever. It's not like we could ever forget.'

'So what should we do?'

'Think about it for now,' said Hamish. 'Once we're back, then we'll have to make a decision, but until then, he's not going anywhere.'

***

Virtual World

The psychiatrist looked up as Alex appeared in the chair opposite her. Immediately, she registered the change in his body language. There was an aggressive restlessness about the way he sat forward in the chair. After a few seconds he got up and started to pace the room.

'Why did you call me?' he demanded angrily. 'I'm busy.'

The woman didn't respond immediately, but sat perfectly still, watching him.

'What?' he shouted impatiently.

Eventually the woman replied: 'I have some good

news for you, Alex,' she said.

'News? You could have sent me a thought message!'

'I thought you might want to see what I have to show you,' she continued patiently.

'You're wasting my time. What do you want?'

'I don't want anything, Alex,' she replied. 'But I thought you did.'

'What?' he demanded.

'Your mother, Alex. The process is finished.'

Without hesitating, he said: 'So?'

'At least, I thought it was finished until a few minutes ago,' she added.

'What the hell does that mean?'

'Your attitude, Alex. I haven't seen you like this before.'

'What attitude?'

'You've always been equable, pleasant, even-tempered. But today, you seem - '

'I haven't got time for this!' he shouted. 'You say my mother is ready - great. What about my father?'

The psychiatrist paused, almost as if she could feel surprise at his words.

'You have never expressed a desire for your father to be recreated,' she replied evenly. 'In fact, you have always given the impression that you never wished to see your father again.'

'What do you know about what I want?' he growled.

'A great deal, I think,' she replied. 'Is there anything you want to tell me?'

'Why should I want to tell you anything?'

'Because it would help me to understand.'

'I couldn't care less whether you understand or not,' he retorted. 'Your job is to bring them back to life - all of them.'

'All of them?'

'My mother, my father, my uncle - they killed him too, you know.'

'And the girl, Ann?' she asked softly.

'Who the hell is she?'

***

Quantum Entangled Virtual Space

'I checked Alex's emotional parameters,' said Prem. 'There's quite clearly been a change in the values.'

Raj pursed his lips. 'From what you've said about sudden mood swings, I'm not surprised. But knowing the cause doesn't explain how they came to be changed. Have you checked the logs?'

'Not yet,' replied Prem. 'But there's something else: the actor reported that Alex's behaviour had changed radically. She was about to show him the world where his mother would appear, but he didn't react at all as she would have expected.'

'What happened?'

'He insisted he wanted to recreate his father,' Prem replied. 'The AI said he'd never shown the slightest interest in having his father back. In fact, he told her at one point that he could never forgive him for what he did to Ann Mitchell.'

'That's odd,' mused Raj. 'Changes in the emotional parameters shouldn't cause a complete about turn in his fundamental desires. At least, I've never seen it happen before.'

'She said that his whole demeanour was different. He seemed to have a deep-seated anger that kept welling up inside him. She'd never detected that from him before. She said it was almost as if he'd had a complete personality change.'

Raj was silent for a moment. 'I was trying to think of a scenario where that might happen, but I can't think of anything that would cause such a change. I don't suppose he's been messing with his own parameters, has he?'

'I don't know. But I guess I can find that out from the logs.'

'Under normal circumstances, I'd suggest that we did a complete reset on his personality settings, but as he's now a superuser, that wouldn't be possible without him knowing.'

'There was one more thing she noted, Raj.'

'What was that?'

'In addition to mentioning his father, he also said that he wanted his uncle back.'

'His uncle?'

'Yes, according to the AI, he'd never mentioned an

uncle before. He actually said: *they killed him, too.'*

'What on earth - ?'

'I know, it's weird. But it gets worse. According to the AI, she's researched all his relatives and neither his father nor his mother had a brother.'

***

Chapter 11

The White House, Washington DC

The person most surprised was Vice President Rossi. The last thing he had ever expected was to become President. Of course, he'd thought about it now and again, but Greenbaum's health was fine, he kept himself fit; there was never a suggestion that he wouldn't serve his full term.

But to Vincent Rossi, whatever the White House press release had said about the resignation, the phrase 'for health reasons' did not ring true.

When he saw Greenbaum at the handing over ceremony, it was true that he looked nothing like the man who had transferred power only a few days earlier. He appeared shrunken, a haunted look about him, as if the whole of his world had suddenly collapsed.

There had been rumours, of course: there were always rumours, But until he had fully taken the reins of power, no one - least of all the Vice President - had any idea of the catastrophic events that had lead to the President's resignation. The seriousness of the allegations had almost taken Rossi's breath away. That a sitting President could contemplate fomenting a war between two other nations was, at least to all decent persons, unthinkable. And to have initiated a covert attack on the territory of a long standing ally like Israel was almost beyond belief.

But the shocking truth would have to be dealt with. Rossi had spoken to the Israeli Prime Minister immediately he had been inaugurated, and he was waiting for his call to the Israeli President to come through. That first conversation had been harsh and angry, and he expected nothing different from the subsequent one.

And what could he say? Greenbaum had resigned. He would retire to obscurity, to live out his days in disgrace and humiliation. That Randolph Clinton had also been involved was almost beside the point; the man was immune to any consequences in the virtual world. No doubt, whoever was now in charge would deal with the problem. There was nothing anyone in the real world could do about it.

The possibility of legal action against the former President had already been raised in the media, but so far, no one seemed to have the distance and objectivity to decide what laws, if any, had been broken. It was a topic that would no doubt rear its ugly head in the not so distant future, and Rossi hoped that the Department of Justice would find a way of making sure the whole affair wasn't dragged endlessly through the court system. But he knew in his heart that the court of public opinion would prove to be far more intractable, and the trust in the office of the President had suffered a severe, if not fatal blow.

It was Rossi's fate to weather the storm of international condemnation, and to try to find a way to re-establish confidence in the executive, and indeed the Presidency itself. He shuddered at the scale of the task in front of him, and wished with all his heart that he had never accepted the offer of the vice presidency.

***

CIA Headquarters, Langley, Virginia

'Dammit, I didn't know he was an impostor,' shouted Markie. 'How could I? He looked like Greenbaum. He sounded like Greenbaum. As far as everybody was concerned, he *was* Greenbaum!'

Kominsky sat back in his chair, casually examining the general's florid face. General Clarke had been right, he thought: the guy's blood pressure must be through the roof, and carrying all that weight…

'I can't believe that you had no suspicion that anything was untoward when he started quoting Randolph Clinton's ideas on the future of military warfare,' he stated calmly. 'It speaks volumes for your underlying attitudes that you were so easily swayed by the theories of a man who was dishonourably discharged from the service because of his inhuman conduct on the field of battle. A man who thought nothing of deliberately killing innocent civilians in the pursuit of possible targets - not even confirmed targets.'

‘You don’t understand,’ protested the general. ‘This was the President! The Commander in Chief! How could I disagree with what he was saying?’

‘Have you forgotten your military history, General?’ retorted Kominsky, suddenly angry. ‘I seem to remember that the Nuremberg trials wouldn’t accept the excuse that Nazi officers were ‘only obeying orders’. And I don’t see any difference now! Where was your humanity, General? Where was your common sense of decency? Those bombs would have destroyed thousands of lives - innocent lives. There was no legitimate military target. There was no provocation. There was no legitimate justification. There was no ‘clear and present danger’. This was an act of state terrorism, and you were the perpetrator!’

‘I was ordered - ’

‘You were lead by the nose, General,’ Kominsky went on angrily. ‘Because you fundamentally agreed with what Greenbaum was feeding you. You didn’t raise any objection because you believed what he was telling you: that a Middle East war was inevitable, and that it was in the interests of the United States to incite Iran and Israel to attack each other. You might not have come up with the idea of a covert terrorist attack yourself, but you signed right up to it because you thought it would bring about the sort of wholesale destruction that would bring the whole of the Arab oil producing machine to its knees, and reassert the power of the West in the region. And all with no risk to US lives. General, you are a contemptible human being.'

'I didn't know - '

'At your level of seniority, General, naïvety is no excuse. You are responsible. And no matter what justifications you may use to convince yourself of your innocence, you will have to live with the consequences of your actions for the rest of your life.'

***

Quantum Entangled Virtual Space

'Do we know what will happen to the girl?' asked Raj.

'Jennings' friend, Kominsky, has been very clever, I think,' replied Hamish. 'Despite all the atrocities we know she's committed, he was aware that all the life-log evidence we could supply would be inadmissible in court. So she'll face trial for the murder of Clinton. She admitted it in front of the CIA agents who were sent to arrest him: she was holding the smoking gun - literally. And even though she may try to claim now that she was obeying orders she couldn't refuse, I just think that whatever she says, no one will really believe that she wasn't a willing participant - especially after the fact that General Clarke himself proved that it was possible to act against Clinton's direct orders.'

'What will happen to her?'

‘I have no doubt she’ll be convicted,’ replied Hamish flatly.

‘But then what? They won’t recycle her into another Clarke clone: that was made illegal ages ago. And they won’t send her here.’

Hamish shook his head. ‘Once Clinton had found the way to create his clones, there’s no doubt he carried on doing it - whatever the United Nations might have said, or how illegal it was. No, she won’t be brought back. And no, she won’t be allowed to come here. They’ll execute her, and that’ll be the end.’

‘How do you think Alex will react to that? Ann Mitchell will be gone forever.’

‘I think he’s already recognised the inevitable. That might have something to do with his erratic behaviour. It might just be part of the grieving process.’

***

United States Penitentiary, Terre Haute, Indiana

Peter Kominsky couldn’t get comfortable. The chair was unyielding plastic, and the air-con in the claustrophobic, windowless room struggled against the heat of the morning. Next to him sat the governor of the prison who appeared to be totally relaxed despite the oppressive atmosphere. Kominsky wondered if it was the occasion that was causing him to sweat profusely; maybe the governor was used to such events, but he doubted she had officiated over a Federal death sentence before.

In front of him, separated by a glass window, the execution chamber was empty. Kominsky looked anxiously at his watch. Apart from himself, the governor, a couple of US Marshals and the blank sightless lenses of the official recording devices, the viewing room was empty.

Right on time, the gurney carrying the Clarke clone was pushed into the centre of the adjoining room. The girl, her eyes wide open, was staring directly at the ceiling.

'The Bureau of Prisons hasn't had an execution for years,' whispered the governor, leaning in to Kominsky. 'Ever since the introduction of the virtual prison system, they've all been transmutations.'

'She's a special case,' replied Kominsky. 'Went all the way to the Supreme Court. They were very specific: because of Clinton's influence over the virtual world, they couldn't guarantee that she wouldn't be extracted from a virtual prison. The court ruled that Clarkes were effectively automata, and therefore couldn't feel remorse. The rehabilitation that the virtual prison system was intended to provide would prove totally ineffective on her. So they decided the only solution was to execute her.'

'That's why you're here, Mr Kominsky? We rarely see someone as senior as you in this neck of the woods.'

'I drew the short straw,' replied Kominsky. 'Once the doctor declares her dead, I have to accompany the body to the crematorium. The President wants assurance that she can't do any more damage.'

The Governor raised her eyebrows in surprise. 'As high as that?'

'He needs justice to be seen to be done,' replied Kominsky. 'After Greenbaum, there's a lot of trust to be re-established.'

The doctor connected the clear plastic tubes from the automatic drug dispenser to the cannula on the back of the girl's hand. Her face remained completely expressionless.

Then he stood back as the machine delivered the first drug: the anaesthetic phase which would render her unconscious. The girl's eyes closed. The doctor continued to watch his monitor. After a few minutes, he glanced up, looking directly at Kominsky. Kominsky gave a slight nod of his head, and the doctor walked away, leaving the girl alone.

'I understand they'll give her the other drugs

remotely,' said the Governor quietly. 'When they confirm she's flat-lined, they'll check that there's no brain function.'

Kominsky's face was grave. He nodded his understanding.

After what seemed an eternity, the curtains in front of them closed, cutting them off from the sight of the dead girl.

'That's it,' said the Governor flatly. 'If you'll excuse me, I'll leave you to get on with the rest of your unpleasant duty, Mr Director.'

***

In the darkened room, Kominsky waited patiently.

After a few minutes, the double doors opened and the doctor wheeled in the gurney carrying the girl's body.

'Is she - ?' asked Kominsky.

The doctor nodded. 'I'll leave her in your charge now, Mr Director,' he said. 'Everything went as expected.'

As the doctor closed the doors behind him, Kominsky rose and crossed to the girl's side. He looked down at the face. In repose, it looked younger than when he had last seen her in the courtroom. He looked at her hands, and noticed that the cannula had been removed. He looked at his watch: the undertakers would arrive at any minute, and he would need to supervise the removal of the casket.

It was not in his nature to feel remorse, but when he looked into the girl's face, he came as near to regret as he ever had. Had it been a failure? Had the girl's life been wasted needlessly? Had there been another way to track Clinton's whereabouts?

Angrily, he thrust the doubts from his mind. What was done, was done - and there was no way he could change the past.

***

Online Gaming World

'Christina just called,' said Hisako. 'She confirmed that the clones for Hamish and Rajesh have completed the first stage of their maturation.'

'So that means we're ready to go,' said Prem nervously. 'This better work.'

'It will work,' replied Hisako confidently. 'It's the only logical option left.'

'So what do we expect to happen?'

Hisako sighed. ‘How many more times do I have to explain it?’

‘Okay, okay. I get it,’ replied Prem. ‘I’ll make sure the reception area is running on a quantum machine, and then we’re ready to go.’

‘You need to check that the avatar database is completely up to date, and that both Hamish and Raj have their clone flags set correctly.’

‘I’ve already done that.’

‘Then all we have to do is to start AltLife running in the reception area, and they can just walk out of there,’ said Hisako.

‘Except they need to be asleep, right?’

‘It was just a turn of phrase, Prem,’ she replied. ‘They know what to do. Go tell them to get ready.’

***

Virtual World

‘Hello, Alex,’ said Hamish, as he and Raj materialised.

‘Who the hell are you?’ demanded Duchovny.

'I'm Hamish McAllister, and this is Raj Singh,' replied Hamish.

'They told me you were dead,' muttered Alex accusingly.

Hamish grinned. 'That's true: but if I'm going to be really pedantic, all three of us are dead.'

'They told me Clinton had erased you,' Alex retorted.

'As you can see, that wasn't quite true.'

'So it was you two pulling the strings all the time.'

'Not directly: we had a lot of help from Prem,' replied Hamish, ignoring the aggressive tone in Duchovny's voice. 'But we also had a lot of help from you. There were things that Prem couldn't have done on his own, and I wanted to thank you - '

'I don't need your thanks,' interrupted Duchovny. 'Just leave me alone.'

Hamish and Raj exchanged glances.

'Is something wrong, Alex?' asked Raj. 'You seem a little - '

'What could be wrong with me?' demanded Alex angrily. 'I'm an avatar. I'm perfect.'

'It's just that according to the AIs, your behaviour has changed,' added Hamish. 'And we're concerned to find out why.'

'Just mind your own business. You've got plenty to be getting on with now Clinton's not around. Just leave me out of it.'

'What about your mother, Alex,' asked Raj. 'I understand she's waiting for you.'

'That's not my mother.'

Hamish raised his eyebrows in surprise. 'But isn't that what you wanted? To recreate her?'

'And what about my father? And my uncle? I need to bring them back.'

For a second, there was silence. Then Hamish asked: 'What's your uncle's name, Alex?'

'Edward,' replied Duchovny. 'Uncle Eddie.'

'What's his second name, Alex?'

'Clinton - Eddie Clinton.'

***

'When exactly did he start behaving like this?'

demanded Hamish.

'According to the avatar logs, his emotional parameters changed right in the middle of Clinton's transmutation,' replied Prem.

'I need to know exactly when,' added Raj.

Prem scanned the log entries in front of him. 'It was exactly at the point he saved the copy to his home directory. There was an error message concerning permissions, and then he realised the macro had changed his user to yours, Raj.'

'That's got to be it, Hamish,' cried Raj. 'It was because his superuser was connected to his own home directory and not to mine. That's when it must have happened.'

'I don't understand what you mean,' said Prem anxiously. 'What happened?'

'I don't understand exactly how it happened, but I suspect the permissions on those directories may be different. In some way, the copy of Clinton's personality - some of the algorithms, at least - have leaked into Alex's avatar database entry. I don't think the file was there long enough to create a complete copy before he moved it, but maybe enough of the algorithms to cause the sort of erratic behaviour we've seen.'

'Edward Clinton was Randolph's uncle,' explained

Hamish. 'He was a fireman in New York. He was killed in 9/11 when one of the twin towers collapsed and crushed him under thousands of tons of rubble.'

'So we were talking to Clinton himself,' said Prem.

'A small part of him, I suspect,' replied Hamish. 'But we have no way of knowing whether that part is growing, and having more and more influence over Alex. It obviously doesn't recognise us - not yet, at least - but it seems determined to bring back both of Clinton's parents - and the uncle.'

'So what can we do?' asked Prem.

'We could try to erase him,' suggested Raj. 'But he's a superuser now. He'd recognise immediately what we were trying to do.'

'We can't do that. There must be another way.'

'What would happen if Clinton took Alex over completely,' asked Prem.

'Then we'd have the real Randolph Clinton back in the virtual world, with all the powers of a superuser,' replied Hamish. 'And that's something none of us wants to contemplate.'

***

'Even if it's only a part of Clinton's persona, how

aware would he be of what's happened to the rest of him?' asked Raj.

'I don't think it's a matter of knowing where we've hidden him,' replied Hamish. 'As a superuser, he could find out easily by checking our logs.'

'The AIs have reported that his eccentric behaviour is getting worse,' said Raj. 'So I think we have to assume that the personality algorithms are regenerating themselves.'

'What does that mean?' asked Prem.

'It mean that we don't have much time to stop him,' replied Raj.

'Is it possible for those algorithms to completely take over Alex's avatar?' asked Prem.

'I don't know,' replied Raj.

'If we assume that they can't take over completely, and there'll always be some part of Duchovny's personality in there, then the only way for it to become complete again would be to free Clinton from the virtual prison we made,' said Hamish.

'So, maybe our first task is to dispose of Clinton,' suggested Raj.

'But how?' asked Prem.

‘That’s where we need to be creative,’ said Hamish.

‘And quick,’ added Raj.

For several moments, the three were silent, each trying desperately to think of a solution to their problem.

At last, the hint of a smile appeared on Prem’s face. ‘I think I may have an idea,’ he said. ‘But I need to speak to Hisako.’

***

National Center of Neurology and Psychiatry, Tokyo

Hisako’s cellphone rang. The image of Prem appeared on the screen.

‘Things must be getting back to normal,’ smiled Hisako. ‘You wouldn’t have dared to call me directly a few days ago.’

‘Hisako, I need to talk to you about AltLife. Urgently.’

‘Okay - what do you want to know?’ she answered, surprised at his uncharacteristic directness.

‘You remember when you used AltLife to try to find out about Alex’s life? When we had very little data to give it, and it came up with some strange results?'

'I remember,' she replied. 'AltLife predicted that Alex would get some sort of medal. But it projected three different scenarios, with three different presidents presenting him with the award.'

'How unusual is that?' asked Prem.

'You mean to predict the same outcome, but with three distinct people playing a major role?'

Prem frowned. 'It's not necessarily about the three people,' he said. 'But to get similar results with such a consistently low level of probability?'

'It's highly unlikely,' she replied. 'At least, in a real world situation.'

'But for AltLife to come up with millions of alternative worlds?' Prem prompted her.

'Like I said, it's almost unheard of. It was definitely caused by the fact that we had so little for AltLife to go on. With more data, it would never have happened.'

Prem pursed his lips in thought. 'What if we supplied it with the same level of data for someone else? Someone we know a lot about about, but restricted AltLife's access to it?'

'Same result, Prem. There could be millions of

possibilities. But AltLife couldn't generate them all - it would require far too many resources.'

'But if you stopped it before it used up too much in the way of computing resources, and chose one particular solution?'

'Then AltLife would fill in the gaps and predict forwards.'

'And if you placed the subject in that alternative world, they could live forward along that timeline?'

'In theory,' she replied cautiously. What *was* he driving at?

'Would they recognise it as a fake?'

'Not necessarily,' she replied. 'It depends on how familiar it was, and how much AltLife knew about it as an environment.'

'What if it was a prediction based on the virtual world?'

'Then AltLife would create a perfect model,' she replied.

'Because it has a hundred percent understanding of the virtual world?'

'That's right.'

'And what would happen if the subject recognised it as a fake?'

'I'd just let them out, as usual.'

'But if you didn't let them out? Could they get out by themself?'

Hisako frowned. 'I don't know,' she said. 'I've never left a patient there alone.'

'But if you did?'

'Prem, what are you getting at?' she demanded in frustration.

'I'm just trying to understand the mechanism. If they were left there on their own, realised that the timeline was not real, could they think themselves out?'

Hisako thought for a moment. 'No,' she replied. 'They'd have to obey the rules of whatever world AltLife had created. You can't just think yourself out of the virtual world and into the real one - you have to be transmuted. You can only think yourself from one virtual world to another.'

'So to get out you'd have to be transmuted?'

‘It doesn’t really work like that, Prem,’ said Hisako. ‘Don’t forget, I run AltLife in the real world. When I go in there with a patient, we’re both wearing immersive VR suits. We can’t get stuck. There’s no question of thinking your self anywhere.’

‘But what if you were running AltLife from VR?’ insisted Prem.

‘I don’t do that.’

‘But you used to - when you were developing the system. You were in VR; the AltLife simulations were also within VR.’

‘What are you getting at, Prem?’ she asked suspiciously.

Prem grinned. ‘Suppose you ran a simulation in VR. You give it some sketchy data. It comes back with millions of low probability solutions. You pick one and insert a subject into that time line. Because you’re in VR, there’s no headset, no VR suit. How do you get out?’

‘I used to create a portal,’ she replied without hesitation.

‘Are there portals in the production version?’

‘No, of course not,’ she replied. ‘There’s no need for them.’

‘So if you ran the production version of AltLife from inside the virtual world, there’s no way of getting out.’

‘No - ’

‘So if you inserted someone from VR into that simulation, once they were inside, they definitely couldn’t get out.’

‘Not until we stopped AltLife.’

‘And if you didn’t?’

‘They’d be stuck there,’ she replied. ‘Prem, why are you asking me this stuff?’

‘And they’d think they were in a virtual world?’ he continued, ignoring her question.

‘If that’s what we’d set up. Yes.’

‘So they might *think* that they could transmute out of it into the real world.’

‘Yes.’

‘And if they tried to do that?’

‘AltLife would create a version of the real world, and swap them into that.’

‘But they’d still be within AltLife?’

‘Of course.’

‘And if they realised that the real world they found themselves in wasn’t real at all?’ he asked. ‘If they tried to transmute back to the virtual world?’

‘AltLife would transfer them to a virtual world.’

‘Would it be the one they started in?’

‘No, because AltLife would assume that they’d finished exploring the possibilities of that time line, and create another from the millions of possibilities it had proposed.’

‘So no matter what you did, you could never think yourself out, or transmute yourself to the real world?’

‘No, you’d just jump from strand to strand of the web of possibilities.’

‘So you could end up in there for eternity, just going from one possible life to another.’

‘Yes, until we turned off AltLife.’

‘So it would be an infinite prison,’ he said softly. ‘As long as AltLife keeps running.’

***

Virtual World

'Prem, you're brilliant!' cried Hamish.

'It was your idea, Hamish,' replied Prem modestly. 'When you told me to set up those two worlds, and give the links to Hisako, I didn't know why you wanted them. But then I guessed it was something to do with getting Clinton to flip-flop between fake versions of the real and virtual worlds. I just expanded the idea a bit, and with a bit of help from Hisako, we came up with the idea of enmeshing him in an infinite number of parallel worlds, all generated within AltLife.'

'So what's Hisako doing?'

'She's setting up a version of AltLife in the virtual world, which will include the two copies of the real and virtual worlds I modified, exactly the way you wanted. Then she's going to add just enough of Clinton's background so that AltLife will struggle to give any definitive projections, but will generate lots of alternative time lines. Once she's done that, we add the world where we're holding him into the system, and transfer him into the fake virtual world.'

'Definitely an improvement on my first idea,' said Hamish. 'At first, he won't recognise it as a fake, and he'll think he's back in the 'real' virtual world. He'll watch the news outlets which will show him what he expects to see - a series of small scale nuclear explosions, attributed to terrorist groups on both sides. And then the whole scenario will escalate into war between Iran and Israel, and finally all the Gulf States will be drawn into the conflict.'

'And that's as far as I modified the world,' said Prem.

'It won't take him that long to realise that he's being shown what he expects to see,' said Hamish. 'Once he suspects, he'll try to see what's happening directly using the girl's life-log.'

'I managed to fake quite a lot of that by editing, but it's a loop: he won't be convinced for long,' added Prem.

'If he's suspicious of what he's being fed, the next thing he'll do is to try to get himself transmuted back to the real world,' Hamish went on. 'And as soon as he does that, he'll see exactly the same sort of news media as he saw in the fake virtual world, and he'll realise pretty quickly he's been fooled. But if our delaying tactics have worked, by that time AltLife will have generated thousands of alternative timelines, and he'll find his only choice is to get transmuted again back to the virtual world where he believes he has all the power.'

'But the virtual world he returns to won't be the one he started in,' Prem added. 'It'll be entirely generated by AltLife, and will have no connection to the reality he wants to get to.'

'What happens then is entirely up to him,' said Hamish. 'And as long as AltLife continues to run, he can never escape.'

***

'AltLife is up and running from within the virtual world,' confirmed Raj. 'I noticed that Hisako has made sure it's running in the background, so LDS won't notice any degradation in service. It's locked into their quantum computers,' added Raj.

'So long as the machines don't go down, Clinton will be stuck forever.'

'Hisako's made sure LDS's machines are configured for hot standby so if one goes down, the other takes over immediately, with no loss of service,' explained Prem. 'The chances of both going down simultaneously is so small that it's not worth thinking about.'

'Even so,' replied Raj, 'I'd like to find a way of making sure it never happens.'

'That's tomorrow's problem,' said Hamish. 'What we need to do now is get Clinton in there as soon as we can, so we can get back to dealing with Alex.'

'We're all set to go,' said Prem.

'Then let's do it.'

***

AltLife: Clinton timeline #1

Clinton opened his eyes and looked around him.

'You're back safely, Professor,' said the transmutation technician.

'What just happened?' demanded Clinton.

'I don't understand,' replied the man, surprised. 'We brought you back from the real world, just as you ordered.'

'It was different,' said Clinton accusingly.

'Different, sir?'

'I've done this before. I know what it feels like,' said Clinton. 'This was different.'

A look of puzzlement crossed the technician's face. 'In what way was it different?' he asked.

'I saw images,' replied Clinton. 'Things that couldn't be.'

'What exactly did you see?' asked the man carefully.

‘First there was a shimmer in reality,’ replied Clinton frowning. ‘Then I was inside what looked like a church - it was all cherubs and gold - ’

‘Could it have been a Catholic church?’

‘I couldn’t care less what sort of church it was - it was what was inside it,’ shouted Clinton. ‘The people - their eyes were full of hate. And then there was him - ’

‘Who, sir?’

‘Singh - he was there - just for a second. And then he was gone - like a ghost.’

For a split second, the technician looked sceptical. Then before Clinton could notice his expression of disbelief, he disguised it with a frown, trying desperately to think why anyone would see images during their transmutation.

‘I’ll just check what sort of machine we’re running on,’ he said, looking down the log on his monitor.

‘Well?’ demanded Clinton impatiently.

‘We’re running on a quantum machine,’ replied the technician, anxiety replaced by relief as a possible solution hit him.

‘So what?’ retorted Clinton.

'I've not seen this before,' said the technician, 'but my colleagues have reported that when someone transmutes from the real world onto a quantum based virtual reality, the difference in speed can manifest itself in subliminal images.'

'Difference in speed?'

'Quantum computers are so much faster than classical ones. The transmutation process was built on classical architecture, which is why, in the majority of cases, no one notices the actual transition. But when you arrive on a quantum machine, there can sometimes be a jolt - a bit like stepping off a moving train.'

'But why the images?'

'Because of the discrepancy in speed, we have to use many more temporary files to transfer the personality information in parallel to the new quantum host. A lot of these files haven't been used for a long time. They contain fragments of old versions of worlds, test data, parameter settings - could be anything. That's probably what you thought you saw.'

'But I saw Singh. Why did I see him?'

The technician thought for a moment. 'It might be something to do with Miss Myamoto,' he said.

'I know Miss Myamoto. What about her?'

'She's still running tests on the quantum machines at LDS. She and Mr Singh were close, I understand, so it's possible she was using Mr Singh as a test subject.'

Clinton's frown deepened.

'It's not surprising that images of Singh have been left lying around. He was central to everything - and when you ordered the restore, we did the minimum we had to. Singh wouldn't have let us get away with that. He'd have insisted on getting each world back to its original state. As it was, we just did the basics, and left the people to get back to the state they were in on their own.'

'What do you mean? The minimum?'

'Houses that had been built were no longer there, redecoration reverted to its old former state - nothing desperate, but it must have been unsettling to close your eyes then open them to find everything was different.'

The technician assured himself that his explanation had been satisfactory. 'Anyway, that would explain the slight jolt and the residual images. I'll make out a report and send it in to development. They'll probably be working on a fix for quantum transmutation as we speak.'

***

Clinton smiled with grim satisfaction.

The newscast showed the smouldering remains of the old city of Jerusalem. There was little left to identify the place as the focus of religious faith for Christians, Jews and Muslims over the centuries. The majority of the holy places had been completely levelled.

All that was left were vast piles of radioactive rubble pierced in places by the gaunt skeletons of melted steel structures from more modern buildings.

The media were quick to speculate on the cause of the devastation. From the radiation readings, it had become clear very early on that the bomb had been a small nuclear device. That alone narrowed the field of likely perpetrators: Iranian terrorists and Hamas were the two that stood out, but the conspiracy theorists had already decided that it was an Israeli plot to trigger their own plans for retaliation against enemies who had been a thorn in their side for too long.

A nuclear attack was acknowledged as the ultimate affront, and would allow the Israelis to remove any constraints they had previously imposed on themselves, and retaliate to the full extent of their military power.

The question was: which of the two would they attack?

The answer came quite quickly: two more detonations - both small nuclear devices. One destroyed much of the centre of the Iranian town of Qom. The other devastated the Israeli settlement, Modi'in Illit, the largest Jewish settlement in the occupied West Bank.

The choice of Qom as a target raised enormous speculation in the media. If the Israelis were responsible, why not attack the capital, Tehran? Qom was not even a very large city.

But when the commentators looked more closely, they found that the relatively obscure city was significant as a distribution centre for petroleum products, as well as having major natural gas and crude oil pipelines running through it.

As an economic target near to Tehran, it would send an unmistakable message to the Iranian government that whoever had planned the attack was starting to prepare the battlefield for a complete annihilation of the Iranian State.

But the economic headlines were rivalled by the fact that Qom was sacred to Shi'a Muslims, home to the shrine of Fatimah bin Musa. The city was the largest centre of Shi'a scholarship in the world, and a significant destination for over twenty million pilgrims each year. Did this point to an Israeli planned attack, calculated to offend everyone of the Shi'a faith?

As to the destruction of the Israeli settlement, there seemed to be little doubt that the two main suspects remained Hamas and their Iranian counterparts.

Delight flickered in Clinton's eyes. Despite Israel's

Iron Dome defences, it was only a matter of time before the missiles came scything down to reap the whirlwind of hatred that he had sparked.

***

Chapter 12

AltLife: Clinton timeline #1

It had been more than twenty four hours, and the newscasts had all changed. The emphasis had moved from the devastation the explosions had caused; now, the concentration was on the political realities. Each side was poised its finger on the nuclear trigger, but who would blink first?

Clinton busied himself preparing the database of potential assassins that he had destroyed the virtual world to get his hands on. It had taken many hours to find what he wanted, but eventually the search engine located the database in a backup copy of the development environment that Singh had missed in his final desperate attempts to erase all traces of the information that could prove deadly to so many.

Now, there was no one to stop him sending out the message to the tens of thousands of life-loggers that would unlock the fake memory of loved ones being massacred by Islamic extremists. And with the database of those thousands of visitors to the Holy Land Theme Park who had been infected with the fake memory in his hands, there was nothing to prevent him from unleashing the religious genocide he had dreamed of for so long.

He waited, as did the whole world, for the inevitable next step in the escalating conflict. To his surprise, he found he was content to wait, knowing that everything was now in his own hands, and that as soon as the nuclear missiles started to hit their allotted targets, he could initiate the apparently random acts of individual violence against the followers of Islam with no possibility of the two series of horrific events being linked either to one another, and least of all, to him.

The waiting did not last long. The newscasts almost simultaneously reported the first of Iran's rockets being intercepted by Israel's Iron Dome anti missile defences. The Israeli reaction was immediate. Nuclear detonations started to decimate Tehran and the major Iranian port cities.

The United Nations had been in constant session for days, but their condemnation of the attacks did nothing to stop the bombardment. Impotence quickly gave way to a shift towards partisan support for one side or the other. And as Israel continued to wipe out Iranian airports, communication systems, sea ports and government buildings, individual governments started to prepare for the inevitable escalation of the conflict into neighbouring states. But Iran's missile capacity had been underestimated, and eventually, the Iron Dome was overwhelmed, and Israel started to suffer the same degree of devastation as its enemy. The concept of mutually assured destruction was being graphically demonstrated in front of the whole world.

Satisfied with the progress of the devastation he had initiated, Clinton casually pressed the button that would send out the deadly messages to the myriads of waiting life-loggers, filling the minds of their unsuspecting owners with the horrific memories of what they would now believe had happened to their children and loved ones, and turning them into an army of mindless killing machines.

At last, Clinton was to achieve his ultimate desire: millions would die in revenge for the death of his family.

***

Virtual World

A rare feeling of well-being swept through Alex Duchovny. His mood lifted as swiftly and unexpectedly as the recent feelings of paranoid anger had crept up on him.

For the first time, he thought about what McAllister had said to him. He'd thanked him - at least as far as Alex had let him. Thanked him for what he'd done. And all he'd done in exchange was to be rude and churlish. He knew he needed to apologise for his behaviour, but suddenly realised that he had no idea why he had behaved the way he had. It was so unlike him. One of the things he'd always prided himself on was his ability to keep a cool head. It had even been noted in his reviews at the NSA. So what had changed? There was nothing he could think of - unless something had upset his emotional parameters.

His first instinct was to open his avatar database record and look up his parameters. But he realised that without knowing what they should be set to, he wouldn't be aware of any anomalies. He frowned. There was only one person he could turn to for help - and he was one of the two he had seriously offended.

For a second, he hesitated. Then he thought: *where is Raj Singh?*

***

AltLife: Clinton timeline #1

The newscasts all confirmed the escalation of the war in the Middle East, but Clinton's attention was focussed on the first newsflash to report the isolated outbreaks of attacks against individual Muslim targets: a single reporter's first hand audio description of an attack on an Islamic mosque.

The building had been surrounded and burned to the ground, killing all those sheltering within it. Retaliation to the outrage had been swift: gangs of Muslim youths roamed the streets, attacking anyone they came across.

But without warning, they found themselves confronted by hordes of everyday citizens armed with any makeshift weapons they could lay their hands on. The crowds increased in number, and then, seemingly unconcerned for their own safety, ploughed into the young Muslims, killing and maiming indiscriminately.

Clinton's eyes gleamed with delight at the success of his plans. But at last his patience wore thin: a single eye-witness account of one of the first massacres was all very well, but there must be a way to find out more without waiting for the other news gathering organisations to jump on the bandwagon and start recording the thousands of similar attacks that would be spontaneously happening all over the western world.

Surely the White House would be receiving more up to date reports from its operatives all over the world, he thought. And with that, he turned to his keyboard and searched for Clarke's life-log.

The desire to see the confusion and panic in Greenbaum's Oval Office at first hand was overwhelming.

***

Virtual World

'Of course,' said Raj carefully. 'If that's what you want.'

'Yes,' replied Alex. 'I behaved badly. Not like me at all. I think it may have something to do with my emotional parameters.'

Raj called up the avatar data and examined Alex's profile.

‘Well?’ asked Alex. ‘Is there anything?’

Raj thought carefully for a moment, then said: ‘They’re not normal.’

‘What’s normal?’

‘There are default settings that every avatar is set to when they’re created,’ explained Raj slowly. ‘Most people never change them because they don’t need to. There are occasions when we change them deliberately, but they’re for very special circumstances.

‘I can count on the fingers of one hand how many times I’ve had to intervene,’ he said, thinking specifically of the apparent insanity that had affected General Clarke after his death. ‘It needs super user permissions,’ he started to explain.

‘And I was the only super user at the time,’ Alex went on. ‘You think I changed them?’

‘I have no idea,’ replied Raj cagily. ‘We can look at the logs - ’

‘Go on - ’

‘I don’t need to,’ said Raj quietly. ‘We’ve already looked. It wasn’t you. At least, not deliberately.’

‘What do you mean?’

'I think you ought to sit down,' said Raj. 'What I have to tell you might come as a shock.'

***

AltLife: Clinton timeline #1

Clinton opened the life-log data and rewound it a short time into the past. To his surprise, the view through Clarke's life-logger showed Greenbaum sitting at his desk, reading what looked like a sheaf of briefing notes. The man seemed completely calm as he leafed slowly through the pages. Clinton continued to watch as the door opened and a secretary appeared. Without speaking, she retrieved some documents from the President's out tray and left the room, closing the door quietly behind her.

Clarke's gaze never shifted from Greenbaum. The telephone on his desk rang, but Greenbaum studiously ignored it, and continued to read the document in his hand.

Why was the man so calm? Why was the room not filled with advisers updating the President as to the state of hostilities? Where were the news reports filling the video screens? Why wasn't the place in an uproar?

Clinton fast forwarded the life-log data. When he pressed PLAY, the images were exactly the same: Greenbaum was leaning back in his chair, a cup in his hand.

This is not right, Clinton thought, *the whole scene is too calm, too - normal. There's no sign at all that the world is facing one of the greatest crises in its existence.*

Instinctively, he called up the metadata associated with the life-log, and scanned the content. Everything looked perfectly normal - except the time code.

Clinton's eyes opened wide: the time code was wrong! It was the wrong date!

The person he was watching was himself.

***

If it had been possible, at that moment, Clinton's mouth would have gone dry. Instead, his emotions ranged from disbelief to anxiety to intense anger. Who had done this? Who had modified Clarke's life-log? And why?

Clinton's face reflected his emotions. For someone to have falsified Clarke's life-log would have required super user status. But there was no one in the virtual world - except himself - who had such ability.

For a moment he was confused. For a second he considered the possibility that there could be a fault in the life-log recording system, but he dismissed it almost instantly. Then he checked the list of users. It confirmed that he was the only superuser. If there was no one in the virtual world who could have changed the data, then the only remaining possibility was that the life-log data had been intercepted before it had been saved. And that meant that someone in the real world was sending him false information.

Instantly, he thought himself to the transmutation station. There was only one place to look, and that was back in the real world.

***

Virtual World

'I've got part of Clinton inside my avatar?' said Alex slowly.

'We think so,' replied Raj. 'It would explain why you've been behaving so erratically. It wasn't just Hamish and I who noticed - the AIs are designed to report anomalous behaviour. And rejecting the opportunity to bond with the mother you've worked so hard to create counts as anomalous.'

'What can I do?' asked Alex.

'We don't know,' replied Raj. 'Our first thought was to ensure that Clinton was safely enmeshed in his prison, to make sure he couldn't escape back here. We thought that once he was totally removed from the virtual world, his influence over your personality would cease completely. But those parameter values would suggest otherwise.'

'Can't you just change them back?'

'Of course, but I suspect the effect would just be temporary. You see, the algorithms that have infected you are similar to self motivating avatars, they have a prime objective. They were designed to be like any other life form: their fundamental objective is to reproduce, and so ensure the survival of their - I suppose you might call it their 'species'.'

'So even if you change my emotional parameters, it won't make any difference?'

'I think it's more complicated than that,' said Raj. 'I think your moods are being affected by Clinton's.'

'How can that be?'

Raj paused, not sure how much information to disclose.

Eventually, he said: 'It's only a theory, but it's all to do with what kind of machine your avatar is running on.'

'I don't understand.'

'Clinton's avatar is running on a quantum computer. It doesn't matter how or where, but it is. When your avatar is also running on a quantum machine, the algorithms which have seeped into your avatar will be aligned with the same routines within Clinton. So if he's happy, so are you. If he's angry, so are you.'

'And at the moment?'

Raj smiled. 'At the moment, either he's happy, or your avatar is running on a conventional machine. The problem is: I don't know which it is.'

***

Alex's meeting with Raj had left him with more questions than answers.

Why would Clinton be happy in a prison? Why would Raj claim he couldn't tell which of his theories was correct? Surely it was easy to tell what sort of machine his avatar was running on? And if his personality was being infiltrated by elements of Clinton, what would become of him if they continued to propagate? Would he become more like Clinton? Would Clinton's personality take over completely?

And then, suddenly, he understood why Raj had been deliberately vague: they expected Clinton to take him over completely.

Alex contemplated the consequences: a second Clinton in the virtual world; one with super user access, seeking revenge for what had been done to him. No wonder Raj had seemed vague: he knew absolutely that his quantum computer scenario was untrue; he knew that if left unchecked, Clinton's personality would eventually take over Alex's whole being. He must also understand what that would mean for the virtual world.

The only conclusion that Alex could draw was that Raj was being kind to him, knowing that eventually his personality would be eclipsed by the evil nature of Randolph Clinton.

But surely, there must be something they could do to prevent the inevitable? This was the virtual world, anything was possible. Then he realised, quite suddenly, that the only solution was his own annihilation. Raj and Hamish must already know that in some way, they had to erase him from the virtual world. That they had to somehow remove his super user status so that they could erase him from all existence.

For a long time, he sat quite still, trying to feel the changes taking place within him. But all he could feel was the emptiness of knowing that the end of his existence was being determined by someone else.

For a second, the thought depressed him totally, then as if out of nowhere, he heard a voice in his head:

Don't give in, whispered the voice. *You have to fight for your existence.*

At first, he was startled. Then his surprise turned to

confusion: the voice he had heard was Hamish McAllister's.

***

AltLife: Clinton timeline #2

Clinton opened his eyes to find himself in the familiar surroundings of a transmutation unit. But to him it seemed like awakening from a bad dream. The after-images he had seen during the transmutation process had been more disturbing this time. There had been subliminal flashes of alternative realities he didn't recognise, people he had never met, talking to him in languages he didn't understand. He had tried to metaphorically close his eyes to the images, but when he did so, other scenes appeared before him, all equally strange and unfamiliar.

'It happened again,' he said.

'Just like last time?' asked the technician standing next to the trolley.

'Worse,' replied Clinton, turning to look at the other man. 'You're the same guy,' he said accusingly. 'The same guy that was there when I transmuted to the virtual world.'

'That's right, Professor,' replied the man. 'That's my avatar you saw. They changed the way we do things these days - thought it was less stressful for the customer to see the same person at both ends.'

‘But that’s not possible.’

‘Sure, it is,’ replied the man. ‘Just because we keep our customers in stasis while they’re away on vacation in VR, doesn’t mean the technical staff have to.’

‘But what about merging life-log data? When they got back, they’d have two sets of memories.’

The man laughed. ‘Only if the avatar and the real person get to merge. In my case, I’m never gonna get together with my alter ego, so it’s no problem.’

Clinton swung his legs off the trolley. ‘Where’s the nearest newscast monitor?’ he demanded.

‘Right next door,’ replied the technician. ‘But it’s the same news they have in VR.’

Clinton ignored him, and rushed through to the next room. He found himself in a waiting area facing a video wall. The screen was showing a live ice hockey match.

‘News channel,’ barked Clinton.

‘Please specify what sort of news you require,’ responded the video control system.

‘World.’

The screen instantly changed to images of the

destruction left by the bombings in Jerusalem and Qom.

A ticker tape scrolled across the bottom of the screen: *** *Hate crimes increase by 77%* *** *Latest attacks on mosques unprecedented* *** *Christians run riot in Muslim ghettos* ***

'Change channel,' ordered Clinton. 'US News.'

The video wall changed again. This time the images showed aerial footage of the White House. The drone zoomed into the gates to the building, showing the angry, chanting crowds. There was no audio, but Clinton could read some of the placards being waved: *Greenbaum out! US Jews support Israel. Resign!*

Clinton's face showed his consternation. How could it have got out? How could the people have found out what he had been doing? Someone must have talked - but who?

It was clear from the angry scenes that there was no sympathy from the American people for what had happened, and that they blamed Greenbaum. But Clinton was still confused as to how anyone could have found out what was going on. Clarke would never have talked, and if Markie had showed any sign of weakness or betrayal, she would have dealt with him without a second thought. So what could have happened to expose his foolproof plan?

The ticker tape running along the bottom of the

screen declared the breaking news: *** *Military plot to destabilise Middle East uncovered* *** *President resigns* *** *Greenbaum leaves White House* *** *Vice President Rossi to be sworn in* ***

‘What the hell?’ muttered Clinton.

The images suddenly changed to a courtroom. The camera zoomed into the grim face of the presiding judge. He was clearly speaking, but there was no audio. The shot changed to show the face of the accused, standing in the dock. Clinton felt himself grow pale as he recognised the familiar face of Clarke.

Beneath the pictures, the ticker tape had changed: *** *Personal security to President convicted of murder* *** *death penalty for Clarke* *** *virtual prison denied to killer Clarke* ***

‘How can this be possible?’ Clinton whispered to himself, his eyes wide with disbelief. ‘She couldn’t have betrayed me.’

From off the screen, the ticker tape added a further message: *** *Clarke admits murder of Randolph Clinton* ***

With those words, the truth clicked into place: of course she had admitted it, that was what he had instructed her to do. But then he had proclaimed her a national hero, and promoted her to his personal staff. Surely that was sufficient to protect her from the charge of murder. Randolph Clinton had been the most wanted man in the United States at that point in time, and the fact that she had finally disposed of him was surely an act of patriotism, not a crime. Then the realisation struck him that he had omitted to sign her Presidential pardon. How was he to have known that the tide in affairs could have turned the way it had?

He continued to watch the girl's expressionless face as sentence was passed, and the two guards by her side led her away to her death. For a split second, he felt some regret for her fate. But a word to his people in the prison system would ensure that her body would be diverted to the unacknowledged Clarke clone recycling facility. She would be available for duty within days.

From the edge of the screen, the ticker tape revealed its next messages: *** *Clarke responsible for nuclear attack on Jerusalem* *** *Clone confesses role in destruction of virtual world* *** *Clarke implicates Clinton in murder of late President Winter* ***

Clinton watched speechless as the catalogue of admissions continued.

*** *Clarke admits London hospital bombing* *** *Clarke admits Diablo Canyon nuclear blast* *** *Clarke admits Tokyo hospital attack* ***

Then his face grew dark, and he turned away from the screen.

'Transmute me back to the virtual world,' he shouted

at the technician.

'But why?' asked the man. 'You only just got here.'

'Because someone is playing games with me - and wherever this place is, it isn't the real world.'

***

Virtual World

'Clinton's jumped again,' said Raj. 'He's well and truly lost now.'

'I think we can safely ignore him for the time being,' replied Hamish. 'I'm more concerned about Alex Duchovny.'

'The only solution is to erase him,' replied Raj. 'It won't take him long to work that out, and I'm not sure what he's likely to do once he realises. The thing is, we can't do anything to him without his realising what we're doing. And as soon as Clinton finds out that he's being toyed with, his mood is likely to change suddenly. If Alex is mirroring that mood, the last thing he's going to do is to cooperate in his own destruction.'

'If we explain that we only need to reset him back to the moment before he copied that file - '

'If he's under Clinton's influence at the time, he's never going to trust us enough to do that.'

‘What other option do we have?’ asked Hamish. ‘If he’s not under Clinton’s influence, he might agree.’

‘The AIs are monitoring him from minute to minute,’ replied Raj. ‘The last time I spoke to him, I’m pretty sure he might have agreed, but we have to be sure we pick the right moment.’

Hamish and Raj: Alex has just requested to see his mother, said a voice in their heads.

Hamish looked at Raj quizzically: ‘Can we influence her?’ he asked.

Raj shook his head. ‘It’s too late, Hamish. The actor is fully immersed in the character. If we wanted to influence the mother, we’d have to tear her apart from the actor - and we both remember how difficult, how traumatic that was.’

***

Alex stood looking at the house he had lived in most of his life. As a replica, it and the surrounding neighbourhood were perfect. Hesitantly, he walked up to the front door. Should he ring the doorbell? Or should he walk right in, exactly as he would normally have done? He realised that he was afraid: afraid that he would be disappointed; afraid that he would still look at her as the avatar actor; afraid that it was too soon to accept her as a substitute for what he had lost.

As he raised his hand towards the bell push, the door opened and his mother appeared, smiling exactly as he remembered her, before the dreadful illness took away her sense of joy.

She held out her arms to him and, to his own surprise, without hesitating, he walked into them and held her close. The two stood in that first embrace for what seemed ages. Alex felt the warmth of his mother's body against his, and the scent of her perfume brought back to life the whole of his childhood and teenage years.

At last, his mother held him at arms' length and looked deep into his eyes. 'It's so good to see you, Alex,' she said.

'It's so good to see you, too,' he heard himself say. 'You look - '

'Yes, I feel wonderful, Alex,' she smiled. 'And so glad you came.' She paused, looking him up and down. 'You look thinner. Have you been eating properly? And why are we standing out here?' she asked impatiently. 'Come on in. We've such a lot to talk about.'

As she shut the door behind them, he asked: 'How did you know I was here?'

'New-fangled doorbell camera,' she said, shooing him into the living room. 'Well? What do you think?'

she asked.

'You look - so well,' he replied looking at her, unable to keep the smile from his face.

'Not me - the new curtains,' she chided. 'Just like your father - never notice the important things.'

'Father?' he asked tentatively. 'Where is he?'

'Away on one of his trips,' she replied casually. 'As usual. He'll be back in a few days, and then all he'll want to do is sleep. They seem to work them so hard. But I suppose it's worth it for the money.'

'Who's he working for?' asked Alex.

'The usual people,' she replied evasively. 'But never mind about him - what have you been doing?'

'Same old stuff,' he replied.

'Communicative as ever,' she grinned. 'Want some coffee? There's some on the stove. Your aunt called me the other day.'

'What did she want?' he asked abruptly, his demeanour suddenly changed at the thought of the woman who had abandoned Ann.

'She asked after you.'

'Did she ask after her daughter?' he demanded coldly.

She shook her head sadly. 'Oh, Alex. Are you still angry?'

Alex saw the pain in his mother's eyes, and lowered his gaze. 'I know I shouldn't be,' he replied.

There was a long silence between the two. At last, he said, 'Have you heard from her?'

'Ann? No, not for a long time,' replied his mother sadly.

'You know what happened to her?' he asked cautiously, not yet fully understanding the dynamic between them.

'No, tell me.'

'She went - undercover.'

He felt his mother stiffen. 'What does that mean, Alex?'

'It means that she was doing something - something very dangerous.'

'Oh, no,' whispered his mother.

'Just like - '

His mother looked into his eyes, and in that second, there was an unspoken understanding between the two of them.

It was in that instant that she became his mother.

***

Alex began to recognise the unpredictable shifts in his underlying mood. Now that he had talked to Raj, he was more aware of these changing feelings, and the thought that Clinton was in some way taking over his life terrified him.

Don't give in, the voice had said. *You have to fight for your existence.*

But how? What could he do to fight back? How could he suppress these dark, unwelcome stirrings in his unconscious? And what would happen to him if he tried somehow to confront them? Was Clinton aware of his existence? Could he feel what Alex was feeling in return?

And if he chose to confront Clinton, how could he do that? Where was he? Where had they hidden him? Was it even possible?

As for Raj and Hamish, he could understand their

reluctance to share the information: the fewer people that knew, the safer they obviously felt. But why was that? How had Clinton escaped the last time they had held him captive? The fact that they refused to allow anyone to know the location of his current prison must mean that it was an individual person who had released him. Had it been a deliberate act? Or an accident? Whichever it was, they were obviously determined it shouldn't happen again.

Alex thought back to the origins of the virtual world. At first, it had been a retreat for the super-rich. But Hamish's vision was never confined to that: to raise the money for the expansion of the virtual world, Hamish had proposed a radical solution for the chronic overcrowding in earthly prisons. The concept of the virtual prison as an opportunity to save money had been seized by governments all over the world, and Raj had devoted much of his effort and expertise in setting up virtual prison worlds for nations around the globe. If there were two other people who knew anything like as much about how to build a secure prison, Alex couldn't think of them.

And if Hamish and Raj were nervous about disclosing the whereabouts of Clinton's captivity, it must surely mean that he was being held somewhere completely unlike a conventional virtual world.

As originally conceived by McAllister, virtual prisons were merely a series of interconnected worlds intended to provide rehabilitation, allowing their prisoner inhabitants to demonstrate their return to being responsible members of whatever society they chose at the end of their journey through the various tests and challenges they were forced to confront. Had Hamish and Raj decided that Clinton's prison would allow him to demonstrate remorse? Would he ever be allowed to be rehabilitated?

Alex thought about the nature of their captive. Clinton was not just any criminal; he was professor of virtual reality, a world leader in the same field as McAllister. With his knowledge, was there any sort of virtual confinement that he couldn't find a way to escape from? To hold captive someone like Clinton must surely demand an extraordinary type of prison.

Don't give in, the voice had told him. *You have to fight for your existence.*

What did that mean? Did Hamish mean for him to confront Clinton directly? If so, he had to find out where Clinton was, and how to get to him.

For a long time, Alex wracked his brains, but nothing seemed to click. If there were clues to Clinton's location, he couldn't see them.

***

'I still blame him,' said Alex.

'Try to understand,' replied his mother. 'Your father

was doing what he thought was best.'

'Best for who, mother?' Alex demanded. 'Not best for me.'

'He saw something in her - '

'Something he didn't see in me?'

His mother fell silent.

'I was never good enough,' Alex went on. 'She was always the one. Why couldn't he see me?'

After a long silence, his mother spoke again. 'I never told you this, Alex,' she said. 'He did see something in you - but it wasn't what he expected. You were never the action hero type. Sure, you played baseball and all that stuff, but there was something more - cerebral about you. He could see that. And that it didn't suit you to be a copy of him.

'But Ann was different. She was a real tomboy. She got a kick out of all the stuff they used to do together. There was never any doubt in his mind that she would fit into the sort of world he lived in.

'But with you - I think he realised that you would never be happy with the sort of lifestyle that he'd made for himself - for us. I think that in his way, he was protecting you - preventing you from making what might have been the biggest mistake of your life.

'And I think he was also trying to protect me. By keeping you safe, he knew that he was in some small way making up for the time he was forced to spend away from me. I suppose he imagined that his sense of duty to his country justified his chosen way of life, but he also realised that every time he went away, it was hurting me. Never knowing if he was coming back, and if he did, would he be the same man that went away.'

'Did you know what he was doing?'

'Not the details, but of course I knew.'

'And about Ann?'

'Yes.'

'Then you lied to me,' he said.

She lowered her eyes, and said, 'I was trying to protect you, too.'

'Then you know what she became?'

His mother nodded silently, her eyes filled with tears.

'I loved her, too, Alex,' she whispered. 'I hated what he did to her as much as you did.'

The two of them sat in silence for a long time.

At last his mother said, ‘There’s something you ought to see.’

And reaching for the remote, she turned on the video screen.

***

Waves of anger welled up inside him as he watched the trial of the girl who had once been Ann Mitchell.

Seeing her order the killing of thousands of innocent civilians had shown him the monster she had become, but to hear all the other atrocities she had committed at the whim of Randolph Clinton laid out dispassionately in front of the court was in a way far worse. This was her existence laid bare: the cold, calculating executioner, the heartless urban terrorist, the soulless automaton, without conscience, intent only on carrying out the orders of her psychopathic megalomaniac leader.

Part of him recognised the justice of the sentence brought down upon her; part of him was revolted by the thought of her existence being brought to an end. That Clarke was guilty was never in doubt, but the sentence that would end the existence of Ann Mitchell brought tears to his eyes.

Perhaps his father had been right all along: he was never made for the harsh, lonely world of the field agent. There was too much of his mother in him.

He turned away from the screen, wretched, unable to put into words what he was feeling. His mother looked on helplessly: there was nothing she could do to lessen the anguish he felt.

‘I have - to go,’ he said at last. ‘There’s something I have to do.’

***

Chapter 13

Virtual World

Was it revenge he wanted? Or was it justice for Ann Mitchell? Either way, the answer lay somehow with Randolph Clinton. But how could Alex get at him? Especially when he didn't know where to start looking.

Eventually he realised that what he needed was to follow Clinton's life-log from the point where he had effectively snatched him from the transmutation process and copied him into Raj Singh's home directory. If he searched the logs, he should be able to see where Prem had created the world that Clinton had been inserted into. Once he had that information, he could look for what had happened to Clinton since then.

Alex accessed the system to look for the tiny virtual world where Clinton had been incarcerated. Unsurprisingly, the file was no longer there. Searching through the log files, he found that the world had been deleted by Prem, but not before it had been copied to another location.

Alex frowned: the new location wasn't in the virtual world. Prem had copied Clinton's data to a computer in the real world.

Suddenly, Alex realised he was on the right track.

Wasn't that what the AI had told him? When he'd demanded to see whoever was controlling him?

They're not in the virtual world - at least, not as you understand it.

He understood now that the AI had been talking about Hamish and Raj. But where had they been that wasn't in the virtual world? Had they been hiding somewhere in the real world? Is that why Prem had moved Clinton's world to a machine in the real world? Was there something significant about the particular computer he'd chosen?

Alex looked up the address of the machine to discover it was a quantum computer located in Salt Lake City in Utah.

But the bigger surprise was that it belonged to the Church of Latter Day Saints.

***

Alex's mind raced: the girl who'd been testing some software for the Mormons - what was her name?

There were distinct advantages to living as an avatar in the virtual world, memory recall was instantaneous and perfect. Immediately, he knew her name was Hisako Myamoto. She was developing some software to do with family histories, allowing people to become immersed in their relatives' time lines. How did she do it? It was just like the 3D simulation of the speech he'd found, a technique that assembled a virtual world from multiple sources of data - and she'd developed the software in the virtual world, no doubt with the full cooperation of Rajesh Singh.

Alex smiled in satisfaction: at last he was getting somewhere. There was obviously something significant about the software the girl was implementing for LDS. But how that related to Randolph Clinton, he couldn't quite make out.

Then it hit him: it was unlikely that McAllister and Singh would have agreed to let her do her initial development in the virtual world if the purpose of the software was to make a commercial profit. Having met Hamish and Raj, and knowing their history, he realised there had to be some altruistic reason they had allowed her to work in the virtual world using their resources. But what was it?

He accessed Hisako's life-log data, and scrolled back in time. Most of the content showed her hard at work, hunched over a computer terminal, but eventually he came to a packed lecture theatre, an attentive audience hanging on her every word. He scrolled to the beginning of her talk, and pressed PLAY.

As he watched and listened, he started to understand how the software had come into existence to help Hisako's patients to confront episodes in their past life which might help explain their subsequent actions, and help them to understand how they might change their behaviour based on the new insights they had gained. Of course that was why McAllister and Singh had helped her! It was all so obvious!

But it did nothing to explain why Prem had moved Clinton's tiny prison world to the LDS machine.

Except that the software was called AltLife.

***

Was that it? Had they created an alternative life for Clinton? How was that possible?

He thought about it for a long time, examining the information he had discovered, trying to make sense of what he had learned, analysing various scenarios that would fit the facts as he knew them.

If they had placed Clinton into some alternative reality, that world would not only have to involve time past, but also the ability to simulate time going forward. Such a world would allow Clinton to live a life based on whatever surroundings the software could generate. But surely the software couldn't be so sophisticated that it would fool a technically knowledgeable captive such as Clinton?

Not unless it was based on reality.

Not unless it was based on Clinton's own life-log.

A wave of dark suspicion welled up in his mind.

Why hadn't they told him? Why were they keeping it a secret from him? Didn't they trust him? Had they ever trusted him? Was it because they suspected that part of him was now Clinton?

What were they planning? Now that Clinton had been secured, what further use did they have for him? As far as they were concerned, he was now entirely dispensable. So why did he hear that voice in his head? Was it really Hamish he'd heard? Or could it have been someone else?

If it wasn't Hamish, then who could it be? Was the message even intended for him? Could it have been Clinton? Could he have heard what Clinton was thinking? Had Clinton's persona crept so far into his, were they so intertwined that he was able to tune into Clinton's thoughts?

Or was it the other way round? Could Clinton's thoughts, like his anger, spill over into Alex's conscious mind?

***

It became very clear to Alex that for McAllister and Singh to protect the virtual world, he could not be allowed to provide a way for Randolph Clinton to re-establish himself as an independent entity - especially one with super user capabilities.

He tried to consider rationally what options Raj and Hamish had open to them. Whichever way he looked at it, finally, there was only one solution: in order to stop Clinton from gaining a foothold back in the virtual world, McAllister and Singh had to erase Alex Duchovny from existence.

A deep vein of anger ran through him. It was irrelevant now whether his feelings were his own, or whether they were reflections of Randolph Clinton. All he knew was that he had to use those emotions to protect himself from whatever attack Raj and Hamish might plan.

Don't give in, the voice had said. *You have to fight for your existence.*

No, he had been mistaken. That had never been Hamish's voice. It was Clinton, telling him to do what he knew he had to do: remain alive until Clinton's persona took over his whole being and allowed him to exist again in the virtual world.

Far from confronting Clinton, he had to allow him to gain control over him. He had to be his conduit back to the world he was destined to control. And surely, he would be rewarded for his sacrifice. Yes, Clinton would realise, and would reward him.

No matter what traps Singh and McAllister might set for him, he would evade them. No matter what they tried to do to him, he would resist. He was equally as powerful as they were: why should he be concerned? There was nothing they could do to him.

And once Clinton was back in the virtual world, whatever prison they had created for him would be irrelevant.

Suddenly, the anger within him subsided, and a strange calm settled over him. The rational part of his mind reasserted itself.

What *had* he been thinking? Ally himself with Randolph Clinton? He must really be crazy!

When he thought of what the man had done, the evil he had instigated, Alex shuddered at the thought of what might become of him if he were drawn into his web of destruction.

It was clear to him that all the paranoid thoughts that had passed through his mind just seconds before were directly attributable to Clinton. The man was a monster, and his influence was growing stronger. Alex knew that it was only time before it became so great that he would no longer be able to resist.

He had to do something. But what? Who could he turn to?

***

'The AIs are reporting that Alex's emotions are

varying wildly outside the accepted parameter settings,' said Raj. 'If we don't do something soon, Clinton's influence may have increased to such an extent that he may be able to control Alex's actions. If that happens, goodness knows what he might do.'

Hamish thought for a moment. 'Is he having any lucid periods?' he asked.

'Some.'

'We need to get him to allow us to erase him,' said Hamish. 'We can recreate him from just before we captured Clinton.'

'But how do we convince him to trust us?'

'I don't know - but we need to try,' replied Hamish. 'Get him here.'

***

'What do you want?' asked Alex warily, feigning ignorance of what he knew must be coming.

'We want you to let us erase you,' replied Hamish. 'It's the only way to keep Clinton from gaining control over you.'

'You want to erase me?'

'Yes. Then we can recreate you the moment before

you copied the file with Clinton's persona in it.'

'You're telling me you want to erase me?' repeated Alex, as if in disbelief.

'Yes. You're the key to this, Alex. If we don't do this, it's only a matter of time before Clinton replaces you completely. And once he's free in this world, keeping him in the prison we designed for him won't matter a damn. He'll be free to wreak havoc exactly as he's done in the past.'

'And you're saying if I don't, it'll all be my fault?'

'It's nobody's fault, Alex. But the consequence of doing nothing is that you'll soon cease to exist, and Clinton will be free. We can't force you do this, but if we don't do it soon, it will be too late.'

'If I agree, it'd make things really easy for you, wouldn't it?' retorted Alex petulantly. 'But I have no way of knowing that you'll recreate me. Why should I trust you? All along you've been using me for your own ends.'

'We had no choice,' Raj interrupted. 'We had to remain hidden. It was the only way.'

'Same as erasing me is the only way?' demanded Alex bitterly.

'You've seen what Clinton has done in the past,'

said Hamish. 'You know what he's tried to do, and how grave the consequences might have been. You've seen how he used Ann Mitchell.'

'It wasn't Clinton, it was the CIA who used her!' shouted Alex. 'I saw what she'd become. I heard the terrible things she did. How does erasing me help her?'

There was a silence.

At last Hamish said, 'We could recreate her. Just like you recreated your mother.'

For a second, Alex hesitated. 'If anyone is going to recreate her, it's me,' he retorted.

'To do that, you have to exist,' replied Hamish quietly. 'And I think you already know there are times when you're not in control. And it's going to get worse, Alex. I don't think you have time - '

'I'll take my chances, McAllister,' snarled Alex. 'I've heard your solution. Maybe I'll ask Clinton what he thinks.'

'And how do you propose to do that?' asked Raj.

'I can get into his timeline. The AltLife thing - '

'You know about that?' asked Raj in alarm. 'But how - ?'

'I can do my research as well as you can.'

Raj and Hamish exchanged glances. If Alex saw the fear in their faces, he ignored it.

He smiled grimly. 'I can get into Clinton's little world,' he said. 'And when I do, I can go back to the point before Ann agreed to do what those bastards at the CIA forced her to do.'

'It's not her timeline - ,' started Raj. But Hamish held up his hand to stop him saying any more. 'If he wants to try, Raj, it's not up to us to stop him,' he said slowly. 'He has to make his own decisions.'

'But - '

'You won't find the answer there, Alex,' said Hamish. 'We're the only real option you have.'

***

'I think I preferred you as the Japanese professor,' laughed Kominsky.

'And I prefer you as a hologram,' retorted Jennings, 'What do you think, Barbara?'

'I think I agree with Peter,' she replied, mockingly. 'I was hoping some of Sato's dignity and charm would have rubbed off on you, but no such luck.'

‘To what do we owe this pleasure?’ asked Jennings. ‘Do you want our help in replacing somebody else?’

‘No, we’re fine back here in the real world, thanks. Rossi seems to be growing into the job, and the legal system is handling the others.’

‘Yes, we saw Clarke’s trial,’ said Jennings grimly.

‘And the execution,’ added Barbara.

‘Justice was seen to be done,’ said Kominsky gravely. ‘But that’s not why I got into this silly VR suit.’

‘And I thought it was the pleasure of our company,’ teased Jennings.

‘We’ll look forward to that when your clones are ready,’ replied Kominsky. ‘I need you to pass a message on to Duchovny for me.’

‘Is that the Duchovny you denied having heard of?’

‘That’s the one.’

‘So what’s the message?’

‘The operation he was preparing for has been cancelled. You can tell him to stand down.’

‘Really? So what’s he going to do here? He’s not

just a visitor, you remember: he died to get in here.'

'Come on, Jennings, don't you know me better than that?' said Kominsky. 'We've got his DNA ready to grow a clone for him to return to. As soon as it's matured, he can come back whenever he likes.'

'You're all heart, Peter,' replied Jennings. 'Did you tell him that before he volunteered?'

'Well - no.'

'Then that's going to come as a complete surprise to him. I suspect he might feel a little - upset that you didn't tell him there was a way back.'

'I have a sweetener for him,' replied Kominsky.

'You do? And what's that?'

'There was something else we didn't tell him.'

'Oh, really? And what was that?'

'We kept Ann Mitchell's life-log data,' replied Kominsky. 'Clarke appeared to be executed, but the doctor switched the lethal injection for an anaesthetic. Once the media had broadcast the death sentence being carried out, we smuggled her out of the prison in a casket, switched it at the crematorium, then transmuted Ann Mitchell's life-log into her old body.

‘Ann Mitchell is very much alive.’

***

Over and over, Alex asked himself: could he trust Raj and Hamish? Did he really believe that they would recreate him? And even if they did, how was he any better off?

At least if he chose to confront Clinton, it would be his own decision, his fate would be in his own hands. And if the world that they had created for their prisoner was anything like the virtual world, there was no way that Clinton or anyone else could harm him. Was it not better to live out his existence in a world where Ann Mitchell existed?

As convincing and real as she was, the mother Raj and Hamish had allowed him to create wasn’t as real as the Ann that continued to live in Clinton’s life line.

Was that his real motivation? Was Ann the reason he was prepared to risk meeting Clinton? Had that been his real purpose all along? To get Ann back in some way, no matter how dangerous to himself?

But he understood that to confront Clinton, he would have to find a way into that same world, an artificial world created entirely by AltLife. And his heart froze when he realised that somewhere in that same timeline would be the monster that Ann Mitchell had become.

There was no possibility that she could be avoided: to encounter Clinton was to come face to face with her.

In the back of his mind a thought nagged at him: what had Raj meant when he said ‘it’s not her time line’?

No obvious answer came to mind. Was there something about AltLife that he didn’t understand? Was there something he’d missed? He dismissed the thought from his mind: there just wasn’t time. He had to make a decision while he was still able to. He would face whatever consequences there might be: it would be worth it to see and talk to Ann again.

Suddenly, his face grew pale: there was one conclusion to his proposed action he couldn’t avoid: if Hamish and Raj were convinced that Clinton could not escape from their prison, then neither could anyone else.

Once he had found his way inside, he could never leave.

***

‘I’ve just spoken to Peter Kominsky,’ said Jennings. ‘He wanted me to pass on a message to Duchovny, but I thought it might be better coming from you.’

‘What’s the message?’ asked Hamish.

‘Kominsky wants Alex to stop whatever he was doing here. The project’s been cancelled and they want him back in the real world.'

Hamish raised his eyebrows in surprise.

'Did Alex know they had his DNA?' he asked.

'Kominsky omitted to mention that fact to him,' replied Jennings. 'I guess he thought that just being able to be create his dead mother was enough of a lever to get him to volunteer.'

'It seems he was right,' mused Hamish. 'Are they growing a clone for him?'

'Yes. But there's even better news: Ann Mitchell is alive and well.'

Hamish raised his eyebrows in surprise. 'That's another thing your friend Kominsky omitted to mention to him?'

Jennings acknowledged the reproof in Hamish's tone. 'I know, Hamish. But he's got a tough job. Sometimes he has to do things he's not proud of.'

Hamish frowned.

'You don't seem too pleased, Hamish.'

'I'm not sure what to do,' replied Hamish. 'We have a problem with Alex, and depending on how much influence Clinton has over him at any given moment,

I’m not sure what effect this news will have on him.’

‘Hamish, you need to tell him,’ said Jennings. ‘He has to know.’

‘Yes, I know - you’re right. But I need to think about exactly how to tell him. I need to talk to Raj.’

As Hamish spoke, Raj suddenly materialised in front of the two men.

‘Hamish!’ he cried. ‘It’s Alex - he’s disappeared.’

***

‘Where is he?’ demanded Hamish.

‘I’ve traced him as far as the LDS machine,’ replied Raj.

‘Can he find a way into AltLife?’

‘I’m not sure,’ replied Raj. ‘I’m looking at the logs right now, and I’m guessing he’s copying the method that Prem used to incorporate Clinton into his world.’

‘But Prem was able to do that because he was outside the process. How could Alex do it to himself?’

‘I think he’s set up a routine to carry out Prem’s actions automatically,’ said Raj, his eyes intent on the screen in front of him.

‘What would that mean?’

‘Once he started the routine, it would take his avatar data and store it in a miniature virtual world. Then it would copy the data to the LDS machine, and merge it with the AltLife time line we chose for Clinton.’

‘Can we stop it?’ demanded Hamish.

Raj shook his head. ‘It’s too late, Hamish. The routine has completed and closed down. Assuming it worked, Alex is inside Clinton’s world.’

Hamish’s face was grave. ‘Then there’s nothing we can do,’ he said.

***

AltLife: Clinton timeline #1

Alex opened his eyes to find himself back where he started. At least, it looked like the virtual world where he started. But he was aware that it couldn’t be; that it was a perfect copy generated by the AltLife software from Clinton’s life-log data, supplemented by innumerable other sources of information.

The only difference Alex could see was the world was completely static. Nothing moved. There were no other people, and the screens he could see around him in the transmutation room showed no sign of life.

For a moment he lay completely still, fearful that he had made a dreadful mistake in assuming that AltLife could create a world in which time existed as he understood it. He thought back to Hisako's lecture: she had been quite explicit that any of LDS's potential genealogy customers could enter a chosen world and see exactly what had happened to their relatives and friends. That meant there had to be some simulation of time passing.

So why did the world appear completely sterile?

Alex suddenly recognised that the fact that he was thinking at all meant that time was moving forward. He decided to try to move. Without effort he swung his legs off the bed and stood up. Instantly, the monitors on the walls burst into life, and a transmutation technician materialised in front of him.

'Where did you come from?' asked the man in surprise. 'I wasn't expecting any more clients.'

'I'm a test,' replied Alex quickly. 'Just checking out the system.'

'Hisako still checking things out? She's very thorough,' commented the technician approvingly. 'Where are you headed?'

'I'm not sure,' replied Alex. 'Hisako suggested I wander round to see what I could find.'

‘If you need any help - ’

‘You haven’t seen Randolph Clinton?’

‘Sure, I transmuted him back to the real world,’ said the other man. ‘Then the strangest thing, he was back again within minutes. Claimed I’d sent him to the wrong place.’

‘What did you do?’

‘Transmuted him again.’

‘Did he come back?’

‘No, not seen him since.’

‘You said you sent him to the real world?’

‘That’s right. But he didn’t seem to think it was the real world. He wasn’t pleased, I can tell you. To be honest, I was glad to see the back of him.’

The man paused. ‘I checked the logs to make sure I hadn’t messed up, but it was definitely the right place.’

‘Can I see the logs?’ asked Alex.

‘Sure. Use the terminal over there,’ he said, pointing across the room. ‘There’s nothing confidential in there.’

Alex crossed the room and signed in as his super user. The logs scrolled up the screen. At the top of the list was his own appearance in the world. He noticed that his transmutation didn't have a start point.

He scrolled down to view Clinton's latest entries. Apart from his first entry into the world, each of his subsequent entries had start and end points.

The odd thing that Alex noted was that the end point of each of his transmutations was different. Maybe Clinton was right: his transmutation hadn't taken him to the real world at all. And when he'd come back, the second time he'd transmuted had been to a totally different end point.

Alex frowned. Where were these other end points? Were they just different locations in the real world? Or was it something different? Were they different worlds altogether? And if they were, where were they?

Alex turned to the technician. 'When you transmute someone back to the real world, do you specify the end point?'

'No, it defaults to the place you transmuted from,' replied the man. 'People usually want to go back to their own bodies,' he added with an ironic grin. 'Why? Is this one of Hisako's tests?'

'That's right,' Alex lied. 'Just wanted to check. I

need to be transmuted again, so if I give you the end point - '

'No problem,' he replied. 'And when you get there, say hello to my avatar for me.'

***

AltLife: Clinton timeline #2

Alex opened his eyes. 'Have I moved?' he asked.

'You've just been talking to my avatar, haven't you?' said the technician, jokingly. 'Happens all the time. Some people find it reassuring to see the same person at each end. Others just think it's confusing.'

'I'm just doing some testing for Hisako,' said Alex. 'Can I check your logs?'

'Be my guest.'

Alex opened the log file. The latest transmutation record showed his start point, and the end point he'd specified at his previous transmutation. So wherever he was, he knew now it was possible to control the destination of the transmutation process. He guessed that Clinton hadn't yet worked out how to navigate between the worlds - if they were worlds at all.

Alex scrolled down looking for Clinton's latest transmutation. When he found it, he noticed that the end point was set to yet another code. So Clinton had jumped again, but this time to somewhere else.

‘Where am I?’ Alex asked.

‘Real world,’ replied the technician. ‘Why? Where did you think you were?’

‘Just checking,’ replied Alex. ‘I’ll just have a look outside - need to make a call.’

‘You coming back?’

‘I’ll be a few minutes, then you can transmute me again.’

Alex left the room and found himself in the plush surroundings of a health spa. Nothing unusual in that, he thought, looking round at the clients making their way to and from the various treatment rooms leading off the main corridor.

‘Can I help you?’ asked a voice from behind him.

Alex turned to see a smart young woman wearing what looked to him like white surgical scrubs.

‘I was just looking for the - ’ Never having been to a spa in his life, he struggled to think of an appropriate treatment. ‘ - those tank things - where you float.’

‘The flotation tanks? We call it Zero Environmental

Stimulation Therapy - ZEST for short.'

'That's the thing - '

'Just follow me. Is this your first time? Do you need any help?' she asked politely.

'No, if you just point the way, I'll be fine.'

'The ZEST centre is the third door on your left.'

Alex smiled his thanks and headed along the corridor. As he opened the door she had indicated, he looked back to see the young woman smiling back at him. He flashed a brief smile and hurried inside.

He'd heard about sensory deprivation tanks, but had never seen one. Curious, he lifted the lid of the first pod and looked inside. Instantly, he gasped, dropped the lid and stumbled backwards against the wall.

For a moment, he found he was pressing himself hard against the wall behind him, his breath coming in short gasps. Then after a few seconds he recovered himself sufficiently try to process what he had seen inside the tank.

Or rather, what he'd not seen. Cautiously, he lifted the lid for the second time to confirm that he hadn't been imagining things. As he stared inside, he realised he was looking at - nothing. Or more precisely, nothingness - the absence of everything.

As his mind tried to take in what he'd seen, he understood exactly what Clinton had been describing.

This was most definitely *not* the real world.

***

Virtual World

'Assuming Alex made it into Clinton's world, can we find out where he is in the time line?' asked Hamish.

'Not without going in there ourselves,' replied Raj. 'And I don't think that's advisable. The only hint we have is that each of the worlds generated by AltLife has an activity level associated with it. If there's no one in it, the activity level would be effectively zero. That's how we can tell when someone transmutes between the various strands of timeline.'

'If Alex merged with Clinton's initial timeline, then he's safe for now,' said Hamish. 'Clinton's transmuted twice since then. What are the chances of Alex transmuting to the same world as Clinton?'

'I don't know,' replied Raj. 'You'd need to ask Hisako. She may be able to give you a more definitive answer.'

Raj paused, looking at his friend. 'Knowing where he is won't help, Hamish,' he said gently. 'He can't get out.'

'Why did he do it?' murmured Hamish. 'Why didn't he trust us?'

'I don't think it had anything to do with us, Hamish,' replied Raj. 'I think it was to do with the girl. I think the option of being able to create a replica of her wasn't enough for him. He didn't know that she's alive again. If he had, I don't think he'd have gone to look for her.'

'You think that's what he's done? Sacrificed himself for the chance to see her again?'

'I don't think he'd see it as a sacrifice, Hamish. He's alive. She's alive. That may be enough for him.'

'The timing was awful, Raj. If only we'd known sooner. We could have stopped him.'

'It may not be so bad, Hamish. He's safe enough.'

'As long as he doesn't get into the same world as Clinton.'

'Even if he does, Hamish, Clinton won't know who he is. As far as I'm aware, they never met. They have nothing in common.'

'Unless you count Clarke - '

Raj fell silent.

'If he's looking for Ann Mitchell, that's the way he'll try to find her,' said Hamish. 'He'll try to follow the timeline backwards. And if he does that, he's bound to find Clinton along the way.'

'Is that a problem?'

'Not in itself,' replied Hamish. 'But unlike Clinton, Alex is aware that the two of them are living within AltLife. If Clinton got to understand that, he'd recognise the implications and do what you or I would do.'

'What's that?'

'He'd make sure he got super user privileges, and then try to find a way to make a portal out of AltLife.'

***

'How much does Alex know about AltLife?' asked Hisako's hologram.

'As far as we know, very little,' replied Hamish. 'I'm surprised he managed to get in there at all.'

'I should never have left my logs lying around,' said Prem. ' I feel such a fool.'

'Don't be so hard on yourself, Prem,' said Hamish. 'It's not your fault. How could any of us have known Alex would decide to throw himself into the lion's den?'

‘Alex hit on a clever solution,’ said Hisako, ‘copying what you did, Prem. But all it means is he’s stuck in there, exactly the same as Clinton.’

‘As you say, Hisako, it was clever,’ said Hamish. ‘But if he’s clever enough to do that, is he clever enough to find a way out?’

‘There is no way out,’ replied Hisako shortly.

‘Could he find a way to build a portal from inside AltLife?’

‘There are no software tools inside AltLife,’ replied Hisako.

‘But isn’t it a copy of the virtual world?’ asked Prem.

‘Only in the sense that it’s created from images of the virtual world collected by the people who’ve been there,’ she replied.

‘It doesn’t work the same way as the virtual world - there’s no infrastructure behind it. It may appear to have the sorts of things that we’d take for granted in the virtual world, but they’re just illusions, images. There are portals, but they don’t work.’

‘So how can it fool anyone into thinking it is the virtual world?’

Hisako grimaced. 'It was never meant to. Just as it was never intended to be a prison. It wasn't supposed to take the place of reality. It was merely a tool to get people to examine their past decisions. The fact that some of it is so realistic is merely a result of the hundreds of sources that AltLife can gather together.

'When it does that, it can certainly give the impression that it's real, but you just have to open a cupboard, or a door that wasn't opened when these images were gathered, and you'd realise straight away that it is just an illusion. And as for using software tools - '

'But it's possible to move around within the AltLife timeline.'

'Of course, that's built in to the system,' she replied. 'But don't confuse it with the way you can think yourself to any location in the virtual world. You can only go backwards or forwards along the single timeline.'

'But you can transmute?'

'Again, that's an illusion,' Hisako replied. 'What actually happens is you move from one AltLife possibility strand to another. AltLife generates the destination of the transmutation at random, so you end up in another potential future. From outside, we can only tell if someone has moved from one strand to another.

And that's the only way we can keep track of where Clinton - and now, Alex - have ended up.'

'What's the probability that Alex will meet Clinton?' asked Hamish.

'Infinitesimally small,' replied Hisako. 'Unless - '

'Unless what?'

'Unless Alex is much cleverer than we thought.'

***

Chapter 14

AltLife: Clinton timeline #25

Alex looked around him. Yet another transmutation suite: the same equipment, the same monitor screens, but more significantly, the same technician.

'This getting annoying,' Alex said. 'It's always you.'

'The other guy is my avatar,' replied the technician with a smile. 'I'm the real thing.'

'Of course you are,' murmured Alex, standing up from the bed. 'I just need to check your logs.'

'Inspection?'

'Just doing some testing,' replied Alex. 'Hisako's being thorough. I see Professor Clinton's been through here.'

'He's been back and fore a couple of times. Always seems in a hurry to get somewhere. Doesn't say a lot. Not what you'd call friendly.'

Alex made a note of Clinton's destination point.

'I'll just grab a coffee,' he said. 'Then I'll be back.'

‘I’ll be here,’ replied the technician.

I’m sure you will, thought Alex. *I’m sure you’ll always be here.*

As soon as he left the building Alex knew immediately that he was *not* in the real world, but also that Clinton would have recognised the fact, too.

All his previous transmutations had arrived where Clinton had originally started - in Washington DC. But this place was clearly not Washington. Alex stared at the streaming traffic, the neon signs, the hurrying people. This was New York.

But there was something quite different from the New York he was familiar with. For a moment he was confused, but then he recognised the fundamental difference: this New York was unbelievably noisy.

Gone were the silently gliding autocabs, the pedestrianised streets. Instead he was aware of the constant noise of internal combustion engines, the impatient blaring of horns, the roar of buses and trucks, the wail of police and ambulance sirens. This was emphatically *not* the New York that Alex knew.

With the unrelenting tumult came the growing awareness that what he was seeing was not the New York of the present, but the pollution choked New York as it had been many years previously. It would be easy to confirm his suspicions: he walked across the sidewalk to a news stand, grabbed a copy of the Wall Street Journal and checked out the date.

Alex's face grew pale as he read the words: September 11, 2001.

'What time is it?' he shouted to the news seller.

'Eight forty,' the man replied. 'Hey! You want a paper or not?'

But Alex was already running, looking upwards into the blue September sky. He kept running until he saw the twin towers of the World Trade Center sticking up above the other skyscrapers that dominated the Lower Manhattan skyline. He stopped and stared mesmerised as American Airlines Flight 11 struck the North Tower. It was 08:46 am.

Alex closed his eyes and turned away. He started to walk slowly back to the transmutation suite, ignoring the growing sounds of awareness as people in the street started to react to the fact that an unprecedented disaster had started to play out around them, and reluctant to witness the second horror he knew was coming seventeen minutes later.

'You don't look so good,' said the technician. 'Lousy coffee?'

'No.'

‘I just remembered something about Clinton,’ the man went on. ‘He was complaining about seeing stuff during the transmutation. Visions, he said they were. Could be a fault. You see anything?’

‘No,’ replied Alex. ‘I’ll check it out. Just get me out of here. Here’s the destination code.’

***

AltLife: Clinton timeline #43

‘Back to the virtual world?’ asked the technician.

‘Just use this code,’ Alex instructed, handing the man a piece of paper where he’d scrawled Clinton’s next destination.

‘That’s the virtual world,’ confirmed the technician, frowning. ‘Just like I said. Say hello to my avatar for me.’

Alex shut his eyes.

How many more times would he have to go through this same procedure, he wondered. He’d lost count of how many different transmutations he’d followed Clinton through. Thirty? Forty? And still the man was out of reach. Would he ever catch up?

***

AltLife: Clinton timeline #44

Alex opened his eyes to find himself in an identical room, but this time, the technician was different. Alex swung his legs off the bed, and repeated his excuse of carrying out some testing for Hisako. The technician shrugged his disinterest as Alex paged through the transmutation logs, looking for Clinton's next destination.

Sure enough, Clinton had moved on, and Alex copied down the new destination and handed it to the operator.

'You only just arrived,' he said in surprise. 'Don't you want to look round?'

'No, just send me to that address.'

'Back to the real world?'

'If that's what that address is,' replied Alex.

The man gave a cursory glance. 'Yes, that's the real world,' he confirmed. 'You want to go now?'

'Yes, right away,' said Alex. 'There's someone I'm trying to catch up with.'

'Not that professor guy?'

‘Yes - you remember him?’ asked Alex in surprise.

‘Don’t forget someone like him,’ replied the avatar. ‘Most people are pleased to be here. He was furious. I was glad to see the back of him. Kept insisting this wasn’t where he was meant to be, as if it was my fault.’

‘So what did you do?’

‘Sent him back to the real world,’ said the operator. ‘And they’re welcome to him.’

‘How long ago was that?’

‘About thirty minutes.’

Alex hesitated. He was close now, he was sure. But what would he do when he found himself in the same world as Clinton?

‘Send me now,’ he said quickly.

***

Virtual World

‘From the way he keeps switching from one strand to another, he’s definitely found a way of following Clinton,’ said Hisako. ‘I think we might be underestimating Mr Duchovny. The question is: how is he doing it?’

‘I’m not so interested in the *how,*’ said Hamish. ‘What I want to know is what he intends to do if he catches up with him.’

‘The *how* might be significant, Hamish,’ replied Hisako. ‘From what I can see, Alex is moving very quickly from strand to strand. That must mean that he’s found some way of tracing Clinton’s movements. And if he can do that, he can find his way back to the original world they were merged with.’

‘And if they do?’

‘I don’t know,’ she replied doubtfully. ‘Maybe if they could find their way to the exact moment their world was merged with the AltLife strand - ’

Hisako paused. ‘No, I really don’t know, Hamish,’ she said. ‘I need to look at the actual code. There may be an instant when both worlds are open to one another.’

‘If they got into that world again, they’d no longer be in AltLife.’

‘No, they’d be in a discrete virtual world file within the LDS computer.’

‘How many people have access to that machine?’ asked Hamish softly.

Hisako grimaced.

‘Thousands,’ she said.

***

AltLife: Clinton timeline #45

Alex opened the latest transmutation logs: he could see no record of Clinton moving on. At last, they were both in the same timeline.

‘Where did the professor go?’ he asked.

The transmutation operator shrugged. ‘Didn’t say.’

‘How long ago was this?’

‘Thirty minutes, maybe,’ replied the technician. ‘I did try to warn him - ’

‘Warn him?’

‘Yeah, about the gangs.’

‘What gangs?’

‘The streets aren’t safe - not even here. As if we didn’t have enough problems.’

‘I don’t understand - ’

‘How long have you been away in fairy land?’ asked

the technician in disbelief. 'Don't you watch the newscasts?'

'Why? What's happened?'

'Well, first there was the war - '

'What war?'

'You really haven't heard?' the other man asked incredulously.

'No, tell me.'

'Well, after the Middle East decided to self-destruct, the Chinese and the Ruskies ganged up against the States. Nuked all the major cities in the US. There's not much left of New York and Washington, but we've been lucky here - '

'Where's here?'

'We're in Vancouver.'

Alex's eyes widened, surprise written all over his face.

'Yeah, Vancouver - Canada - British Columbia.'

'Why is that lucky?'

'Because it looks like the Russians are trying not do do any damage to the Pacific North West. What's left of the media figures that when it's all over, they'll be able to annex Alaska. Take back what they sold to the States all that time ago.'

Alex looked blank.

'For the natural resources,' explained the technician. 'That's why they haven't nuked us - or Alberta. Seattle's been lucky, too.'

'You said something about gangs?'

'Yeah, the gangs.' The man paused for a second. 'I suppose we've been lucky there, too,' he said. 'There's not many of them in BC. But the ones there are - '

'Go on - '

'Killing every white person they come across. You need to get yourself across to Vancouver Island. They say Victoria is still safe. The floatplanes are still running.'

'But who are they - these gangs?'

'It's like someone told them to all rise up at once and start killing everyone who wasn't one of them.'

'But who are they?'

'Muslims - followers of Islam. And people like you and me - we're targets - we're infidels, see?'

***

Clinton pressed himself back against the wall. Hiding in the shadows, there was little chance that the marauding groups of Muslims would see him. He was painfully aware that his over-riding emotion was not fear - after all, this was clearly a virtual world, and nothing could really harm him here - but anger. But this anger was unfocused and undirected. He had no idea who could have created this world - a world devised exclusively to taunt him. And it had been the same in so many of the worlds he'd found himself in. The only common factor was a connection, however indirect, to his own life.

After the last of them passed by the entrance to the side alley, he waited before deciding to move. Cautiously, he inched his way back towards the main thoroughfare: there was no traffic on the deserted street. Suddenly, the unnatural silence was broken by the raucous roar of an aero engine bursting into life. From his vantage point, Clinton saw the group of youths change direction and start to run, heading towards the harbour side.

The seaplane sped away from its dock, leaving the angry mob shouting and screaming their hatred. Through the tiny windows in the plane their intended victims stared back in horror and relief to have escaped their inevitable fate.

The plane accelerated noisily away, leaving behind its signature wake across the surface of the bay, and then, freeing itself from the grip of the water, lifted off very slowly into the cloudy sky before turning west towards Vancouver Island and safety.

Clinton took his chance and raced across the deserted street towards the bulk of Canada Place. As he reached the entrance to the World Trade Center, he hammered on the plate glass doors. Inside, a security guard rushed to let him in.

'You were lucky, friend,' said the guard, dragging him inside and securing the doors behind him. 'Now get out of sight. The last thing we want is for them to think there's anyone in here. It's the craziest thing - they don't seem to be searching us out. They only seem to go insane when they see a person they don't recognise as one of their own. As long as we keep out of sight, they don't seem interested in looking for us. Why do you think that is?'

Clinton shrugged his shoulders. 'Damned if I know,' he replied, gasping for breath.

It was all too clear to Clinton what was happening. It was the complete inverse of everything he'd ever planned for: here, in this world, the Muslims were the hunters, everyone else was the prey. Somehow, he knew that every one of then had been infected with some false memory of terrible atrocities perpetrated against them or their families, and that these had been activated by some signal that turned each and every one of them into mindless assassins. It was a ghastly travesty of his own plan for religious genocide.

And it was all too obvious that this whole world had been generated from one of his own thoughts. He couldn't remember thinking of this exact scenario, but he had certainly imagined the same mechanism being applied to other religious groups. In particular, he remembered an occasion when he had been particularly infuriated with Giuseppe Romano, and had indulged his sense of irony by contemplating the annihilation of the Pope and the whole of the Roman Catholic community, using the exact same method.

And it had been the same in so many of the worlds he had found himself in: a single thought expanded into a nightmarish reality.

He had found himself in the midst of the scene of terror and anguish on board American Airlines Flight 11, forced to watch his parents and all the others onboard die as the Boeing 767 hit the eightieth floor of the North Tower of the New York World Trade Center.

He'd watched Osama Bin Laden and the other principal architects of the 9/11 attack forming their plans, their fingers stabbing at detailed maps of New York and Washington, the table spread with airline schedules. He'd seen the 9/11 terrorists undergoing their suspiciously superficial flight training courses.

And then there had been the worlds and events he had actually experienced: the newscast telling him that Hamish McAllister had beaten him to his goal of creating the first virtual worlds, and setting alight his all-consuming jealousy and life-long hatred for the man; the moment he had killed Rajesh Singh and dragged McAllister back to the world of the living; the moment he had called in the drone strike on the Afghan village that had led to his dishonourable discharge from the military.

He had pondered on the significance of these, and the many other worlds he had found himself in, but had come to no firm conclusion. That they were all, in some way or other, connected to him was obvious. But in some the connection was direct, in others, tenuous, and in yet others, he could only detect the hint of something he may or may not have thought or felt in some fleeting moment of imagination.

How these worlds had come into existence, he had no idea. The one thing that was certain was that no one person could have created them: it would have taken a lifetime of work to come up with such an edifice.

The one firm conclusion he could deduce was that each of these worlds was a variant on his timeline.

***

Virtual World

'Hamish, they're both in the same world,' said Hisako. 'So however he's doing it, he's caught up with Clinton.'

'And how many strands have they been through?'

'More than forty,' she replied. 'It's a pity we can't see what those worlds contain. It might give us some insight into Clinton's character.'

'I have all the insight I need,' replied Hamish grimly. 'The question is: what do we do about it.'

'Do we need to do anything?' she asked. 'Clinton is well and truly enmeshed in AltLife.'

'What if Alex tells him how he managed to follow him?' asked Raj.

'You mean, if Clinton manages to find his way back to the original world?'

'If that happens, we'll have no choice,' she replied. 'We'll have to shut down AltLife. We can't take a chance that between them they might figure out how to escape.'

Hamish's face was grave.

'A long time ago,' he said, 'Elizabeth accused me of playing god. I always said she was wrong. I never took decisions that affected people's lives. I merely gave them the tools to make their lives better. Even the prison worlds were designed to allow the inmates to develop, to change for the better, to show their remorse, to try to make amends, to rehabilitate themselves.

'And the virtual worlds were even simpler. There was never any need for conflict. If people were unhappy, they could recreate their lives, remove themselves from whatever problems they found. There was no crime because everyone could generate anything they desired, no one needed to envy anyone else. They could even create new worlds specifically designed for themselves.

'It really is utopia for those that embrace it. And I had no responsibility for people's lives, other than to provide the tools they needed to do all that.

'But this is different. I have incarcerated the most evil creature I could ever have imagined. But even in that I have tried to give him the opportunity to see alternative futures for himself. I've arranged for worlds that will allow him to change his ways, to live out his existence in a different way, if he chooses. That's the crux of the matter: despite imprisoning him, I've given him almost infinite choice.

'To shut down AltLife would truly be playing god. I

would be judge, jury and executioner. Do I have that right, Hisako?'

Hisako was silent. At last she said, 'And Alex?'

Hamish turned to look at her. 'Alex is not the problem. We can recreate him exactly as we promised, before Clinton started to infiltrate his personality. The problem is my sense of morality.

'Do I have the right to remove Clinton from existence?'

***

AltLife: Clinton timeline #45

Alex looked out of the window over Vancouver harbour. Despite the double glazing, his attention was drawn to the sound of a seaplane taking off in front of him. He watched as the wake from the plane's pontoons decreased as they freed themselves from the grip of the water, and rose steadily into the air before turning to the left and heading out over Stanley Park towards Vancouver Island, and the capital, Victoria.

According to the technician, he was safe inside the transmutation unit, overlooking the harbour. And for the first time since he had emerged into the world created by AltLife, he stopped to think. If this world was as the technician had described, it was far from the reality he knew. How had the software created this world? It seemed almost alien to him, but for some reason, it was a world that had some connection to Clinton.

But it was clearly not a world that had its origins in the real world that Ann Mitchell had inhabited. And Alex knew without doubt that moving backwards in this world's time line would not bring him to the girl he had come to find.

After the dozens of worlds he had followed Clinton through, he understood at last that he didn't need Clinton to be able to follow a timeline backwards to his goal. But he did need to be back in the original timeline where he had entered Clinton's world.

He turned away from the window to speak to the technician, only to find that another person had entered the room.

***

'Who the hell are you?' growled Clinton.

Alex impassively returned his gaze. 'My name is Alex Duchovny,' he replied evenly.

'I've never met you.'

'I know.'

'Then how can you be here?' demanded Clinton. 'This is my timeline. Only people I've had contact with exist here.'

'I don't think this *is* your timeline.'

'I've seen enough to realise what this is: someone's playing games. All these virtual worlds - set up to distract me - '

'They aren't virtual worlds,' replied Alex. 'And no one set them up.'

'Of course they are, you fool!' shouted Clinton. 'Do you think I don't recognise a virtual world when I see one?'

'If they were virtual worlds, you'd be able to think yourself anywhere. And you can't. That's why you've been transmuting yourself between them.'

'If they're not worlds, what are they?' demanded Clinton.

Alex looked at the other man curiously: could he really not have deduced what had happened?

'I think they're strands of potential lives that you might live,' he said.

'That's impossible,' replied Clinton. 'I've been in dozens of them, and none of them makes any sense - '

'That's because they don't need to make sense. No one created them, no one designed them. No one -

except you.'

'That's crazy - I couldn't have - '

'I haven't been here long enough to see as much as you, but what I've seen convinced me that each of these worlds is just an offshoot of something you've done - or something you've thought - in the past. It's multiverse theory played out in software.'

'You can't be serious.'

'I think that every time something has changed in your timeline, another strand has been created. And however unlikely that offshoot timeline might be, it has been allowed to play out here.'

'Here? But where is here?'

'All of this is being generated by a piece of software called AltLife.'

Clinton hesitated. 'AltLife - the girl - Hisako Myamoto - '

Alex waited for Clinton's thoughts to catch up.

'So you see, everything you've encountered since you've been here is some sort of prediction based on something you've done, said or imagined in the past.

'This existence - here, now - is not your timeline. There's only one real timeline - and this isn't it.'

***

'Why are you here?' demanded Clinton.

For a second, Alex looked at the other man curiously. Then he said, 'Because you're the only connection I have with someone I've lost.'

'What does that mean?'

'I needed to find you - to find a girl.'

'What girl?'

'Not someone you knew.'

'Then who? If I didn't know her, you won't find her in my timeline. And certainly not in this one.'

Alex regarded him with a feeling of something approaching pity. Clinton looked haggard, shrunken, haunted: a far cry from the holographic image that Alex had once seen.

Where was the man who had destroyed the virtual world? Imprisoned in a virtual world, and in a sense, one of his own making. Where was the man who had plotted the genocide of the Muslims? Trapped in a world where those very people were hunting him and all those like him. Where was the man who had callously plotted the annihilation of thousands of innocent people? Entombed in a web of his own thoughts and desires, unable even to recognise the structure of the maze that surrounded him.

'You're right, of course,' replied Alex. 'It's not you I need at all. It's what you've done.'

And with that, he turned to the technician who stood watching the two of them without apparent interest.

'Transmute me back,' he said, handing over the destination code.

'Where are you going?' demanded Clinton.

'Back to the beginning,' replied Alex calmly. 'Back to your original timeline.'

'You know how to get out!' exclaimed Clinton, his eyes suddenly alight with a spark of new hope.

Alex shrugged. 'You can follow me if you like. But it won't help you. You can't escape.'

'You know,' growled Clinton. 'You will help me.'

'I don't know anything,' said Alex. 'Except that there's nothing you can do to get yourself out of here. You're caught in a trap of your own making. Every malicious thought, every twisted desire, every paranoid imagining - they're all here - somewhere. Waiting for you in some as yet unvisited timeline. Everything you ever wanted is here - somewhere. All you have to do is keep looking for it.'

'But you're going to find a way out.'

'No, I'm going to find a way to stay here. And following me won't do you any good at all. So, I'll say goodbye now, Professor. I hope we don't meet again.'

***

AltLife: Clinton timeline #1

'You're back,' exclaimed the technician in surprise.

'Many customers since you transmuted me?' asked Alex innocently.

'It's been very quiet,' replied the avatar. 'In fact, none at all. How did you know?'

Alex grinned. 'Well, you can expect another one soon,' he said. 'And when he arrives, tell him he's wasting his time following me.' And then to himself: *But I guess he's got all the time in the world.*

'How do I move backwards in time?' he asked.

'What?'

'How do I move backwards and forwards along the timeline?'

'I don't understand,' replied the technician, looking puzzled. 'This is the real world. There's no such thing as time travel.'

'Of course it is,' replied Alex. 'Silly of me. Forget I asked.'

Alex walked out of the transmutation centre and looked around him. A procession of red autocabs with their familiar grey stripes streamed past him. He recognised them immediately: this had to be the virtual version of Washington DC. This must be the identical copy of the real world location where Clinton had tried to transmute himself when McAllister and Singh had hijacked the transmission and kidnapped him. This had to be the virtual version of Clinton's original timeline.

And if Alex was indeed in a virtual world, he should be able to think himself to any location within it. In addition, from what he'd experienced of virtual worlds, they always seemed to have some sort of transportation portal. Not that people needed them, but he assumed they were there because of the familiarity element. Just like bathrooms that nobody required to use, and restaurants for people who never needed food.

He reasoned that it was likely that transportation portals would be situated in locations that people would find logical. In the case of Washington, Union Station might be a good bet - or one of the airports.

He thought himself directly to Union Station and found himself immediately outside the three grand arches of the station entrance. He walked inside to find himself beneath the vaulted ceiling of the main hall. He looked around to see if there were any clues that would give away the true nature of the building, but everything seemed to be exactly what he would have expected to find in a main railway terminus. He felt a sudden annoyance with himself for even thinking that McAllister and Singh would have been so careless as to create a portal that advertised itself as such. But he was still convinced that he was on the right track: it seemed such a natural place to choose for a portal.

For a second he paused: was there a hint in the words *the right track*? Perhaps if he tried to board a train there might be some hint, some sign that he could interpret.

He headed for the Amtrak ticket counters. For a moment, he hesitated: which train should he pick? Where would Clinton be likely to travel to? Alex remembered that Clinton's tenure as a Professor of Virtual Worlds was at Princeton. Maybe that was a good place to start.

Hesitantly, he asked for a coach class ticket to Princeton.

'Would you like to face forward? Or would you

prefer to have your back to the engine?' enquired the clerk.

For a second, Alex hesitated: had the man placed a slight emphasis on the words *forward* and *back*? Or was he imagining things? At last, a slow smile spread across Alex's face. 'I'd like to face backwards,' he replied.

'Departing from Gate D - just over there,' said the clerk indicating the way.

Alex walked towards the designated gate. If he was right, by choosing the direction of travel, somehow he should move back along the timeline. But how far? And how would he be able to tell how far? He shrugged mentally: there was only one way to find out.

***

As he passed through Gate D, an attendant looked up from his screen.

'I see you requested a rear facing seat, sir,' he said. 'The train will be a few minutes, so perhaps you'd like to wait in the executive lounge. There's a video console for your use.'

Alex looked at the man in surprise. 'I didn't know there was an executive lounge,' he said.

'Reserved for backward facing passengers only,' replied the attendant with a smile, indicating a door to his left.

Inside the room, Alex found himself alone. He seated himself at the console and read the instructions on the screen. *So that's how it works*, he smiled, pressing the button on the touchscreen marked 'Rewind'.

The date and time on the screen instantly started to move backwards in time. At the same time a series of images flashed up on the video display. How far should he go back? He had no idea when the Clarke girl had started to work with Clinton, but he guessed that it had to be at least a couple of years. When the time code display had moved back sufficiently, he pressed 'Pause', then 'Play'.

The scene showed Clinton at work at a desk. There was no sign of anyone else in the room, so Alex pressed 'Rewind' again. As the images flew bye, he thought he glimpsed a figure in combat fatigues, and he pressed 'Pause' and 'Play' again.

This time, the scene was a different location, and he could see Clinton speaking to the girl. Mentally, he noted the date and time, then pressed 'Rewind' again.

He repeated the process a number of times until at last he zeroed in on what he thought might be the first time that Clinton had encountered his new assistant. For a moment her stared at the screen, not knowing what to do next. Then he got up from the console and opened the door to the station platform.

To his surprise, he found himself in the room he had just been observing on the screen. Clinton sat at his computer, showing no awareness of Alex's presence in the room. Alex realised instantly that that was exactly what he should have expected: he was merely an observer of a part of Clinton's timeline, generated from his life-log entries by AltLife. And if he had chosen the date and time correctly, all he had to do was to wait to see the first meeting between Clinton and the Clarke girl.

As he was contemplating what to do to when the girl appeared, there was a knock at the door. The girl who entered and stood to attention was completely recognisable as Ann Mitchell. All that had changed was the combat clothing and the short blonde hair beneath the forage cap.

For a moment, Alex stared at her, trying to differentiate between the Ann Mitchell he had known, and the cold expressionless monster he knew the girl in front of him to be. Then he set his mind to the task of how to follow the girl's timeline back to the period before her execution when she had been his Ann Mitchell.

He needed to jump to the girl's timeline. But how? There was no obvious answer to the question, but he wondered whether he could cross over by pre-empting the girl's actions. Now he knew which door she would enter by, if he could open the door before she arrived, surely that would put him into her timeline, and then all he had to figure out was how to move backwards to the time before her execution.

He opened the door back to the executive lounge and rewound the images to before the girl arrived. Then he re-entered Clinton's room and moved to the other door. He turned the handle and pulled the door open.

In a fraction of a second, his heart sank: outside the door was that same nothingness that he had seen in the sensory deprivation tank. Nothing existed outside that door until the instant the girl appeared through it.

In a flash, the meaning of Raj's words became clear: *it's not her timeline.* Whatever Alex had hoped for, Raj and Hamish had known it was impossible. Clinton's timeline and the girl's may have coincided for large periods of time, but fundamentally, they were always - would always be - discrete. There was never any way of crossing over from one to the other.

Alex's dreams were always doomed to failure.

***

Virtual World

'They're together again, Hamish,' said Raj quietly. 'Clinton's found out how to follow him.'

'We can't be sure they're working together,' said Hamish. 'It may be a coincidence. Maybe Clinton thinks that Alex knows a way out.'

'They both moved directly to Clinton's original timeline,' said Raj. 'At the very least it means that Clinton has recognised that what he's experiencing is a parallel skein of potential timelines, and he's made the assumption that Alex wouldn't have entered AltLife voluntarily unless he knew a way to get out. So even if they're not working together, Clinton's going to stick with Alex just to see if he can use him to escape.'

'If only we knew exactly where they were in the timeline,' muttered Hamish.

'Hisako's looking to see if there are any weaknesses that Alex might exploit,' replied Raj. 'As far as she can see so far, the only potential is the instant that Alex merged himself into Clinton's original timeline.'

'Or the point at which we merged Clinton into his timeline.'

'That's far less likely,' replied Raj. 'Clinton wouldn't have any memory of the event, so identifying one particular instant in a lifetime would be much harder than finding the proverbial needle in a haystack.'

***

AltLife: Clinton timeline #1

Alex closed the door on nothingness. Clinton worked

on in silence at his desk.

'So it was the girl,' said a familiar voice. 'I should have known: *cherchez la femme.*'

'I told you I wasn't trying to escape,' said Alex. 'Why did you follow me?'

The second Clinton smiled coldly. 'Because whatever you chose to do, escape or remain, you're the only one of the two of us that knows how you got here. And somehow or other, you're going to tell me something - anything- that might get me out of here.'

'That's never going to happen.'

'I wouldn't bet on that,' replied Clinton, his eyes cold and detached. 'Now I know how to follow you, you'll never be free of me. Besides, from the look on your face, it looks like your little plan to follow Clarke's timeline has come to nothing. Though why you'd want to follow her timeline - a murderer - '

Alex smiled wanly. 'Shows how little you knew, Clinton,' he said. 'She was a plant. They used facial recognition software to track her every move. It was a way of keeping tabs on you. She was CIA. The whole murder backstory was fabricated.'

Clinton was silent for a moment.

'Well, well, well,' he mused, 'so it was a love story

after all. For whatever reason, you couldn't get her back in the real world, so this was the only place you thought she'd still exist.'

He paused. 'And now you know what you planned isn't going to happen, what are you going to do? I don't see much point in staying here, do you?

'I suggest that we put our heads together and work out how to get out of here.'

***

Virtual World

'Yes, I found a way they could get out,' admitted Hisako. 'But it relies on the fact that the virtual world that was merged with the timeline is still there.'

'And is it?' asked Raj.

'I just deleted it,' she replied. 'There's no way out now.'

'Put it back,' said Hamish suddenly.

'What?'

'Reinstate it. At exactly the point that Alex merged himself into AltLife. He deserves a way out.'

‘But what about Clinton?’ demanded Raj. ‘If they’re working together - ’

‘I don’t believe they are. I don’t believe Alex would collaborate with such a man.’

There was an awkward silence between the three of them.

‘You’re taking a big risk, Hamish,’ said Raj at last. ‘If you’re wrong – if they both get out - ’

‘If they do, the two of them would find themselves in a featureless virtual world where they have no powers,’ replied Hamish slowly. ‘A world that’s completely under our control.’

‘And then what?’ asked Raj dubiously. ‘We’d know where they were, but how does that help Alex?’

‘We could let Clinton go,’ replied Hamish. ‘Then we could retrieve Alex.’

‘Have you gone crazy?’ said Raj in amazement. ‘How can you even contemplate letting him go?’

For a second, a twisted smile played at the corners of Hamish’s mouth.

‘Trust me,’ he said quietly.

***

AltLife: Clinton timeline #1

'If you think I'm going to help you escape from here, you're more deluded than I thought,' said Alex.

'I don't think you have any choice, my friend,' replied Clinton calmly. 'Where you go, I go. What you do, I do. You can't evade me in here. You have no choice at all.'

Alex looked at the other man, immediately recognising the truth of what he had said.

'In that case, I won't try to escape, and you and I will both be here for eternity. We'll see which one of us can stand the monotony. Which one of us cracks first.'

'You won't be able to stand it,' replied Clinton confidently. 'Unlike me, you came here for a reason: to find a girl. You failed to find her here, but somewhere inside you the desire to succeed still burns. You won't be able to stop yourself thinking about it, and if you can't find her here, you'll think of something else, some other existence, somewhere else. Somewhere there might be the possibility - somewhere there might be hope. And when you do - '

Alex's face betrayed his thoughts. Clinton was right: if there was another way to find her, he would find it. And if that meant escaping from this prison, he knew he would have to try.

And inevitably, Clinton would escape, too.

***

Chapter 15

AltLife: Clinton timeline #1

'It looks like I have no choice,' said Alex. 'But there are no guarantees. Despite what you think, I don't know how to get out of here.'

'But you know how you got here, which is more than I do,' commented Clinton, his eyes gleaming with the prospect of escape from the labyrinth he'd found himself in.

Alex's eyes narrowed. Was that the key to it? The way he got here? And if it was, should he tell the other man exactly how he had transferred himself into the AltLife construct that Hamish and Raj had created? And if - and it was a big if - if he could figure out how to use that knowledge to get back, was there a way that he could avoid taking Clinton with him?

Alex recalled exactly what had happened when he had inserted himself into Clinton's timeline. He had transferred himself into the small featureless virtual world, then his automatic routine had merged his world with the AltLife timeline. At the point where the two had coincided, he had opened his eyes to find himself in what he took at first glance to be a static world. But the frozen scene around him had started into life within seconds of his arrival. And it was in those first few seconds that Alex knew the solution of how to extricate himself would lie.

He forced himself to think logically about the mechanism that had placed him in that first transmutation room. The fact that the technician had been surprised by his arrival meant that the normal process of transmutation wasn't the mechanism that had been used. And on each of his subsequent transmutations within the AltLife maze he hadn't been greeted by the static world he'd experienced on his arrival.

The only explanation he could think of was that the virtual world he'd first imprisoned himself in had merged in some way with the AltLife timeline, and that the sheer volume of processing to bring the two entirely different types of worlds together had been such that the visual interpretation of the room had been suspended by AltLife for the first few seconds after his arrival.

If that was the explanation, what could he deduce from it? For those few seconds, were the virtual world and AltLife sharing the same space within the quantum computer? And if they were, would it be possible to run time backwards for those few seconds to create the opposite effect?

But the biggest unknown of all was whether the virtual world was still there.

'Well?' demanded Clinton impatiently. 'You've

been sitting there for hours. Surely you've come up with something useful?

Alex stared at him for a few seconds. Then he said, 'I have a theory.'

Clinton raised his eyebrows. 'And what is this great theory?' he asked, mockingly.

'I think I know how I got here.'

'You got here deliberately. How could you possibly not know how?' snapped the other man.

'I copied the mechanism they used to kidnap you.'

'What?'

'I copied it. I didn't examine how it actually worked.'

Clinton looked at him in amazement. 'You didn't - '

'I don't need to know how an autocab works in order to use one,' retorted Alex. 'The routine worked on you, I just automated it to suit my purposes.'

'Are you telling me that I could have worked out how I got here?'

'No, but I am telling you that the mechanism might

work in reverse. Do you remember when you first transmuted here?'

'Yes - but what has that got to do with it?' demanded Clinton.

'Was the world suddenly completely frozen?'

'Not that I remember.'

'Are you sure?' asked Alex.

'No - why?'

'Tell me what happened.'

'I went to sleep in the transmutation center, then I woke up in what I thought was the real world.'

'Was there anything strange about the transmutation?'

Clinton frowned. 'Yes, the dreams, the images.'

'What were they?'

'The technician told me they were after-images from previous temporary files.'

'Did you open your eyes as soon as you woke up?'

‘No, I just lay there until the images had gone. Then I got up.’

Alex nodded. ‘I think by keeping your eyes shut you missed the key to getting back,’ he said.

***

Virtual World

‘Hamish, I don’t understand what you’re thinking,’ protested Raj.

‘It’s just an idea,’ murmured Hamish with a faraway look in his eyes. ‘And it might just work.’

‘Are you going to explain why Hisako should reinstate that virtual world?’

‘Because that’s the way Alex will try to escape,’ replied Hamish. ‘And if it’s not there, nothing will happen.’

‘And if it is there, they will both escape.’

‘But where to, Raj? That’s the question you should be asking.’

‘I just don’t understand you sometimes,’ said Raj. ‘You can’t be thinking of leaving the two of them there, that would be sheer torture.’

'Oh no, they won't be there more than a couple of minutes,' replied Hamish. 'Just long enough for me to get into AltLife.'

'You?'

'Yes, I couldn't ask anyone else to do it,' replied Hamish calmly. 'Besides, I think it's my responsibility to explain to Clinton what's happening to him, and to point out his options.'

'He has options?'

'Of course,' replied Hamish grimly. 'I told you I couldn't be judge, jury and executioner. This way, I avoid being the executioner.'

***

AltLife: Clinton timeline #1

'Where are we going?' asked Clinton suspiciously.

'Well, as you can't remember the exact point when you arrived here,' said Alex, 'we'll have to see if we can use my arrival point instead. Besides, I know for certain that yours wouldn't work.'

'How do you know?'

'Because I was the one who deleted the escape pod,'

replied Alex with a wry grin.

‘Escape pod? What the hell are you talking about?’

‘Just my little joke.’

‘You can joke at a time like this? What’s so funny?’

‘Nothing you need know about,’ replied Alex. ‘Let’s just say I don’t know whether there’s room for two in the pod, or whether it’s only built for one.’

Clinton scowled. ‘Whatever this ‘pod’ of yours turns out to be, you’d better make sure I’m the one who gets to use it.’

‘And as you know precisely nothing about what I’m planning, how do you intend to force me to let you go first?’

Clinton’s scowl grew deeper. ‘I won’t forget this,’ he growled.

‘If I leave you here, you’ll never have the chance to forget,’ retorted Alex. ‘What’s it feel like to be completely helpless, Clinton? A novel experience for you, I guess. And if you don’t stop threatening me, I will make sure you stay here, and you’ll have all eternity to get used to being completely impotent.’

‘Alright, alright - just get on with it.’

Alex smiled grimly. 'Very well,' he said. 'The first thing we need to do is to move forward along the timeline to the point just after I got here.'

***

Virtual World

'You should let me switch it off, Hamish,' said Hisako.

'I can't do that,' he replied. 'It would go against everything I've ever believed in. That was why I chose the virtual prison project as the first big venture in virtual reality. It wasn't just the government funding, I could have made much more from the super rich who wanted to live forever. I actually wanted to help people. And not just the patients I was treating, not just the postmortic surgery. And the prison project gave them so much more than eternal life. It gave them the opportunity to assess what they had done, to decide for themselves how they wanted to live, to try to make amends if that's what they wanted. There was never a point where there was no hope for those people. I believed in it then, and I believe in it now. To turn off AltLife with Clinton inside it would be to deprive him of the opportunity to change.'

'Do you really expect him to change, Hamish?' asked Raj in disbelief.

'That's not for me to say, Raj. All I know is that I can't deprive him of the chance.'

'But letting him escape - ' exclaimed Hisako.

'I'm not letting him escape, Hisako - '

'Putting yourself at risk - '

'I'm relying on you all to keep me safe.'

'But how, Hamish?' she asked despairingly.

***

AltLife: Clinton timeline #1

Alex looked around the transmutation room. Everything was exactly as he remembered it.

'Where did you come from?' asked the technician in surprise. 'You only just left.'

'Another test,' replied Alex. 'We'll disappear again in a few moments.'

'Oh, it's you,' scowled the man, noticing Clinton for the first time. 'Thought I'd seen the last of you.'

Clinton ignored the remark. 'Well, what next?' he demanded.

‘We need to move back a few more minutes. I’ll check the log to see exactly what time.’

‘And then what?’

‘There should be a window of about thirty seconds. You didn’t see it because you had your eyes shut.’

‘And what do we do in that thirty seconds?’

‘I don’t know,’ replied Alex. ‘But if I’m right, we ought to be able to get into the virtual world at that point. What happens then is anybody’s guess.’

Clinton looked at him in disgust. ‘You call that a plan?’

‘It’s the only one there is. Take it or leave it.’

Clinton glared at him, knowing that he had no choice. In his mind he replayed the other man’s taunts about helplessness and impotence, and he swore to himself that he would somehow find a way to get his revenge.

Alex disappeared from view. Clinton thought himself back to the executive lounge at Union Station. He found the other man slowly rewinding the timeline frame by frame. The images showed Alex’s body lying on the transmutation table, then as he rewound still further, the body seemed to dissolve into nothingness, and there was a blurred image of something moving backwards out of the frame.

'That must be it,' said Alex. 'That must be the point at which the window into the virtual world is open.'

He moved the timeline forward very slowly, watching, fascinated, as the essence that was Alex Duchovny streamed into the room to form itself into the body on the table. He continued to watch, frame by frame, until he saw himself open his eyes onto the static world. A few frames further on, and the world suddenly burst into motion.

'And that must be the end of the window,' Alex murmured to himself.

He turned to Clinton. 'All we have to do is to get ourselves into that room between those two timecodes, and we should find the opening into the virtual world. If I could get in, then we should be able to get out.'

'But into what?'

'Who knows? But whatever it is, it's probably safer than staying here.'

'Why?'

'I don't know how much they can see inside AltLife, but I'm guessing that one of their options is to turn the system off. If they do that, both of us will cease to exist.'

'Who are you talking about?'

'You don't need to know,' replied Alex curtly.

'And why would they - whoever they are - go to all the trouble of generating this - prison - for me if they intended to shut it off?'

'Because they knew you couldn't find a way out. But now that I'm here, they must assume that because I found my way in, I might be able to use the same mechanism to get out. And they're bound to suspect that you and I are working together. If you were in their shoes, would you hesitate to shut down AltLife?'

Slowly, Clinton nodded his head in agreement.

Alex moved the timeline back to the timecode that marked the start of the window of opportunity. As they thought themselves back to the transmutation room, a shimmering wall appeared down the centre of the room. As they watched, an opening appeared, and what seemed to be a semi-transparent cloud in the shape of a humanoid flowed through into the room.

Without hesitating, Alex threw himself through the opening into the empty space beyond. He turned in time to see Clinton follow him as the opening closed behind them, shutting off his final impression of the cloud forming itself into the shape of his body on the table.

Before either of the two had time to take in the

nature of the space round them, the featureless white cube gave a sudden lurch. Alex slid to the floor, as Clinton forced himself to remain standing against the opposite wall, his hands spread against the smooth surface for support.

For a second, it seemed that time was suspended, then the room lurched again, and the opening in the wall opposite Clinton reappeared. Alex could see the astonishment on Clinton's face as he looked through the gap. For a moment, Clinton stood completely still, then he moved forward towards the opening.

As Alex struggled to his feet, Clinton walked through the aperture and into the room beyond. From where he stood, Alex glimpsed what appeared to be a small office. He moved cautiously to the opening and stared wide-eyed at the scene that was being played out in front of him.

Clinton stood watching a man sitting at a desk, his laptop open in front of him. With a single movement, the man reached up to close the laptop, then slid it sideways across the desk away from him.

'Now, Clarke,' said the man at the desk.

As Clinton turned around, Alex saw the blood drain from his face. Instantly, a single shot rang out, and the figure at the desk slumped forward. In surprise, Alex thrust his head out of the opening to see the figure of Clarke holding an automatic pistol at arm's length, a wisp of smoke curling upwards from the barrel.

Clinton stared wild-eyed at the girl, then his eyes turned and locked onto a point just behind her. His face, already pale, turned ashen. It was then that Alex saw another figure in the room.

'You're right, Clinton,' said the figure. 'This is the most significant moment in your life. At least, since the day your parents were killed.'

Alex stared in disbelief. The figure was clearly Hamish McAllister, but there was something almost ethereal about him, a ghost-like transparency quite unlike the McAllister he had encountered in the virtual world.

McAllister turned to him and said urgently, 'Go back, Alex. Go back now. This is not Clarke's timeline. You won't find the girl here.' There was an authority in his voice that stopped Alex in his tracks. How could this be? Was this still AltLife? And if it were, how could McAllister be here?

'You're dead,' whispered Clinton. 'What sort of game is this? Who generated this hologram?'

As Alex backed through the opening, there came the sound of hammering on an outside door, then the unmistakable crash of the door being broken down. Within seconds, the room was full of CIA agents in Kevlar jackets with guns drawn. Alex backed away until he felt the wall behind him. Through the open aperture, Alex watched as the tableau played out as if in slow motion. As he tried to take in the significance of the scene in front of him, the opening closed and inexorably his world turned to black.

***

Epilogue

Real world

'Alex, wake up,' said the gentle voice, somewhere in the deep recesses of his mind.

In the blackness, the voice came again. 'You can wake up now, Alex.'

He reached into his memory to find that the voice was familiar.

'Wake up. It's time to come back to us.'

Alex struggled to move his lips. His mouth was dry, his throat parched.

'Wh - ere?' he managed to gasp.

'You're here - with me, Alex,' said the familiar voice.

'Who?' he mumbled.

'Don't you recognise me, Alex?'

From the darkness, a remembered face crept to the front of his conscious mind.

'Ann?'

He struggled to open his eyes, but even the subdued lighting in the room caused him pain.

'I can't - '

'It's me, Alex.'

'But - '

He felt a hand close over his, and he tried to open his eyes once more.

'Don't try to talk. We have plenty of time for that. It's a long story, and to tell the truth, I'm still trying to come to terms with it myself.'

' You're dead,' he whispered. 'And I'm - '

'Not any more.'

'But - I was - in VR. Can't be alive - need clone.'

'They made a clone for you, Alex.'

'There was - no DNA - '

'Yes, there was, Alex. Viva Eterna retained a sample.'

‘But you - they told me - ’

‘They lied to you, Alex,’ said the girl softly. ‘They lied to you about everything - about you, about me.’

‘Then how - ?’

‘You have friends, Alex. They’ve worked miracles. For me, too.’

‘Can’t be - real - ’

‘It is real, my darling. Just as real as I am. Except this is my original body.’

‘Do you - remember?’

‘Only up to the point where I was executed. All the rest is a blank. It’s only in the past few days that I’ve learned what happened to me - what I did. And what you did.’

‘You know?’

‘Yes, Alex - I know exactly what you did for me.’

***

Washington DC

‘What did happen?’ asked Alex, as they sat together on a bench in Constitution Gardens. ‘I don’t remember anything after I agreed to help kidnap Clinton.'

Ann looked out over the lake. 'It took me a long time to understand. Hisako came to see me, and she tried to explain, but it was so complicated. Then, despite everything, Christina took the time to sit down with me.'

'Who's Christina?'

'She's the person you should be most thankful to. She's the one who created your clone.'

'But who is she?'

'She's Hamish's wife.'

'I didn't know he was married.'

'I don't think you knew very much about him at all,' said Ann quietly.

'What was there to know? He was dead.'

Alex stared into the face of the girl he had searched so long for, the overwhelming emotion of seeing her again blinding him to the sudden look of pain that flashed across her eyes.

'About that,' she said. 'There's something you need to know - '

***

Alex shook his head in disbelief. 'I don't remember any of this -'

'How could you?' she asked. 'They restored your memories up to the point where they knew you hadn't been infected by Clinton's persona. And after that happened, you started to behave so erratically that they weren't sure whether you got into Clinton's world to try to find me, or because you had an irresistible compulsion to become one with Clinton.

'So, after you got yourself trapped in the web,' she continued. 'Raj and Hisako thought the easiest solution was to turn off AltLife. They already knew they could recreate you. And me, of course. But by then you'd gone, and they couldn't stop you.'

'But McAllister turned up - and saved me?'

'Yes, he did,' she said slowly. 'That was the most complex bit. I don't pretend to understand it all, but Hisako told me they thought that Hamish might have used quantum entanglement to project himself into the timeline.'

'Quantum entanglement? Is that even possible?'

'They'd merged you and Clinton with the AltLife timeline at the point where Clinton was shot by Clarke - me - on the assumption that there'd be so much confusion - the shooting, the CIA turning up - and the final straw, seeing what must have looked like the ghost of Hamish McAllister - Clinton wouldn't have time to think about following you back into the virtual world.

'And it worked. Clinton couldn't believe what he was seeing, and the total confusion gave you enough time to get yourself back into the virtual lifeboat, leaving Hamish and Clinton back in the AltLife prison that Hisako created for him.'

There was silence as Alex took in what McAllister had done. 'It would have been easier to turn it off, wouldn't it?' he asked at last. 'If they thought I was compelled to find Clinton – to join with him in some way - '

'Hamish refused. His sense of humanity wouldn't let him. He's a good man, Alex.'

'But Clinton's imprisoned for eternity. He could have just left me there - '

'Christina told me that Hamish's only objective was to provide Clinton with the opportunity for rehabilitation, if he was prepared to take it. He wasn't prepared to condemn you, too – especially as what happened wasn't your fault. But I think you may be wrong in assuming that Clinton will survive for eternity.'

'What do you mean?'

'Hamish wasn't entirely naïve. He was quite aware that eventually something will happen to force AltLife to be turned off on the LDS machine. But at that point, it wouldn't be his decision.

'Raj thought it was quite ironic that the people that Clinton thought he was avenging - or protecting - or whatever he thought he was doing - that it should be a Christian Church that would bring about his end.'

'So the fact that they rewound my life log - '

'They were protecting themselves – and you – from Clinton's malign influence.'

'And this body? The clone? You and me – together in the real world?'

'I think that's their way of saying thank you for helping to imprison Clinton, and for freeing Hamish and Raj.'

'It's me who needs to say thank you - to Hamish. Without him - '

For a second she hesitated. 'That's not going to be possible, Alex,' she said softly.

'Why not?'

The girl hesitated. It was the one question she had been dreading.

'He didn't make it out,' she said quietly.

The End

Also by Nigel Holloway

The Hamish McAllister Chronicles

Second Death

Hamish McAllister is playing god: but the church wants to crucify him.
Elizabeth died: but now that she's alive, who is she?
Geraldine is dying for revenge: but she has to be dead to get it.
Death, life and virtual immortality - at the end of a 13 amp power cord

Hamish Redux

Just like Jacob Marley, Hamish McAllister was undeniably dead. After all, he'd just committed suicide in front of millions of television viewers.

However, in Hamish's world, being dead is far from the end of things - at least, just as long as no one pulls the plug out of the socket. And even though McAllister himself is quite content with his lot, others are far less pleased with the consequences of his very public death, and are very determined they're not going to allow him to go on living the death of Riley. They want him back. In the real world.

Such Heights of Evil

After being dragged back to the real world, forced to assist in the creation of a clone army, then help a rogue priest in his quest to save the Christian religion from annihilation, Hamish is finally free from the forces that were determined to control his destiny.

But despite the outlawing of the invincible clone army by the United Nations, its creator is determined to carry on with his plans for religious genocide.

What price will Hamish have to pay to stop him?

Murdering the Messiah

In the process of transmuting him back to the real world, something has gone very wrong: Hamish's body has been successfully resuscitated, but his mind remains trapped in the virtual world.

Back in the real world, someone – or something – has taken over his body. But who – or what – has inhabited it?

Can Hamish prevent his real self from becoming the spark that ignites a global conflict, or will his nemesis' quest for revenge drag humanity into the ultimate Armageddon?

Sibling

The virtual world is running out of computing resources, and its chief architect, Rajesh Singh, is desperate.

When Japanese psychologist, Hisako Myamoto, proposes to use her AltLife research project to demonstrate how quantum computers could solve their problem, Hamish and Raj jump at her offer.

But Hisako has a darker reason for wanting to use the virtual world's unique software facilities: a second secret project that neither Hamish nor Raj can ever know about.

Entanglement

It's hard to kill someone who's already dead.

In the virtual world, there's nowhere left to run.

To kill McAllister and Singh, the virtual world has to be destroyed.

And someone has worked out how to do it.

Other novels

The Damning of Henry Morgan

Saved from the Inquisition, thrown into slavery to write the only eyewitness account of pirate battles in the Caribbean, can this ruthlessly manipulated French surgeon survive a world of mayhem and torture to be reunited with his first love?

Will his unique tale, cynically twisted and distorted, discredit his friend, Henry Morgan, infamous Admiral of the Brethren of the Coast? Or will another soul be damned?

From the court of the Inquisition to the cesspits of Tortuga and Port Royal, from the jungles of Panama to the royal courts of London and Madrid, with its mixture of exotic adventure and high politics, this is a tale of love, truth, deception and ultimate betrayal.

The young surgeon, his forbidden love, the inquisitor, or the pirate - who will pay the price for damning Henry Morgan?

Scartato

The story of how a discarded violin kindled the spark of love in an absent father for his abandoned daughter, and how his gift of a cast-off, second-rate violin touches the many lives who are drawn in by its mysterious power.

A tale which leads from betrayal in a dusty workshop in Cremona, to death and vendetta in Jamaica; from the first stirrings of the American Revolution in the frozen, rat-infested streets of New York, to treachery in pre-Revolutionary Paris; from the uncertain life of the early colonial theatre, to the harsh commercialism of modern day Chicago.

In the course of its journey, the violin becomes, by turns, an object of jealousy and desire, a symbol of love, and a means of salvation and hope. And for those privileged few who are able to conjure its magical song, a secret gateway into another world.

Bard Boy

Bard Boy is the humorous story of Edward, an innocent young man from a tiny village in the Welsh Valleys, and his journey from naïve valleys' boy to potential leader of the newly rejuvenated and politically assertive Druids.

When his fanatical Methodist grandmother proclaims Edward as the reincarnation of the founder of the Druid Movement, will the Druids' spin doctor seize on this unexpected public relations gift, and accept Edward into the very heart of the organisation?

Will Edward's sudden emergence from total obscurity be hailed as the Second Coming, or will it be necessary to supply a martyr to the Druid cause?

Either way, there's a Methodist hit man coming for him...

Printed in Great Britain
by Amazon

24002836R00258